'I want to w to his publisher – who also happ e Aunt Sheila.

'It's a revolutionary sex book designed for youngsters who want to bonk like rabbits but are so hung-up and inexperienced they'd have more fun eating rabbit pie. It won't be a "guide" or a "manual", more of an illustrated personal record.'

'You mean you're going to be in the pictures?'

'With my co-author, yes.'

'And who's that going to be?'

'I haven't found her yet. She must be young but experienced and shaped like a real woman, not some impossible glamour model. There's one other thing.'

'Yes?'

'She must have no shame.'

'Just like you, dear nephew.'

'Quite. Are you going to take your knickers off yourself, auntie, or do you need a hand?'

Also available from Headline Delta

The Lusts of the Borgias
Love Italian Style
Ecstasy Italian Style
Rapture Italian Style
Amorous Liaisons
Lustful Liaisons
Eroticon Dreams
Eroticon Desires
After Hours
French Thrills
In the Mood
A Slave to Love
Amorous Appetites
The Blue Lantern
Sex and Mrs Saxon
The Wife-Watcher Letters
Fondle on Top
Fondle in Flagrante
Fondle All Over
Kiss of Death
The Phallus of Osiris
High Jinks Hall
The Delicious Daughter
Three Women
Passion in Paradise
A Man with Three Maids
A Man with More Maids
Exposed

Shameless

Jennifer Cross

First published in Great Britain in 1994
by HEADLINE BOOK PUBLISHING

A HEADLINE DELTA Paperback

10 9 8 7 6 5 4 3 2 1

ISBN 0 7472 4487 1

Typeset by
Letterpart Limited, Reigate, Surrey

Printed and bound in Great Britain by
HarperCollins Manufacturing, Glasgow

HEADLINE BOOK PUBLISHING
A division of Hodder Headline PLC
338 Euston Road
London NW1 3BH

Delightful task! to rear the tender thought,
To teach the young idea how to shoot.

The Seasons, James Thompson

Chapter One

Lying on my stomach, I brought my head up and looked into the enormous mirror fixed to the wall in front of me. It was tilted upwards at forty-five degrees and perfectly adjusted to reflect the images from the equally enormous mirror fixed directly above me on the ceiling.

On the tilted wall-mirror I saw the naked me, myself, my back view (the right way around because of the double reflection!).

The whole of my skin, from ankles to shoulders, was bright pink. This was no surprise. I was tingling everywhere, pleasurably tingling almost to the point of slightly hurting but not quite.

Moira put the Weasel down. The Weasel was a bundle of nine – it had to be nine – thin green sticks. They were about two feet long. She got them from the garden centre, of all places, where they were sold to support pot plants.

Moira says you can't get birch twigs very easily in Bristol, and if you buy expensive leather tawses – nine thongs, see – they are always going missing, or the customer asks if he can have the tawse to take home for his wife. Which comes to the same thing. Money down the drain.

So, Moira experimented and came up with the Weasel. It makes a loud rattling noise as you use it, and sometimes little bits break off the sticks, but the customers love it. The garden centre simply cannot understand why sales of thin green sticks have shot up so.

Anyway, back to the session. For the last twenty minutes, Moira, dressed like a kind of nightmare Catwoman, had been beating me gently with the Weasel. I hadn't expected to like it, but I did. My noble sentiments of self-sacrifice in The Cause had been exposed as hollow. Instead of grinning and bearing it, I was grinning and loving it.

She had hit me hundreds of times, each time with a loud rattle and each time making me slightly pinker. She had gone over every inch of the back of my legs, my back and shoulders, and had paid special attention to my bottom.

Regular readers of this feature will by now be familiar with my bottom. There's no picture of it this month because we have pictures of Moira instead, in her skin-tight shiny black vinyl pants, her wide leather belt with the rhinestones, her Dick Turpin mask and black skull cap, and her tits bare except for the gold and silver chains.

But my bottom's been in before, and it will be again in two months' time when I tell you about my experiences in the Newcastle strip club.

Anastasia Wrench-Burton, real name Jane Smith, leaned back in her office chair and reached for her cigarettes. There would be no need to make anything up on this feature, no need to gild the lily at all. Enough had happened at Moira's to fill an entire issue of *Sir Lancelot*, never mind one 2000-word feature. She'd have to negotiate a bit more space with Murdo.

Murdo Sinclair was the editor and Anastasia, called Staz around the office, was one of the two deputy editors. The other was Camilla Tickell, known as Frenchie.

Sir Lancelot was an amazing magazine. It had shot from nowhere and was now poised to overhaul *Men Only*, *Penthouse* and *Playboy*, which it closely resembled in many respects, to become the top-selling top-shelfer.

There were two main reasons for its success. The first was this. Instead of the usual, daftly prurient, captions accompanying the centrefold series of pictures, *Sir Lancelot* had a 3000-word article by the editor. It described, in considerable and frank detail, what had happened when the said editor, Murdo Sinclair, had taken the centrefold girl out to dinner and then into bed.

Running this monthly regular a close second in popularity was the bi-monthly series which Murdo had wryly christened 'Work Experience'. Anastasia Wrench-Burton would go and spend a week or so at a different kind of sexual establishment every two months, and then write up her notes. The last one had been about a massage parlour in Sheffield. It was dynamite. This one was about Moira's place in Bristol, variously known on the grapevine as The Miss Voltage School of Correction, The Rubber Scrubber, or just plain Moira's.

Staz put her fag out in the ashtray and once more began tapping at her word processor.

> Why was my bottom pink? Why were its generously rounded hemispheres suffused with a glow I could both see in the mirror and feel, with or without hands? I'll tell you why. It was for the benefit of Stefan Something-or-other-owic, or -ovitch, a Czech devotee from the Khlysti. I'll tell you what the Khlysti are in a minute. Meanwhile we'll concentrate on my bottom, because that is what Moira was now doing.
>
> Stefan was on the other side of the two-way. I knew that. He didn't know I knew.
>
> Moira now put down the Weasel and took out Mr Sharkbite. Mr Sharkbite, Moira told me, was unique in the world. One of her customers from way back had been the wealthy owner of a high-class maker of fishing rods. Salmon and trout rods, she hastened to add, not your hoi polloi jobs for the canalside.

He'd brought one along to a session. He cut the bindings that held the rings on it, and then gave her the ringless top joint to beat him with. It was fine for a while, then it broke. The split cane, so carefully trimmed, bound and glued by craftsmen, was not meant to take, or administer, such punishment.

Next time he came he brought Mr Sharkbite. It was about the thickness of a rod's top joint but it had a cork handle like a bottom joint would have, only not so big.

It had, the customer proudly told Moira, an inner core of fine steel, then fibreglass, and the split cane was built around that. Instead of a brass ferrule on the business end it had ornate and engraved silver, and the whole thing, about three-foot-six long, was uniformly dimensioned. It didn't taper.

Moira had wanted to know how he persuaded his craftsmen to make it. He said he didn't. He was as good a craftsman as they were. He'd made it himself.

Apart from revarnishing and rebinding some of the threads, Mr Sharkbite had had no need of maintenance or repair and it had become famously identified with Moira and her School of Correction. Now, it was to be applied to my pink, glowing bottom.

Was I looking forward to it? Yes, and no.

The first stroke didn't hurt at all. The pink glow absorbed the shock and sent no messages to my brain, at least not immediately.

I looked in the mirror. There was a sharply defined, diagonal red stripe across the pink. Then, just as I saw Mr Sharkbite begin to descend for his second snap, I got the pain of the first. Christ. I clenched my hands together, closed my eyes and bit my lip.

The second impact of Mr Sharkbite was felt, but not yet the full agony of it. I made myself look up into the mirror. Moira had made an X on my arse. The second stroke had made an X with the first.

And now the pain shot into me, making me heave

my bottom into the air. I wanted to get off that leather bed.

Moira spoke. 'Stay still, you silly bitch,' she hissed. 'Imagine it doesn't really hurt.'

I collapsed back and lay, quivering. Moira put down her weapon and began belting me in. There were leather belts fitted to the bed. I realised then what that bed was. It was one of those trolleys they use to shift dangerous madmen around Broadmoor, strapped in.

I was soon strapped in, too. There were two over my legs, one over my waist and one over my shoulders. My arms were pinned in to my side by the two upper straps. My tits were flattened into the leather and I could feel them pressing against my arms.

Only with great effort could I look up into the mirror as the next four blows came whistling down in rapid succession. My imagination was working overtime but I have to tell you, dear reader, that it hurt like fuckery.

I awoke from my reverie, looked, and saw a star. Moira had given me six strokes in the form of an asterisk. The centre vertical began in the small of my back and disappeared in the valley between my cheeks. There was no blood. She had been extremely careful not to cut me. The marks were red enough, but they were very long, very thin bruises, not raw, weeping slashes.

The pain by now had receded into the background. It was there, alright, and very much there, but it was like the noise in a car. You can't hear the noise of travelling at ninety miles an hour if you've got the stereo turned up loud enough.

In my case the stereo was Stefan. In the full-length vertical wall mirror, next to the angled one, I saw him enter the room. He had on a tall hat like a bishop's mitre and an embroidered sort of scarfy shawl thing over his shoulders. (I've looked it up; it's called a chasuble.)

In one hand he carried a kneeling cushion, the kind you see in church which are made and decorated in tapestry stitch by the local WI. (I don't need to look this up. It's a hassock.)

In the other hand he carried a pole, a metal pole, about nine feet long, with a six-pointed gold star on the end.

Another pole made of stiffened flesh, stuck out in a curve in front of him. From it hung a loop of ribbon, and from the ribbon hung another star. Apart from this, all he was wearing was the hat and scarf.

Moira undid the two belts around my legs but left the others where they were. She took the cushion from Stefan and slid it under my stomach. Swiftly she took one leg and tied my ankle to something I couldn't see, then walked around the bed and did the same on the other side.

Thus I was pinioned and spread, my bottom with its star of pain raised in the air.

Stefan began speaking, in Czech I assume. It had a formal ring to it, ceremonial even, and it went on for quite a long time. He was standing at the foot of the bed. I could see in the mirror that Moira was kneeling beside him, giving his prick some occasional stimulus with her hand and her tongue.

The address was complete. Stefan, still in mitre and chasuble, handed his long pole to Moira and climbed on to the bed behind me. He removed the ribbon from his cock and placed it on my buttocks at the centre point of the star. He put one hand on either side of me next to the edges of the hassock and, without pressing himself at all onto my scarred flesh, entered me.

His cock slid in without hindrance. I was feeling very relaxed now. The clouds of pain were numbing all my sensations with an effect not unlike a drug. He shagged me there and then. His movements were rapid and functional. In, out, in, out. No finesse, no attempt at variation. In a couple of dozen thrusts he came, and at that point he withdrew and the semen showered from his cock-end onto my buttocks.

If he was aiming at the centre of the star he was not a good shot because he sprayed the whole of my rear. Then, as if it was an afterthought, he suddenly lunged forward, crushing me beneath him, making my pain sear and flash through me as he penetrated my anus. His last spurt went home there, and he lay on top of me, satisfied.

After he'd gone, Moira undid my straps and quietly crept out. I did what she obviously expected me to do. I slept.

Later, dressed in sweater and slacks, she came in with some tea. She helped me to one of the bathrooms and put me in a warm, not hot, bath with many powerful scents in the water. I lay there with the tea while she told me about the Khlysti.

Apparently they're some kind of reverse-side Christian sect. Instead of ordinary sex in marriage, they do without, and then let it all go in religious orgies. They have men being Jesus and women being Mary, and they all bonk like mad while whipping each other.

I said it sounded like incest to me, and Moira said that if that was the case, I was the Virgin Mary and I'd just been had by my son who was twenty-five years older than me.

Stefan is a bishop in this sect, you see, and is not welcome in his home country. So, he has to pay Moira to fix up his services for him. How much? I asked. Never you mind, she said. You're getting paid by *Sir Lancelot*.

Chapter Two

Murdo Sinclair sat forward, elbows resting on the polished patina of the green leather which topped his antique partners' desk. Chin resting on cupped hands, he absent-mindedly contemplated the naked female who stood in extravagant pose about twenty feet away from him, and wondered why it was that the acme of female pulchritude should be such an improbability.

Murdo thought in phrases like 'acme of female pulchritude' rather than 'ideal bird' because he was classically educated and of a literary bent. Some of the people he met for the first time during the course of his work found this quality in him surprising. They had been expecting the editor of *Sir Lancelot*, the most talked-about and soon to be the biggest men's magazine in the UK after only six months of publication, to be a different kind of character. More flashy, perhaps, more obviously macho. They expected the gold chains and bangles, the Rolex Oyster with diamonded bezel, designer chest hairs, leather jeans, and a white BMW with double spoilers and 36 TIT number plates.

Instead they found a cultured gentleman, no more than twenty-five years of age, dressed by establishments with a single retail outlet in Savile Row or St James's. He drove a 1958 Aston Martin on special occasions and a 1979 Land Rover for knocking around where he lived, and would not have seen himself dead in anything as vulgar as a white car with spoilers. There were no chest hairs allowed to be visible except on the beach and in bed. His wristwatch was a stainless steel clockwork Accurist which had belonged to his late father, and the only gold to be found decorating his person was in his cuff links.

He was handsome enough, indeed very much so, and if he himself was the acme of any kind of pulchritude it was of the British aristocratic variety, with a touch of dark Scottish brooding and a hint of ancient clan brutishness.

People much older than him, who might have had some of the old 1960s paperback editions of James Bond novels on their bookshelves, thought he looked not unlike the artist's illustrated impression of 007 on the cover.

Murdo Sinclair would have been amused and pleased by the comparison because, inside, he had a lot more in common with Bond the sensual adventurer than he had with the pompous farts of the Establishment, who somehow expected a person with his tastes and background to be just as pompous as they were.

He was dressed in a high-Tory dark blue suit, sewn by a little old man who sat cross-legged on a table in a back room up an alley off New Burlington Street. He wore a handmade shirt and silk tie. His socks were Scottish wool, and his shoes were individually produced for him, the left shoe differing from the right as his feet did, by another little old man, this one in a green cotton-duck apron.

As the girl changed position and the photographer's flash bounced off the white umbrellas, Sinclair put his well-trained mind onto the startling improbability presented to him by her shape.

She was tall, long-legged, narrow-waisted, small-hipped. Her ribcage also was narrow, perhaps of the depth you might expect on a lightweight girl of five-feet-three rather than the five-feet-ten which she obviously was. And yet, to go with the unlikelihood of the long legs and the small hips, of the well-above-average height and the well-below-average waist, this girl also carried on her small but perfectly formed ribcage two very large and near-perfectly-formed breasts which stood out as if held by an invisible bra.

Her measurements were 42-22-36, he noted from the data on his computer screen. How anatomically curious, he thought, when placed horizontally on a vertical of seventy inches. Usually, girls with a forty-two-inch bust had at least thirty-six inches of it in ribs and backbone. Not this one, nor most of the other girls who were pictured in his magazine.

They all conformed to the unusual and special type which was sought out for sudden exposure from hidden corners, beside factory benches and shop counters, in farmyards and school classrooms. They were the one in a thousand. Why, then, did the male of the species judge such a rarity to be the one he most wanted? Why put your expectations on a body at 999 to 1 against?

Why not believe the Western female standard pear-shape to be most desirable, when it was so much more probable that a pear shape would be what you'd find under the disguising raiment of whichever female you were mentally or physically undressing?

How much built-in disappointment there had to be when, with the ideal in your mind as portrayed in *Sir Lancelot*, each time a woman disrobed she revealed the small breasts and large hips, or large breasts and huge hips, which occurred in 999 of 1000 cases.

Murdo looked around the office area of the long room in which he sat, spacious enough to suit forty or fifty middle-ranking, open-plan executives or just one wealthy editor. On the walls were floor-to-ceiling enlargements of early pin-ups and postcards. A viewer could start at one end of the display with sepia and black-and-white portraits of partly dressed actresses from the turn of the century, and progress in time around the office to finish on the first Penthouse Pet to show her pubic hair.

The editor looked academically at two of the earliest. Lillie Langtry and the American, Lillian Russell, like all their near-by companions, had large hips and thighs, and the kind of face which said its owner enjoyed a drink and a laugh and a plateful of something filling, as well as a roll on the palliasse with an admirer. These were the kind of girls who made Prince Edward twirl his moustachios. Why had man's ideal changed so drastically?

The Gibson girls, the American ideal woman as designed by Charles Dana Gibson in *Life* magazine in the early 1900s, had an exaggerated bust and a ridiculously narrow waist, but they still had the big hips and thighs of a real woman.

Photographs from the twenties and thirties showed naked flesh, breasts thrust forward but with coyly covered nether regions, in poses from 'art' magazines. The publicity pictures of film stars were more coy still, but clearly revealed with their swimming costumes or carefully placed feather boas that Clara Bow, Louise Brooks, Jean Harlow and the rest were all, to a woman, pear-shaped.

These were girls who ate a proper breakfast, girls who displayed themselves for profit in a more censorious age and not a single one of them showed the slightest embarrassment about the size of her arse.

Things began to change, Murdo noted, with the Petty and Varga drawings in *Esquire* in the forties. On the wall was a page from a Varga calendar showing a girl drawn almost to the standard of detail of a photograph, but she could never have been in front of a camera. She had impossibly long legs, slim thighs, buttocks which would have been small on a nine-year-old and, beneath a tight blouse, breasts which defied gravity unaided.

Murdo looked again at the real life nakedness across the room and wondered how evolution had managed so well in such a short time. That real-life English girl over there, now standing on her toes, her hands holding a straw hat decorated with ribbon behind her, her pelvis thrust forward and her shoulders back, was far, far closer to a Varga illustration than to the photograph of Jean Harlow in a one-piece woollen swimming costume.

Miss Harlow, her hips almost square with their bulk, her thighs round and sturdy, her breasts well developed and large enough but not dominating, was the girl the pre-war man of taste and discrimination would go to bed with in his dreams. She would be good fun to take away for a weekend, and she would know all about having a marvellous time, in and out of the sheets. But very few copies of *Sir Lancelot* would be sold with a naked equivalent of her on the cover.

Perhaps he would write a feature on it: The changing shape in your dreams. Meanwhile, over in the studio section of the room the photographer had finished and was fiddling with his Hasselblad and his lights, preparing for tomorrow's session. His assistant, a pert little thing who fitted her jeans and T-shirt perfectly, was collecting up props. This had been a Hawaiian set-up, with palm trees and grass skirts. There was, for some reason Sinclair couldn't quite fathom, a white plaster bust of Gladstone, over which the model had been pictured placing a garland of flowers.

Two maintenance men came in and began removing the palm trees. Nine months ago, when the boss, Mr Sinclair, had set up the magazine with his own money tripled by a bank loan, and the first issue was being compiled, these same maintenance men got erections every time they saw a model, like this one today, walking across the studio in the buff. Now they just gave her a cursory glance and the working man's inventory – size and jut of tits, length and colour of nipples, graspfulness of arse and note if the colour of the welcome mat exactly matches the barnet.

The girl – Amanda by name, Mr Sinclair saw on his day's schedule – was walking towards him, putting on a discarded garment from the shoot, a lurid orange and blue short shirt of the kind worn by holidaying Americans. She stood, embarrassed, awkward, naked from the navel down, until Mr Sinclair motioned her to a chair. Seated, she crossed her legs by habit, then thought that this might be unladylike and uncrossed them. She sat holding her knees, her breasts hanging enormously under the loose shirt.

Her embarrassment was not due to her nakedness. Over the last two days in this place she had become used to that, even though nobody before had seen her naked since she was a little girl except her seventeen-year-old boyfriend, and that was always in the dark, in her room at home or in the back of his car. No, she was concerned about what was to happen next, later, that evening.

She knew what had to happen, because she knew why *Sir Lancelot* had shot from nowhere. Mr Sinclair pressed a button on his telecoms set and spoke.

'Amanda has finished. Take her back to her hotel and see that she is rested, and that she approves of one of the outfits selected for her. I shall be calling for her at seven, so get the hairdresser there by six and the make-up artist there by six-thirty.'

A secretary came in, a prim-looking Scandinavian type wearing heels to pierce your foot with and eyes to freeze your balls with. Murdo nodded, smiling and comforting, to Amanda, who rose and was marched away by the cold fish of the fjord.

Murdo's idea, of the editor describing a night with the Damsel of the Month, was a brave one. Although the girls were contracted not to give any information to the press about any aspect of their work for *Sir Lancelot*, there was really not much to be done to stop a determined girl from selling her story to the tabloids.

> 'Lance-a-bit flopped with me,' by centrefold Trudy!
> 'Sir Droopalot's no bonking good,' says Disappointed Damsel!

The headlines were doubtless already written.

They would never be used because Murdo Sinclair had a gift. He was a stayer. The woman wasn't born who could wear him out and, as the centrefold girls were rarely more than seventeen years old, few of them had sufficient experience even to make a decent try at the task. In the Playboy-ese language of pre-Murdo men's magazines, Sir Lancelot's champion always rode full tilt through the night and was fresh and ready for a fourth and fifth charge atop the sprightliest mare at the morning's tourney.

That evening, at two minutes to seven, an immaculately black-tied Murdo strode through the foyer of the Westmorland Tower Hotel in Mayfair, the leather soles beneath the spotless black gloss of his shoes clipping the parquet in fine marching rhythm. He knocked on the door of Room 211 at precisely seven o'clock and was greeted by a stunningly beautiful girl. Amanda was perfectly and professionally coiffed and made up. She had on simple but expensive jewellery, and was in a floor-length white silk gown, tightly fitted, with a low but not indecent neckline. Her figure, in this shimmering sheath, was a triumph of the unlikely over the commonplace.

She tried a smile but it came out crumpled. She was nervous as hell.

Murdo, instead of escorting her to the lift, gestured her back inside.

'The photographer can wait,' he said in his Anglo-Caledonian way, the Scottish edge on his consonants and vowels influencing his English just sufficiently to make it distinctive. 'You need a stiff drink, and I need to have a fairly stiff word.'

While he poured her a gin and tonic, he laid down the law.

'The first part of the evening is for the public. They want to see pictures of you and me enjoying ourselves in expensive and fashionable surroundings, in the full knowledge that in a few short hours we'll be sweating and heaving and having a rampant fuck.

'We'll be photographed leaving the hotel, arriving at the restaurant, at some point tête-à-tête during the meal and then, most important of all, leaving the restaurant. In all of these pictures you are to appear beautiful, of course, which you will have no trouble doing, but you must also appear happy. You are enjoying your evening. You are looking forward to the whole of it. The camera records it and does not lie.

'As to what really happens later – well, I am a writer. I have poetic licence, so don't worry about it. Now, if you have finished your drink' – which she had, in two gulps – 'we'll go. And if you want some motivation, just remember that your future as a professional fashion model depends far, far more on the photographs tonight, than either the ones you've already done or the fucking to be done later.'

Amanda, braced by the gin and pepped by the talk, grasped his arm firmly and walked. She could walk in that dress by reason of it having a slit to the waist. Beneath it she was wearing absolutely nothing.

The chauffeur-driven Rolls took them to Le Jardin Galacien, a restaurant where – as Mr Sinclair's Nordic secretary described it – they would give you all you could eat for two hundred quid.

Amanda said she liked fish, so they started with Quenelles de Brochet and a half bottle of a very crisp and flinty Pouilly Fumé. Murdo, like many Scotsmen, could drink with the capacity of a Titan, but very few of the girls could. They were therefore rationed, not from any puritan, Presbyterian streak in Murdo, but because the picture editor always got furious if, as he put it in his Catford twang, the little tart had got rat-arsed and so had eyes like bastard pissholes in the snow.

Amanda had never had Quenelles, and didn't know that pike was a fish. She came from Shrewsbury, where her father was a painter and decorator and her boyfriend was an apprentice mechanic. She had worked in a large creamery on the cheese packing line until being spotted one night at the Top Cat nightclub by one of Murdo's many scouts (practically every local newspaperman in the country was on the look-out for Damsels; they got £500 if they found one who made it to the centrefold).

After the fish she thought she might like a fillet steak. Murdo, ever polite, kept her company although he would rather have had a thick slice off the rump, or a Barnsley chop come to that, real mutton, not watery New Zealand lamb frozen at six months old.

With the steaks they had a Gevrey Chambertin, and with the wild strawberries a little of an old Sauternes.

Time to go. Amanda kept her newly professional face immaculate, and managed a flaunty, swaying, waist-slit walk from the restaurant that had every man in the place goggling and every woman narrow-eyed with envy. She fell silent during the journey back to Murdo's flat in Chelsea, and still hadn't spoken a word by the time he returned from his dressing room, wrapped in a green and black striped towelling robe, to find her lying naked in his bed.

He adjusted the dimmer, slipped off his robe, and slid in beside her. He kissed her on the forehead as she looked up at him, not a little frightened, and then kissed her on the neck, and ran his hand across her magnificent bosom. She didn't move, not even when his finger strayed across her stomach to the tightly knit curls of black hair which carpeted the way forward.

By now he was beginning to be worried. Amanda was behaving like a scared child. He took her small, cool hand and placed it on his erect member, hot and hard. The hand didn't resist being placed there, but it made no effort to grip or move.

Murdo had had a difficult week. In an attempt to starve him out, the other major magazines had got together and offered all his main advertisers cheap space. Murdo and his advertising manager had been pulling every string to keep at least some of them from deserting. Now, with another day of the same creeping and crawling looming, and then the weekend to write his 'Damsel of the Month' article, he could see himself having to make up every single word of it instead of just having to imagine about half, as usual.

He tried to remember how privileged he was, having one of the most beautiful young women in the country lying naked beneath his sheets. He moved his hips, so his cock would slide in her hand. It didn't. She let go of it.

'For fuck's sake,' he heard himself say, and immediately admonished himself for allowing the words to slip. The girl turned over, scrunched herself up into the foetal position and burst into tears.

Murdo got out of bed, replaced his towelling robe, and went over to the drinks tray. She could drink what she liked now. There would be no more photography. And he could have the extremely large Glenfarclas he had been wanting all night. He also lit a couple of cigarettes supplied by Clode and Whittaker, the last tobacconist in London which would make cigarettes especially to personal order.

He sat on the edge of the bed beside the sobbing girl. With a kindly hand he fluffed up the pillows, raised her up, placed a large Gordon's and Canada Dry tonic in her shaking fingers and tucked the duvet up and around her breasts, giving each a light kiss as he did so.

She pulled hard on the cigarette and tapped the ash fiercely into the gunmetal ashtray he had placed on the bed. Murdo sat in the bedside chair and drew at his whisky.

'You never mentioned that you were a virgin,' he said.

'I'm not,' replied Amanda. 'At least, I've done it, I mean, I've done it quite a lot, but only with one boy. He just gets on top of me and it's all over in half a minute. I don't enjoy it much. Well, not at all, really. And so, you see, I was kind of frightened of not being pleasing to you, of not being able to . . .'

By an exercise of will which impressed the editor, the girl managed to stop herself breaking down again. A furious puff on the cigarette was followed by the glass being drained. Murdo rose to get another.

As he poured, he spoke. 'Would it help you to know that I also am nervous? What would happen if I failed to please you? Imagine what the papers would make of that.'

'Oh, I'd never . . . I mean . . .'

'And would it also help you to know that most of the girls are like you? Now, let's see, you are going in Issue Nine in three months. We had one pilot issue to show advertisers which never went on sale, so that's ten Damsels of the Month so far. Of those, only one was fairly experienced, having worked for a summer in a bar in Spain. Most of the rest were like you, only had sex with one or two boyfriends, and generally that was the selfish sort of sex you describe.'

'I'm willing,' said Amanda. 'I've made myself be willing. But it was this side of it which almost made me say no.

Not the actual sex, I mean, but being sure I would make a mess of it. I've read those articles. The girls all sound like red hot lovers. You make them sound as if they're brilliant experts at it.

'And I knew I wasn't, and the thought of being shown up was almost enough to make me turn down your money, which I tell you is an enormous amount to me, and all the other stuff, you know, the modelling and that. I nearly didn't do it because I had to get into bed with someone who would be expecting me to know what to do like those other girls.'

'And now you see I'm expecting nothing of the sort,' said Murdo, finishing his whisky and deciding to hell with it, he'd have a refill. 'Now, we'll have another cigarette, and finish our drinks, and then I've got something I'd like to show you. It's called The Murdo Sinclair Guide to Utter Bliss. It's not written down anywhere, or taped. It's only in my head, and from there I shall transfer it to your body until you are a quivering communion of helpless sensations.'

Amanda took another big gulp of gin. She had never been a quivering communion of helpless sensations before.

'You don't need to do anything,' he continued, 'except lie back and enjoy it. You don't need to think of England, or Shrewsbury, but only of yourself. You can close your eyes if you wish' – he took her glass and removed the ashtray – 'but above all try to relax. I'm not guaranteeing anything but, Amanda, I shall be doing my very best.'

Murdo walked around to the other side of the bed, dropping his robe on the floor. He climbed up beside Amanda, being careful not to crowd her.

Gently he pulled down a corner of the duvet, revealing the swelling, curving magnificence of her left breast. He bent over her and breathed gently on the nipple, and then gripped it even more gently between his teeth, and caressed it with the very tip of his tongue. His lips closed round it and his tongue worked from side to side. His hand came up to help, sensing the undercurve of the breast and tracing its line, and then fondling the firm mass of it.

His finger traced the many minute undulations of the aureole as he pursed his lips and applied pressure to the nipple. At last he got his reward. It sprung up, like a flower opening in a speeded-up film. It seemed to leap at him, to burst forth, and as he renewed the stimulation with his tongue tip he heard the little groan, the little gurgle of enjoyment he wanted.

His other hand moved to the right breast. Now he grasped her more firmly, his hands working the big mounds of firm flesh. He switched his tongue to the right nipple, touched it once, and up it sprang.

Now he stepped up the pace slightly, kissing her breasts and stomach, moving his hands more freely over her. Her arms came up so she could stroke his back and his neck. As his kisses moved nearer and nearer the black curls, her thighs moved. She opened them, and thrust up her pelvis, anxious by instinct for his lips and tongue to reach within.

Murdo ignored the sign for the moment. He would wait until she was frantic. His mouth traversed back up to her breasts again, and then down to her tummy button, then up to her nipples, then down to the fringe of her black curls, then up to the secret niches below each breast.

His hand lightly stroked the inside of her thighs, now open even wider in gasping expectation. He allowed his index finger to move up to trace the pinkish-brown folds of skin which were warm and damp with desire, then to her hard mons, and softly stirred his fingertip in among her curls, as if trying to wind on the hair.

He bent his head to the cleft of her, and searched with his tongue into the little hem of skin which hoods over that part which, he guessed correctly, she didn't know existed. She had never even found it for herself, in the bath, in bed alone, and now it lay there in wait.

His tongue touched the *sanctum sanctorum* and found the altar's offering within. The girl cried out in surprise as well as gratification, a sort of half shout, rather as if someone had trodden on her toe while giving her a million pounds.

Sinclair felt the little organ stir and stiffen. He rasped it with his tastebuds, and thrust two fingers into her vagina, pushing in and out slowly in time with his massage on her clitoris. Her knees were jerking, her hands were scrabbling hopelessly at his back, her head was flipping over this way and that, and within moments she would reach her first ever orgasm.

Sinclair wanted that to be with him inside her, so he lifted his head from its work, shuffled up her body and presented the head of his cock to the gaping gate. He was not massively endowed. Women didn't cry out in fear when they saw him erect. Well, he couldn't have everything. But Mother Nature had given one of her most enduring sons quite enough to satisfy. It is, as he so often reminded himself, what you do with it that counts.

He pushed home, keeping the shaft well up in her so that the stiff clit could feel the movement. He knew it would not be a long time. After a few slow thrusts he felt her becoming more urgent. Her hands gripped his neck. Her legs wrapped themselves around his hips, unbidden by any conscious thought but driven by a completely instinctive and irresistible need to come, and to come now.

She pushed herself up against him in a wild sequence of rapid movements and brought herself to a climax in a great rush of sound and trembling, her voice making noises as ancient as the species, her body searching madly for, and finding in supreme pleasure, the goal of every rousting, rutting animal.

Cleaving to him in gratitude, and slowly returning to a form of waking attention, she was astonished to feel him still thrusting. In all the sex she had ever had, the boy had come almost as soon as he put his cock in, and there was never any question of going beyond a dozen strokes.

Of course, the boy was usually ready for another inside half an hour, but that was just as brief. And here was the mysterious man who had just made her reach a place she never knew about, pushing his hard rod into her again and again, thirty, forty, fifty times, and so steady, and so strong, she could feel the sensations beginning to build up in her again!

He timed it perfectly. Once more sensing the involuntary, galvanic movements of her legs and arms, and feeling the nails dig into his skin, Murdo began to accelerate. His own moment was approaching too, and so he let go the reins and went for it. With a huge heaving gasp, her back arched and her heels kicking, the girl came for the second time in her life as she felt the gush of fluid speed into her innermost regions. Sinclair pushed right up in his final spasm, and they fell together back onto the bed. She uttered a three-word obscene blasphemy of deepest satisfaction and lay still in amazement.

Murdo looked down at the girl beneath him, her beautiful face a picture of serenity, her eyes closed in utter bliss as promised, and her bosom now slowing its rise and fall towards a more sustainable tempo. And, at that instant, he had the most brilliant idea.

Chapter Three

Murdo sat down to his computer terminal in determined mood. He had phoned a publisher he knew, one who was very strong on marketing, and outlined his brilliant idea. The woman was very enthusiastic and demanded lunch that day.

'And a good lunch, Murdo dear. Not one of your office jobs with tins of lager and beetroot sandwiches.'

Murdo, who had never eaten a beetroot sandwich in his life, said she should choose and book, and he would pay.

By the time the morning editorial conference was over it was half-past ten. Lunch was at one, which meant leaving at half-twelve. He had three hours to write his minimum of 5000 words about the encounter with Amanda. It had to be done today, and it couldn't be done this afternoon after a lunch with Sheila, he knew that. And tomorrow, well . . . who knew what he could be doing? If Sheila's enthusiasm was anything to go by, he might not have time for writing articles in the office.

Murdo spoke to his secretary on the intercom. No calls, and he meant none. Coffee to be brought to him every half hour. He also needed a fresh pack of Gitanes. (He had this quirk, did Murdo. Couldn't write without a constant supply of Gitanes cigarettes. Something to do with a film he'd once seen.)

He opened the Damsel file on the screen and keyed in the title he'd just thought up.

'Abandoned Amanda, the dirtiest Damsel of all!'

The Nordic robot he called a secretary brought the Gitanes and the first coffee instantly. He lit a cigarette and inhaled the smoke.

Not a lot of facts and real action to go with this one, he thought. Not that there usually was a great deal, but normally there was at least something to give him a start. But poor Amanda! Well. And oh well. Here goes. His fingers moved to the keyboard and began tapping.

You will know that when your correspondent goes forth to do his duty on your behalf, a certain nervousness generally attends. The girls are always so very beautiful and look so poised. Amanda, this month's Damsel, is stunningly all of this and more – a princess royal, even by our own high standards.

Damsels are also physically perfect. They are dream girls. Amanda is 5 feet 10 inches tall and her horizontal measurements are 42-22-36. These are the figures of heaven, of a man's remote imaginings. How else, then, could I approach our night together other than with trepidation? Could I match Amanda's ideals? Would the young goddess pictured so enticingly in this issue of *Sir Lancelot* find spiritual and carnal sufficiency in a mere mortal?

I forced firmness into my knock on the door of Room 211 of the Westmorland Tower Hotel, which is a rather swish little twenty-floor pub in West One where a suite of rooms for one night costs as much as your average bank manager earns in a month.

The door opened and there stood Amanda. She had a glass of *Sir Lancelot*'s private-cuvee champagne in her left hand. In her right she held a bundle of black and white contact prints, made from the two-and-a-quarter square colour transparencies which had been taken that afternoon. The actual trannies from the Damsel session are kept under lock and key, but we let the girls have an early glimpse of themselves in monochrome.

Perhaps without the due deference which should

have been shown to such an important editor person as I am, Amanda threw the contacts on a table and said, 'Get an eyeful of these, baby. If they don't make your cock stand, I don't know what will.'

While I gave the pictures a rapid perusal, from professional interest only, you will realise, Amanda went to pour me a glass of bubbly. She had another herself, and was clearly feeling rather jolly. I couldn't help noticing that when she bent down to the drinks fridge, her short, white, judo-style dressing gown rode up over her exceptionally well-defined buttocks, revealing that she had forgotten to put her knickers on.

She walked towards me with a very broad smile on her face, gave me my drink and put the hand grasping her own champagne round my neck. She drew me towards her. Her mouth was a fine rosebud, her eyes pools of fire. I thought she was going to say something poetic, but that's not our Amanda's style. Her free hand went to my crotch and felt the rearing bump which had been gradually growing since I walked into the room.

'What time's dinner?' she said.

'Plenty of time yet,' I managed to gulp out, trying to sip champers, speak intelligently and stop myself bursting the buttons off my flies all at the same moment.

'Time? Time for what?' said Amanda.

Her hand stayed behind briefly on my trousered truncheon as she turned and walked, majestically, to the bedroom door. There was a small table there, Regency, I should have said, with a polished circular top supported by a single central leg which splayed at the end into three feet.

Feeling that my own central leg would shortly also attain three feet, I tried to keep my jaw from hitting the floor as she placed her glass on the table and shrugged off her judo outfit, retaining only the black belt in her hand. Trailing this over her shoulder, a night-time ribbon falling over the moving white of her daytime curves, she walked stark naked away from me towards a bed I couldn't yet see.

My glass joined hers on the table top, a few drops spilling in my haste. I was through the door now. I could see Amanda lying on the bed, one knee raised – the one nearest me – and an arm placed casually across her chest so that only one nipple was visible.

She held the end of the black belt to her lips. The rest ran casually down her body and disappeared between her thighs.

My own clothes, which had taken half an hour to put on with accompanying brushing, combing, shaving and perfuming, were on the floor in twenty seconds flat. I lurched towards the bed, my man standing stiff for me like a Clydesdale stallion's.

I could see a slight look of disappointment on her face. I don't have the biggest one in the world, as you know. But as you will also know, not even a Clydesdale could perform as many services in a night as I can, and each one infinitely extendable. I'd soon have that look wiped off her face.

In my eagerness I tripped slightly as I attempted to get on the bed beside her. She whipped away and bounded on top of me, her knees on my arms, her hands gripping my wrists. Quick as a flash she pulled the far end of the black belt up from below (and I have to say I failed to resist her as I watched the strip of black cloth move across her thigh and past my waving flagpole).

Keeping the other end in her teeth for the moment (and how brightly her eyes were shining, I noticed) she tied my wrists together. She finished the job with a hard granny knot and sat back on my stomach. Her hand reached behind her and confirmed with a grip and a couple of pulls that there was a rod of iron waiting to rule her should she so desire.

She lowered herself towards me, offering the nipple of her enormous left tit first. I sucked it and kissed it and felt it rise up in my mouth. She grinned, and murmured her approval. Now she brought her right nipple to my lips. I soon had that hardened too, and her smile became a little wider.

She slid down my body until she was sitting on my shins. She grabbed my cock firmly in her right hand and placed a blob of her own spittle first on her left index finger, and then on the end of my cock. She wiped the spittle around the rim, lubricating the widest point of the shaft. There wasn't enough. Her finger went back to her lips, and more spittle was conveyed to a piston almost hot enough to evaporate spit as fast as it was put on.

Briefly, I thought the lubrication would have been better applied direct, without the intermediary of a finger, but before I could develop the idea she had moved up my prone person with a double-leg shift not dissimilar to that employed by a sumo wrestler when settling down to face his opponent.

This particular sumo, of the rounded bottom, narrow waist and vastly suspenseful tits, didn't shout 'Hoogah! Haggoh!' or whatever it is they say, as she walked on her knees past my cock and then sat back onto it. In fact she didn't shout anything at all. She just sighed.

Now she was gyrating and thrusting, her pelvis making a series of well-practised movements. Had it been possible to trace them onto paper, they would have produced one of those marvellous graphic flowery circle designs you make with different coloured pens and a pendulum.

Talking of pendula, Amanda's amazing breasts were swinging too, in opposite and similar directions as she assaulted my sword of fortune with the most complex strategy ever devised by a quim and a pair of thighs. Round, up, across, down, along, repeat, do it differently, up, down and round she went, each movement producing a new surge of delicious sensations in both of us.

Her eyes had been looking directly into mine, her hands on my arms. Now she shifted her hands to the black-belted wrists and pushed them above my head as far as they would go. Her own head sagged as she pushed against the black-belt tie as if it were an exerciser, you know, dynamic tension, that sort of thing.

She changed her angle from sitting to a half raised kneeling. Her movements became more exaggerated. She pushed with her hands and stretched with her torso. I was a human multi-gym! This was Amanda's version of the rowing machine, upside down and back to front!

Her breasts were nearer to me but my hands were not free. Eagerly I tried to reach a summit or two with my tongue, my nose, anything! If only I could touch that swinging flesh as Amanda accelerated. Her breath was coming in short snorts. Suddenly she changed up into fifth gear and her beautiful arse, instead of performing artistically varied and circuitous undulations, went into smooth, regular, reciprocating mode.

She was fucking me, and with what energy! Faster and faster she went, her mouth now open and issuing cries from the wilderness. Still faster she shoved, harder and harder, and I felt my own moment approaching as she could obviously feel hers.

I pushed up into her as she came to her final fling. Her head went back, her mouth was wide, and she sang out with the gusto of an opera soprano on the final note of her most dramatic aria just before she dies. The note was flat, or sharp, I'm never sure which. It was squeaky rather than well rounded, but it was high, very high.

One, two, three, four, five deep thrusts I made as I felt her quim quivering and contracting on my cock as she came, and my own hot juices spurted into her.

She collapsed onto my chest, her lovely head beside mine, her delectable breasts crushed against me. 'Fucking hell,' she said. 'That was something else. But don't expect me to do all the work next time.'

Twenty minutes later, with me restored to my former gentlemanly cut and bearing, and she with make-up and hair adjusted by the waiting professional adjusters, we greeted Salim the chauffeur. I watched his eye travel up and down Amanda. She was wearing a clinging white number with nothing whatever underneath it, and Salim's mental cinema was showing blue movies all the way to the restaurant.

The door of the Rolls opened, Salim saluted, and we stepped out. The understated lights and entrance of Le Jardin Galacien beckoned us and the head waiter, Jean-Pierre, an old friend of mine, ushered us to my favourite corner table.

Looking back in my editorial records I see *Sir Lancelot* has never done a review column about Le Jardin Galacien. I imagine that is because the prices are beyond our food writer's budget. Tough titty for him. Nothing, however, could be too good for Amanda.

That Olympian creature can sit in a chair like an angel and stop all conversation in any restaurant ten times the size of Le Jardin. She can arrange a leg so that her waist-slit dress falls open entirely by accident to reveal long expanses of impossibly desirable thigh. She can narrow the eyes of every woman in the place, and make every man groan with frustrated longing. But she doesn't know the first thing about food.

You see, no woman in the world is flawless. Of course, you may say food-ignorance is a small flaw. Would I rather a connoisseur gourmet with impeccable taste, who was a stunted dwarf with a face like a prune, a figure like a bean-bag and all the sexual drives of a tin of spam?

Or, would I rather have fish, chips and mushy peas with Amanda?

In fact she said she wanted fish, so I suggested Quenelles de Brochet. She said what were they, so I ordered a bottle of a dramatically incisive Pouilly Fumé to keep us going while I explained the art of poaching gently the delicate mounds of pounded fish mixed with egg yolks, cream and so on.

'I thought pike was meat,' she said, knocking back the Pouilly like it was a steelworker's first pint at lunch time (although I believe they call it 'dinner' time in Sheffield).

The quenelles came, risen and dainty in a velouté sauce. Amanda tried them, hesitantly, then cleaned the lot up faster than you could say 'boiled black pudding on saucer'.

She declared them 'quite nice, really' and changed her leg position to give a bald-headed chap over on the other side of the room a view of her inner thigh with – I imagined from his reaction – a fleeting glimpse of pubic curlies.

Baldy began coughing and water had to be sent for. He drank some, but it just ran down his nose. His wife looked as if she was going to stab him there and then with the two-pronged fork she had been using to deal with her portion of a Chateaubriand.

While the poor man subsided, the wife glared at Amanda. Our Damsel merely smiled sweetly, scratched herself lightly with one finger across the top of a generously swelling right tit, and said, 'What's next?'

I'd wanted something fairly simple and robust for main course after the pomp and calories of the quenelles, so I'd ordered Kidneys Robert. The mustard and lemon would give me the tang I was after and kidneys, especially new season English lambs', are as well known for their flavour as they are for their beneficial effect on the circulation of blood to the nether regions.

Be that as it may, Amanda knew what kidneys were so I had no need to deliver another Cordon Bleu lecture. Instead, while we waited, she told me something of her life. She had been to Brighton College of Art as a foundation-year student, but her parents then broke up and there was no money. Rather than give up her course she began to pay for it by modelling in life classes for the senior years.

Two male students were expelled for masturbating behind their sketch pads and her modelling career came to an immediate stop. Two lecturers, both mid-twenties and single, offered to take her into their flat. She slept alternate nights with them, and both on Sundays, and they paid her way through college.

Unfortunately her appetites were not satisfied and she became involved with several fellow students. The final straw broke the camel's back when the principal of the college, an elderly lesbian who always claimed links with the Bloomsbury set through her father, an unknown poet, came upon Amanda and a few of her friends.

She and two girlfriends had been standing in front of easels painting abstracts. This in itself was good stuff, except that they were naked and were being fucked as they painted from behind by three of the lads. It was an experiment to assess the effect on the artistic faculties of simultaneous screwing.

Even this would perhaps not have been unutterably cataclysmic in the principal's view had it not been for the audience. A dozen or so students had come along to watch the event and of course had become inflamed themselves. Everywhere were naked tits, bobbing arses and bobbing heads. Cocks stood unashamed, and quim lips lay open, steaming, like so many dried peaches after being soaked in boiling water.

They did a deal. Nothing like this would happen again, and nothing would appear in the papers, if they would all be awarded distinctions and whatnot in their qualifications. The only proviso from the college side was that Amanda had to go, and so she did. And her first action was to get some nude pictures of herself done by the local happy snapper, paid for in the currency which Amanda was fast discovering was like pure gold: herself. The pictures she sent to me and the rest is, or shortly would be, history.

Ah, the kidneys. They were finished at the table in a small, antique copper pan by Jean-Pierre himself. He served them to us with tiny new potatoes, still in their skins, wrapped in a linen napkin, and some baby broad beans, skins taken off, which had been merely kissed with steam and then lightly buttered.

We had a Gevrey Chambertin with the kidneys, its generous, rolling flavours meeting and co-operating on very friendly terms with the deep interest of the meat and the Robert sauce.

For a few moments Amanda was quiet. I think she was beginning to understand the difference between sweet and sour pork with fried rice from the Ho Fun take-away, and first class cuisine served in splendid surroundings.

Jean-Pierre as ever was a marvel. He's as red blooded as the next man, and I know because I once arranged a night for him with one of our secondary models, not a Damsel but a corker nonetheless, in return for half a dozen cases of an extremely good Mosel he happened to have come across.

The girl told me afterwards that he . . . never mind. I merely wanted to point out that, despite leaning over Amanda's fabulous décolletage any number of times, and despite her putting her hand on his to thank him for serving the food, and despite her dropping her napkin – which he then had to pick up right next to her totally bare leg – he never betrayed himself once. What a man.

There were wild strawberries afterwards, with thick unpasteurised cream which comes direct from a small farm in Buckinghamshire every day. We had a half bottle of an old Sauternes with that.

I quite fancied a drop of vintage port and a small

piece of one-year-old Gouda, but Amanda was getting a little excited. She had on a fine silver necklace with a pearl pendant. She kept taking the pendant between finger and thumb and wagging it gently just over her cleavage.

It was time to return to my apartment. I'd sent the chauffeur home so we just took a normal cab. In the back, Amanda was inside my trousers straightaway. I didn't know the cabbie, but he might have known me and he certainly wouldn't ever forget Amanda after she gave him a double-barrelled eyeful of swinging bosom and silken thigh as she climbed in while I held the door. The cabbie almost twisted his own head off trying to look behind him from his seat.

Anyway, I managed to keep her under control until we got into the lift. I live in an apartment block which is for men only, in the penthouse flat. We are all working men, of course. No playboys. We are also broad-minded and very discreet, but I fancy the sight of Amanda on her knees with my cock in her mouth would have been widely discussed, discreetly or otherwise, had the lift stopped on the way up and the doors opened for one of my fellow residents.

If she was hoping to have me coming by the end of the lift journey she was disappointed, but not for lack of trying. Her exertions were remarkable. She sucked, she licked, she skinned him up and down, and went at me like I don't know what. The nearest I can describe it is this: imagine a woman mixing bread dough, and kneading it, with one hand. Can you see the pushing, the turning, the revolutions of elbow and wrist, the grasping of fingers and the twisting of the heel of the hand?

Now transfer all those motions into the lips, tongue, cheeks and palate of a beautiful woman kneeling before you on a lift floor. You have your trousers round your ankles and she has the base of your cock encircled by finger and thumb (don't tell me! Of course. Yours is too thick for that). She holds your balls in her other hand.

She sucks and pumps and slurps and tickles. She seems to get the whole of it (sorry, in your case, most of it) in her mouth. You'd spend inside a minute, wouldn't you?

Well, I didn't. The doors opened on my private floor. She disengaged and looked up at me. I smiled knowingly at her. She smiled at me and wiped her lips with the back of her hand as I pulled up my trousers and tucked my shirt in.

'I bet you can't fuck me for half an hour solid,' she said.

'What's the wager?' I replied.

'OK. I have nothing but my body. You can fuck me where nobody's been before, and I'll put that against five thousand pounds.'

'Alright,' I said. 'Five thousand pounds says I can screw you for half an hour. I'll go beyond that. I'll guarantee you will come at least three times and at the end of it I'll come myself – where nobody has been before. And before this night is over, you will have been fucked everywhere it is possible to be fucked, and I shall have come twice in each, and you will have lost count of how many times you've come. Is it a bet?'

Amanda's hand was already on her zip as she walked quickly through the door of my apartment, held open for her by my man Broadhurst. The dress fell to the floor, the shoes were left behind where they were kicked off onto the carpet, the necklace was dumped on a coffee table.

A perfectly naked, perfectly shaped and rampantly eager Amanda turned to Broadhurst and said, 'Which of these fucking doors leads to his bedroom?'

Following his tactful indication she hurled the door open and pranced through. I raised an eyebrow and nodded towards the drinks tray, and Broadhurst, ever the mind-reader, poured me a large Highland Park. This is a whisky I find particularly beneficial in such circumstances, as indeed it is for singing in the bath.

Draining this and clearing my throat, I headed for Amanda. She was lying on her back on the bed – a large Queen Anne four-poster, by the way, recently bought at a Bonham's sale to replace the ill-fated Art Deco circular one (see issue five of *Sir Lancelot*). Her hands (Amanda's, not Queen Anne's) were supporting her divine upper bottom as she did bicycling motions with her legs.

As I approached, the cycling stopped and the legs were spread wide. I put my own hands under her bottom to join hers in keeping her entrance well raised, and at once gave her the full benefit of my adamant organ.

I saw the little bitch glance at the bedside clock! OK, randy Mandy, I'll show you, I thought.

Making a mental note myself of the time – it was five and twenty past midnight, or 00.25 hours in the modern parlance – when my cock slid into her hot pocket and her legs wrapped themselves around my arse like a footballer hugging a colleague who has just put the underdogs one up in injury time.

I fancied I could hear the crowd roar too as I began the long strokes. In I went, up to the hilt, and out until my knob end was just kissing her wet gateway, then in again, long and slow. When I was fully in, she grasped me even more firmly with her legs, then slackened a little as I withdrew.

After about five minutes of this – sorry, I should say, precisely four minutes and forty-three seconds – I could feel her getting impatient. Her passageway was becoming a little more slippery, and her legs more insistent as they pulled me in. She tried to get me to speed up, but I would not.

Another minute of slow thrusting and she was desperate. She was making low gurgles, and half-silent moans. She sounded like a wooden galleon creaking at anchor when the tide turns.

She drummed her heels on my arse. She made incoherent pleas to me to put her out of her misery – but no. I would just keep going at the same pace. If she had to hover on the brink of coming for another hour, that was just too bad. It would serve her right.

But I couldn't be so cruel. As her head rolled and her fingers dug into my flesh, and a pair of dainty heels whacked into my buttocks in time together, and her throat gave out a mournful howl, I suddenly gave her ten rounds, rapid fire.

She squeaked as she came. Eeeeek! I felt her quim tighten in spasm and the rest of her turn to jelly. OK, Amanda, I thought. First round to me.

She flopped back, her eyes closed. Her legs fell from their wrap-around position, and she sighed. I stayed where I was for a minute or maybe even two, then began my slow thrusts again. She groaned in dreaded expectation. She knew what was going to happen, and looked forward to it with fatalistic joy. Once more she was going to be taken to the very edge of consciousness. She would be screaming for me to release her from torment, and then there would be that delicious moment when I did so.

I fancied playing with her tits, so I held her tight in my arms and rolled us on to our sides. I'm not entirely certain how our legs were arranged, but they were lying in some sort of order which was appropriate for maximum penetration, ease of movement, and freedom to squeeze those fantastic mammaries.

Forty-two inches they were when hanging from the vertical. Now they were pulled sideways by gravity and somehow looked even bigger. Our mouths were together now, our tongues intertwined, her enthusiasm for the game reawakened. I increased my speed a little – not too much, but just enough to be different.

I thought she was going to suck all my teeth out, the way she was going for the kiss under the double stimulation of my cock ramming home at approximately 100 revolutions per minute, and my hands roaming over two of the largest, firmest and most voluminous erogenous zones it has ever been my privilege to fondle.

There was a change now in her. She put her mouth in the crook of my neck and gently bit. She knew, I hoped, better than to inflict embarrassing marks on normally visible portions of the editor. Her hands went to my buttocks and pulled me into her in time with my regular strokes.

I was finding it difficult in the position we were to go any faster. I rolled us back into the missionary position, took hold of her legs and put them over my shoulders. She was wide, wide open, and gasping.

Putting the uttermost energy into it I went in deep and hard – but still slow and steady. I bashed myself against her as my cock zoomed in, then pulled out as far as I could, then zoomed in again. Whack!

There were also many slurping sounds as she got wetter and wetter. My cock was sliding in a slippery tunnel. Would I be able to get enough purchase? Would there be enough friction?

Yes, there would. Feeling her reach, at my modestly tempered speed, that point where she would either come with me over the top or slip away from me, I fucked her as fast and as hard as I could. Her arms were round my head, trying to bury me in her tits. Her pelvis was jerking madly, out of control, and her cries of anguished delight would have had anyone but Broadhurst rushing in to the room with a .38 revolver and a first-aid kit.

Bang, bang, bang. She was there. She quivered like a shot pigeon, squealed like a stuck pig – Amanda doesn't holler and shout when she comes. She doesn't moan, 'Yes, yes, yes,' or emit those yowls and whistles that otherwise one can only hear on old fashioned steam radio tuned to short wave. No. Amanda squeaks and squeals. Very unusual, that. Brings new meaning to the expression, 'Fucks like a rabbit.'

Amanda may have been a happy bunny after two tremendous orgasms, but I hadn't come yet and there were still seven minutes of the bet left to go. As she was now semi-comatose I pulled out and went to my bathroom. There I washed my steaming prick in warm water and scentless soap. I stroked it and felt its strength. Good on you, I thought. My old man never lets me down.

Amanda was lying in the foetal position on the bed, her lovely eyes closed, her breathing beginning to get ominously regular. This will not do, I said, grabbing a handful of hair with one hand and lifting her face off the pillow with the other. I presented the head of my knob to her lips. Unenthusiastically she opened up and I began quietly fucking her mouth.

She didn't need to do anything. In fact her relaxed, let-it-happen attitude was beneficial. I could move my cock about in her mouth as I liked, and push up against the back of her throat. She didn't seem to mind.

I did, though, want some participation from her as I approached my climax, so my hand went to her thightop cleft and searched for, and found, her magic mushroom. She made gargling noises as my cock went in and out of her mouth in time with my stimulations on her clit.

Surprisingly quickly she was activated again and her hands were on my behind, gripping the arse cheeks, and her tongue was at work with her face cheeks giving me the go-ahead I needed. I was astonished to find that her own behind was bouncing on the bed, her body reaching for my finger as her mouth sucked and licked.

My own sensations were rapidly approaching climax. My hands went to the back of her head, leaving her quim gaping and unfulfilled, as I went for my own first coming. I moved back and forth in her mouth, keeping away from the throat, until I felt the sperm surging. Then I gave one last thrust and pumped the lot right down her.

She swallowed and swallowed. She had to keep up with my spurts or she would suffocate. Eagerly she coped, her eyes open wide, taking the stuff in and wagging her tail like an orphan lamb taking to the milk bottle.

When it was all out and gone she pulled back and looked up at me and across at the clock. Thirty-nine minutes.

'I've always liked doing that,' she said. 'The only trouble is, it usually means no more cock for a few hours.'

'Not in my case, Amanda,' I replied. 'Look.'

The reason for my confidence was that the thought of – as she put it – fucking where no one had fucked before, had just crossed my mind and I felt a distinct tremor in my limp and hard-pressed member.

It was growing, but not really stiffening. Amanda bent her head and took first my left ball in her mouth, then the right one. Then, she opened her mouth hugely and took both in. Very, very lightly and gently she gave my testicles a wet massage. I reached backwards with my hand again, to find that her legs were still spread and her start button was still there, waiting to be pressed.

Not wanting to induce any sudden reaction from Amanda in her current situation, I played with the opening of her quim and the damp lips rather than that all-powerful miniature prick. Her expertise at the ball-sucking had had a wonderful effect, and the full-scale prick which waved and bounced above her head had assumed regular military readiness.

I raised her head from its task and placed my cock to her lips. She licked it all round, paying special attention to that sensitive spot where foreskin is anchored to glans.

Now at full stretch, I grasped the curved punisher in my hand and told her to turn over.

Her eyes gleamed with excitement and a little fear. Don't worry, I told her. First, I'm going in . . . here!

I had arranged her flat on her stomach, her legs wide apart. Entrance to the front vestibule was simple, and I began pounding away. I took a quick glance at the clock, not for betting reasons but because I was interested technically in how long it would take.

On the one hand was a well-wrung member, fully fucked and sucked, which had been got back to erection but which had very little sensation in it as I rammed in and out.

But, on the other hand, there was the thought of the tighter little hole to come. Every time I allowed that idea to float into my mind, a new enthusiasm suffused my cock. I raised myself a little on my hands and looked down, watching the hard curve of meat going in and out. I looked at the delicious mounds of her bottom, and felt the delectable touch of them as I went in, and watched them vibrate, a symphony in white and cream and pale pink, as I came out.

The extra excitement of new adventure must have been working on Amanda too because she was becoming wet and slippery already. This, I noted from the clock, was after only four-and-three-quarter minutes!

The wetness and slipperiness were what I was after. My cock gleamed and glistened. I watched it again, pumping in and out, and waited for my opportunity.

She was making noises now, a few low grunts. Then, here it was. She began pushing her buttocks up against me, her body raising slightly off the bed and, more importantly, her legs widening each time.

I got into the rhythm and then, all in one movement, withdrew from her cunt and pushed my well-oiled piston into the Other Place. I hit it hard and without hesitation. I was practised at what I was doing, even if she wasn't, and my assertive, decisive method worked perfectly.

In it went, right up her bumhole, like a knife into butter.

She went rigid. She stopped making the noises. She was totally taken aback.

For myself, I felt a new edge of sensation. This channel tunnel was much smaller than the other, and my powertrain was closely gripped. I adjusted my position slightly, making sure I was perfectly poised, and reached under her ribcage to find a couple of handfuls of squashed tit to feel as I moved in and out of her arse for the first time.

The movement induced a further level of rigidity. Her back passage became even more constricted, something which made my member even more excited.

After a few more slow thrusts she began to relax, and then after a few more she began the low grunts again. I was getting confident now. My cock was moving easily in a still tight but more generous groove, and I could also feel the beginnings of my orgasm.

I moved my left hand from tit to clit. There it was, standing up. I twiddled it and twizzled it. Amanda began humping and bumping. I fucked her arse faster. She humped and bumped even harder.

I grabbed her own hand and put it on her clit. I couldn't cope with what was about to happen and her own needs. She diddled herself while I concentrated full time on poking the forbidden fire.

I was ramming into her now at full throttle. My belly slapped against her back. She raised herself slightly, the better to finger herself and the better to give me range and depth. Wham, bam, wham, bam I went, careless of everything except my own impending flush and the need to spend it in the deepest possible recesses of Amanda's gorgeous arse.

And here it came as I sheathed my sword up to the very hilt. I pushed in as far as I could go and spurted three, four, five, six, seven times. Amanda didn't squeak. She sniffed and gargled, like someone testing the bouquet of a fine wine, and then went floppy. She cleared her throat. 'Fucking hell,' she said. 'Bugger me. Fucking hell.'

Chapter Four

The cab ride to Murdo's publisher-friend's office was about twenty minutes. She had a Georgian terraced house in some obscure corner of NW1 up a cul-de-sac called Osric Street. Taxi drivers, no matter how excellently they had conned The Knowledge, never knew where it was. Even postmen 500 yards away didn't know it.

In between giving directions to the cabbie, Murdo let his mind meander over the past. The publisher, one Sheila Simpson, was more than a friend. She was his mother's half-sister. Murdo's mother was dead, killed in a boating accident, and his father lived a lotus-eating, semi-hermit life on the Greek island of Leros, one of the smallest of the Dodecanese. Murdo went over there occasionally, not that he was tremendously welcome, to make sure his father was still fit and his eccentricities weren't alienating him from the locals.

Murdo needn't have worried. He knew that. The locals were as mad as his father, or as tolerant and indolent. All they ever did was milk a few goats, catch a few fish, and sit in the taverna. Murdo enjoyed the life there for three weeks maximum. He could drink the wine, eat the local fetta cheese, swim, go fishing, fuck the occasional female tourist – usually Dutch or German – who was surprised to find such a handsome young Ingleesh on the island.

Then tomorrow would be the same, and the next day. Then he had to get back to modern life and the buzz. His father, however, had had enough buzz. Perhaps Murdo would, one day . . . Now, where was he? Oh yes, his mother's half-sister, Sheila. When the Sinclairs had all been together as a family, Sheila – who'd married Geoffrey Simpson, the MP – had come to stay while her husband was on a parliamentary fact-finding mission to China.

Murdo had been sixteen at the time. Sheila, at twenty-nine a fair amount younger than Murdo's mother, had obviously done something to excite father's libido because she'd only been there a day or two when Murdo discovered them at it in the second barn, the one where they kept the hay.

Murdo was a virgin. He knew what was what, but hadn't yet done the deed, and when he saw his father gruntfuttocking the wife's half-sister, Murdo's step-aunt, against a pile of hay bales at ten o'clock in the morning, her knickers round her ankles, he saw a way in which the situation could be remedied.

He waited until after lunch, which seemed a terribly long time, before asking his Aunt Sheila if she fancied either a game of tennis, a walk in the woods, or a swim in the lake. All three activities were available on the Sinclair estate.

A walk and then a swim would be the ideal, Sheila thought. Sinclair senior had to go into town, mother had a church tea, and so they would have to shift for their own entertainment anyway.

Murdo looked carefully at the demure woman walking beside him. He was a good foot taller than her, and could gaze for as long as he liked on her jutting bosom, fine dark hair, neat little arms, pert features and so on, without her realising. The effort required to turn and look up into his face always gave him plenty of warning to look away and not be caught staring.

Aunt Sheila was not unlike Audrey Hepburn had been in her youth – in the face, that is. In body she was far from being a waif and stray. She had a magnificent bosom and a substantial, well rounded arse of the type which, Murdo had read in books, men liked to maul and mould.

It was hard to remember that this calm, urbane, sweet young woman had but four hours ago been gritting her teeth over such calm, urbane and sweet expressions as, 'Give me the short strokes again, you old bastard,' and, 'Fuck me with your rhythm stick, fuck me slowly, fuck me quick.'

They walked through the sunshine, talking occasionally about this and that, until Murdo suddenly said, 'Who was it who made that record about the rhythm stick?'

'Ian Dury and the Blockheads,' said Sheila. 'Why?'

'It's just that I thought I heard someone singing it this morning. Over by the second barn, it sounded like.'

'Oh, really?' said Sheila, a slight edge to her voice. 'Where was that, I mean, when . . . er . . . who . . .?'

'Thing is,' said Murdo, 'Mama does not approve of that particular song. But I haven't told her yet that I heard it being sung.'

'Yet?' said Auntie Sheila, cottoning on at last. 'So, are you saying that this song should always be sung in private?'

'Absolutely' – second left, driver, and about fifty yards down on the left – 'and I should have thought that grassy bank just over there, the one with the overhanging tree, was the perfect spot for singing it, wouldn't you?'

Murdo asked the cab driver to wait while he got his lunch date out of her office. The receptionist said Mrs Simpson had to hang on for a phone call from America. She would be about five minutes.

Murdo sat with a copy of *Country Life*, but it blurred in front of him as his memories began replaying again.

Sheila sat beside him on the grass, kissed him, and asked him if he'd ever done this sort of thing before. He said no and began getting his tool out.

'I see,' said Sheila, giving the rock-hard erection a gentle caress. 'Not into foreplay then, are we? OK. Listen, boy. I'm here for another ten days. You can have a quick jump now if you want, but I want you to promise me that you'll make the time and the opportunity for me to give you some tuition in the full rites and rituals of the greatest art. Right? Now. Hit me with your fizzing dick.'

He promised that he would indeed attend her tutorials,

as she lay on her back, lifted up her skirt, pushed her knickers down, took hold of his rampant cock and guided it home.

She expected two thrusts and a premature jack. Instead, Murdo remembered with some pride, his first-ever fuck had been almost as long as he could make them now. Sheila had been a raving, dribbling, sex-crazed lunatic by the time he'd finished with her. She'd come three times before he did, at last. Far from being demure, she'd looked like she'd been dragged through a hedge backwards.

Her slightly crazy mein had been intensified by her eyes, which gazed at him in frank disbelief.

'Don't you tell me you've never done that before. No virgin could have made me come three times.'

'My virginity was unalloyed, O aged relative, and I speak only the truth. But I should very much like to do it again.'

'Not a problem, Murdo. The only difficulties will be, (a) finding somewhere soundproofed enough to keep my noise in, and (b) maintaining enough physical fitness to cope with your father who also seems to be after a regular little bit. Now, if you'll excuse me, I shall pull my knicks up and go home, where a hot bath awaits. Come up to my room tonight. Late.'

A door opened and closed behind the receptionist and an extremely smart, shortish, dark haired woman was walking towards him, hand outstretched.

Also stretched was the yellow T-shirt she had on, a lowish cut one, under a leather jacket and short skirt. Sheila was still a cracker even at forty.

Murdo took her hand and put it to his lips. She looked up at him, smiling, knowing, confident but just a little smitten with her rogue nephew.

'Hello, aged relative,' said Murdo. 'You look highly edible today.'

'Murdo, darling, you say the sweetest things. And not so much of the aged. How are you, my little cabbage, after bonking so publicly with all these teenage bomblets?'

She said this nice and loud so the receptionist could hear, who looked up and blushed. Murdo, by now immune to his peculiar brand of fame, gave her a wink which made her blush all the more. He took a business card from his breast pocket and placed it on the desk in front of the girl. Receptionists, after all, should not be the blushing kind.

'Send me some pictures of yourself,' said Murdo, confidentially. 'In the buff. Needn't be anything extravagant. I'll see what I can do.'

'We all know what you can do, Murdo, darling,' said Sheila, taking his hand and guiding him away. 'Now come along. I'm hungry.'

The taxi was requested to take them to the Mumtaz Mahal near Regent's Park where Sheila was a regular. They made an especially vibrant Chicken Jalfraizi just for her, and she was looking forward to it. Her meetings with Murdo, though infrequent these days, generally started off with something spicy and ended with something hot – but illicit, she being married to an MP. They had to be careful. Murdo, the most famous stud in Britain, and the sexy little forty-something wife of a junior minister – well, the headlines didn't bear thinking about.

Of course, it helped with Murdo being a member of the National Union of Hacks, Scribes and Doorsteppers, not to mention the five hundred quid that every shorthand pad in the country was on to find a Damsel, but no doubt there were a few jealous and unscrupulous editors who would relish the story.

But the pair of them were probably safe at the moment, because there was not an unscrupulous editor in Wapping or anywhere else who didn't owe either Sheila or Murdo a favour. Sheila had published several editors' books and Murdo had made sure that any national newspaper editor he came across was well and truly entertained after lunch by what he called his Page Four girls. They didn't just show you their tits; they would also turn over for you.

To business, Sheila declared, after they'd ordered and the pre-starter of poppadoms and pickles had arrived.

Murdo detailed the difference between his largely fictional descriptions of his nights with Damsels and the actual encounters. He told her about Tamsin and Marilyn and Debbie and Caroline and all the others, and most of all he told her about Amanda. It was criminal, he said, that these girls, young and in the very prime and peak of their lives, should be so ignorant about the most interesting act.

There was pressure from all quarters on young people to do it, and they wanted to do it, and they did do it, but they didn't know how to get the best out of it.

Sheila said there were manuals and videos.

'That's my point,' said Murdo. 'Obviously they don't read the manuals or they wouldn't be so ignorant. It's probably because they're all written by doctors and psychologists, or overweight female do-gooding media pundits. Amanda and her chap don't relate to such people. They think the books are for married people who've got bored with Position Three and want to move on to Four and Five.

'If they look at them at all, they see models pretending to do it, with a commentary written by some invisible authority who doesn't imagine his readers might want to know the best way to poke while standing by the garden gate, or in the back seat of a Ford Escort, or in Amanda's bedroom without her mum hearing downstairs.

'All these manuals assume a certain amount of experience and a middle-aged attitude to sex. What the Amandas and the Tamsins need is an instruction book for their time in life, when they want to fuck like rabbits but are so hung up about their inadequacies that they'd get more fun eating rabbit pie.

'And Amanda's boyfriend, well, he doesn't really want to come in ten seconds. He wants his girl to writhe and pant in ecstasy, like he's seen them do on the films. He wants to be the great Latin lover, but he hasn't got a clue where to start.'

'I hear what you say,' said Sheila. 'But what about the videos? They're frank enough.'

'Yes, but they're positioned as porno, aren't they? Everybody knows that the "education" tag is just an excuse to get steaming cocks into people's living rooms. Satellite TV is the same. Young people like Amanda and her boyfriend do not want to sit and watch a stream of come hitting a girl in the eye.'

'So what do they want, then?' asked Sheila, as the shami kebabs and mattar paneer arrived with chapati.

Murdo paused to spoon a small heap of the yellow cheese and peas onto his plate. He took the proffered kebab from Sheila, salted his chapati and tore off a piece. With his left hand he scooped up a bit of kebab and some yellow slush and placed it delicately in his mouth. It was delicious.

Sheila was doing much the same. Good food would not wait on an answer from Murdo. They munched away for a while, then Murdo began to outline his great idea.

'What they want, Auntie Sheila, is not *The Joys of Middle Aged Foreplay* nor *The Encyclopaedia of Positions Achievable By Portly Persons*. They don't even want *The Good Fuck Guide*, because they don't want a school-teacher to tell them what to do.

'What they want is a book positioned as racy, daring, rebellious. They'll learn from it, but without approaching it with that idea. I shall need a female co-author.'

'And who will that be?'

'That's my first problem,' admitted Murdo. 'Having realised that the essential is not to produce something which says it's a guide or a manual, but to write and photograph a personal record, first I must find my partner.'

'Personal record? You mean you're going to be in the pictures?'

'Of course,' said Murdo, wiping up the last of his mattar paneer. 'That's the whole point. The text is written by the same people who are in the pictures. They describe what they're doing and what it feels like. And what they are doing is not all taking place in a luxurious bed in total security and peace and quiet.

'They're doing it where young people have to do it – Janet and John in a single bed, with Janet's room-mate doing it with John's buddy in the bed next to them. Jennifer and Roger among the bushes, in a tent on the school camp, in the prefect's room – under pressure, see? I even remember doing it in the lounge bar of a pub. During opening hours.'

'How did you do that, Murdo? You're a bloody liar.'

'Wait and see, Auntie Sheila. Wait and see. It will be in the book.'

The waiter brought the main courses – the deep cinnabar richness of a rogan josh, the green and white breathtaker called jalfraizi, an orange-brown prawn bhuna, plus tarka dhal, Bombay aloo, sagh bhajia and pilao rice. With it all on the candle-warmers on the table, the waiter placed his hands together, bowed and wished them well.

Ten minutes' silence ensued while they both tried everything and pronounced it good.

'OK, Auntie Sheila,' said Murdo. 'Are you interested? Or not?'

'I was speculating on the size of your ego, nephew. What kind of a man is it who wants to depict his cock from twenty-five different angles in glowing colour, when he doesn't have to? You don't need to do this. You've got your second million on its way. So why?'

'You might be right about ego. You might not be. It might be a combination of reasons – utter frustration with fantastically beautiful girls who are as much use in bed as a chocolate hot water bottle. It could be the wish to be glorified as the man who fucks for his country. The greedy ambition of someone who wants his fifth million before he's thirty.

'Most likely it's just the next stage in a career which started by accident, and with which you had a great deal to do, Sheila dear. Of my friends at school, the one who was the best at cricket went on to play for Cambridge, Kent and England. The best musician became the leader of his own string quartet which has played in China, Russia and all points north, south, east and west.

'One afternoon just eleven years ago, I found out that I was the best at fucking. Someone sitting not a million miles from me at this moment enjoyed it so much that it turned me professional.'

'Quite. The only problem with that is that poor Geoffrey has never been able to make me wriggle since. His latest idea is to stick a carrot up my arse while he pokes me. It's better, but not like my favourite nephew.'

Murdo, who knew something of gardening, smiled at the thought of Sheila with a carrot up her bum and the well rounded Geoffrey Simpson, MP, struggling and squelching on top of her.

'What variety of carrot do you use?' he inquired. 'Autumn Giant, perhaps? Or Amsterdam Forcing?'

Sheila smiled grimly at him and turned her attention briefly back to the food.

'OK, nephew. I'm interested. I'll talk about advances later when I've worked out the first print run. Not that you need an advance, being wealthier than I am, but doubtless you feel it's only right and proper. But what about the partner? She's crucial. All the girls will enjoy looking at your streamlined body, and we can always retouch the cock to make it bigger.'

Murdo nodded in acknowledgement.

Sheila continued. 'But the girl will have to appeal to the boys *and* the girls. I suspect that most purchasers will be female. The boys will be too macho-bound to be seen buying a book which tells them how to do it, even if it isn't ostensibly an instruction manual. Girls won't buy it if Amanda's on the front. It'll be no use having one of your Damsels, with their ridiculous knockers and boy-shaped arses.'

'For once, darling Aunt, I agree with you. She has got to be a woman-shaped woman. Decent pair of tits, a bit of roundness in the belly, tidy arse – big enough, but not too big. The sort of shape that most women almost are, rather than the shape they could never be. She will have to be early twenties, to have had enough experience but not to be too old for the wee girlies to identify with.'

'If you want one fairly young, the source is obvious. You used the word about yourself. Professional.'

'What, you mean a tart? Come off it! The needle holes will show.'

'Don't be such an arrogant pig, nephew. I don't mean one of those poor lost causes who have to make a living wanking off all you fat bastards of men with dandruff who cruise around King's Cross. I mean a call girl. High class.'

'I don't know any call girls. I don't have their numbers.'

'Oh, come on, Murdo, you can be so thick at times. And pompous. Look. Either you can go up to all the bishops and back-benchers in your Pall Mall clubs and ask them for their little black books. Or, you can look up Escort Agencies in the Yellow Pages and take pot luck.'

'Now, Sheila, that sounds really interesting. I could do a couple of articles for *Sir Lancelot* out of it too. Is that all you have to do? Yellow Pages? I never realised.'

'You know, Murdo, for all your being the Masterfucker of Great Britain, I do believe you didn't. On reflection, I suppose you've never needed to. If you're away from home in some godforesaken hotel, the receptionists and the waitresses will be queueing up. No need to let your fingers do the walking.'

'I think some of the girls I've met in hotel bars might have been on the game. But they never charged me anything.'

'Oh shut up, Murdo. You're insufferable. Now, we've finished our meal, we've decided on the business, and only one choice remains. Your place or mine?'

Sheila's Hampstead pied-à-terre – she also had a house just outside Buckingham and a cottage at Walton on the Naze – seemed more convenient, so that's where the taxi took them. Sheila gave her bottom a little extra sway as she walked up the steep stairs ahead of Murdo, and once again Murdo thought of an afternoon long ago.

She had been in first-class nick then, he thought. Two children and eleven years had made the bottom sag, the breasts dangle and the belly swell. There were creases where there never used to be, and the skin wasn't quite so smooth nor quite such a creamy colour.

Still, who cared about that when she knew so much about what she was doing?

Sheila pushed Murdo back onto the bed and removed his shoes and socks. She sat him up and took off his jacket, tie and shirt, undid his trousers and pulled them down, then finally dug both hands inside his briefs and pulled out the mighty conger.

Keeping one hand on it she pulled the knickers off with the other. He was lying near the edge of the bed. Sheila now stripped herself, not for one moment letting go of Murdo's cock. Always she had one hand or her mouth on it. She was either skinning it slowly up and down as she unzipped a skirt or unclasped a necklace, or she was giving it a good slurping suck while both hands were behind her back at her bra fastener.

Murdo watched her tits being released. They were big, especially for a small woman. They hung like a couple of rugby balls in her current bent-over position. When she stood up, naked, her right hand wanking him, her left hand brushing her hair from her face, they returned to something more like their original shape. She was quite a girl, was Auntie Sheila. The pocket Venus. He tried to think of women like her. There were none he knew with her intelligence and business wisdom. The only one he could think of with her shape was that actress in the *Carry On* films, what was her name . . .?

Sheila liked it in. She liked a tongue in her quim, sure, and she liked a certain amount of build-up. But most of all she liked it in, and with Murdo she knew she could put it in with no fears of a jack too soon.

Keeping hold of his cock she swung her leg over his body and placed the knob head just at the entrance. For a few moments she tempted and frustrated herself, exploring her own doorstep with his end. She stroked herself with it, and tickled her cunt lips with the rounded tip of his batterer. Then, with a momentous decision made, she sat on him hard. In he went, through the doorway, up the passage and bang right into the kitchen.

She leaned forward. Her bosoms hung, waiting to be massaged. Murdo grabbed handfuls while Sheila's hair fell around his face, her head bowed, her half-closed eyes watching her own body slide up and down on her favourite magnetic pole.

Her hips were moving in rapid but steady rhythm. Almost imperceptibly she speeded up, her arse bashing into his thighs with ever increasing force. Faster and faster she went, her mouth open and giving out a nameless sound with every in-stroke.

Murdo watched in near detachment as his mother's half-sister drove herself crazy on the end of his cock. Ow, wow, wow, ow, wow . . . woweeeeeeee! Ummmmff.

Sheila flopped on his chest, her first orgasm reached. Should he lie there, and wait for her to recover? Perhaps he could pull out and put it in somewhere else . . . but no. Sheila was on her feet, hand outstretched. She led him to the bathroom where there was an enormous double shower.

When they were both covered in shower gel and lathered up, she knelt and carefully rinsed his still metal-hard prick with a sponge – a pink one, cut in the shape of an elephant. She examined the cock closely, noting the degree of curvature, the strange, purplish colour of the distended head, the curious paradox of bone hardness and silky softness of a shaft covered in movable skin.

She kissed the little opening on its tip, and licked her way carefully over the whole of the exposed part. She opened her mouth wide and took as much in as she could, squeezing his balls gently as she sucked and bobbed her head.

There was no chance, she knew, of him coming yet. She also knew that if she made no special efforts, but rather just had him fuck her and fuck her, she could probably come four or five times before he did. But there was always this curious urge in her to make him come sooner than expected. One day, she told herself, we'll come together at the first occasion. I know I can do it. But how?

She was employing all her skill and experience now.

Her mouth made many shapes, each stimulating a slightly different part of his cock. She moved fast and slow, tight and loose, noisily and quietly. Her index finger scratched at the skin between his scrotum bag and his bum hole. Her left arm went around his hips and pulled his cock further into her mouth. How she wanted to feel that sudden helpless change of action as the spunk came surging. But no. He was just enjoying it like he'd enjoyed his lunch.

Tired, she looked up. Murdo smiled.

'OK, Hercules,' she said. 'On the bath mat.'

She handed him the bottle of shower gel and, dripping wet, she opened the shower door and walked a couple of steps across the thick carpet. She knelt, her bum in the air, her forehead resting on her hands. Murdo knelt behind her and removed the cap of the bottle. Carefully he squeezed a line of gel along the top of his cock. It felt cold. He watched it as it spread itself around his weapon. When he was satisfied that he was properly coated, he put his cock to Sheila's arsehole and whacked it in.

Sheila gave a low, gurgling moan. Had she put enough work in beforehand, she wondered? She needn't have worried. The tight glissandi of the rear orifice was too exciting even for Murdo and within a minute of hard banging he spouted his hot come into her bowels.

This, he told himself as he leant back on his heels, looking academically at his cock disappearing inside the two ample cheeks he now lovingly caressed, was one hell of an Auntie. Perhaps she should do the book with him. Perhaps he need look no further.

No. Husband would never wear it. Of course not. Silly idea. What he needed for his book was a woman with the knowledge and enthusiasm of the aged relative, but also with the body of youth. His readers just wouldn't relate to Auntie S in the buff, well preserved and desirable though she was.

If only he'd had the idea all those years ago, when she was in her twenties and he was a teenager. Ah, but then, he himself wouldn't have known the score beyond one-nil. It was definitely a problem, this. He had stumbled across one of the great truisms. If he'd known then what he knew now, and if she looked now like she'd looked then.

Her breasts had been firmer then, with solidity in them. Her waist had been narrower, her skin without blemish, her tummy just as rounded but with a more artistic curve to it. How she had yelled that first time. She had chortled, even. Yes, positively chortled – with delight, he might add – as his never-tiring boy's prick had fucked her to the ends of the earth and back again.

He remembered her tits in the sunlight, the first pair of tits he had ever had full range over with no impediments. He had put his hand up girls' jumpers, and undone their bras, and felt first one tit then the other. He'd pulled the jumpers up and got his mouth to a nipple, but he'd never had completely free access to a totally naked pair of tits before. And what tits they had been!

The thought made him stir. Sheila, kneeling before him, head on hands on carpet, was snoozing in exhausted bliss, but she felt the Sinclair rogerer stiffen inside her back passage. She came back to earth.

In the instant she had unspeared herself and was up and standing, a bathtowel grabbed from the rail.

'Oh no you don't,' she said. 'Not even I can take that. Go and stick it in the fridge while I make us some coffee.'

Chapter Five

It took Murdo Sinclair a week to get everything set up. He had certain tasks to complete and arrangements which couldn't be broken, but with two such able – and ambitious – deputy editors as Staz and Frenchie, he had fewer worries than he might have had about leaving *Sir Lancelot* alone for a while.

Seven days more or less to the minute after his impromptu withdrawal from between Sheila's generously stuffed buttocks, a taxi was taking him round and up the curling concrete road which leads to the forecourt of the Manchester Piccadilly Hotel.

This spiral staircase for cars, the taxi driver explained, had been famous once, on the telly. There'd been a chat show, years ago, hosted by the disc jockey Simon Dee and, you see, the opening music was played over a film of Dee driving an open-topped car up this very road. In black and white.

Not tremendously impressed, Murdo paid the man and left his cases to be carried in by one of the porters dressed elegantly in long grey coats.

After registering he gave the porter a ten-pound note and asked him if he'd kindly take the cases up and unpack while a refreshing snifter was taken in the bar.

Over a large gin and tonic Murdo surveyed the scene. Sitting at the low tables were mostly groups of business people, mostly men, mostly bald. There were a few very wealthy looking Asians, obviously local, and a table of Japanese, obviously not.

If there were about ten groups of people in the bar, only

three or four included a female. These women all had a defiant air about their faces, their bodies and their severely tailored suits. What was that expression, Murdo tried to recall? Power-dressing, that was it. These women were power-dressing, making a declaration of independence in a man's world of business, hotel bars, morning meetings and overnight stays.

He wondered idly if the two women who had just walked in were in business, or on it. They looked very much more feminine than the grey-suits. They were dressed to attract men, not to put them off. Surely a hotel like the Piccadilly wouldn't permit professional girls in the bar?

The two went over to the table where the Asians were and sat down to an acknowledgement rather than a welcome. Obviously they were regular girlfriends or mistresses, not new for tonight.

To his dismay, Murdo became aware that one of the groups was talking about him. A couple of the men in the group were telling the statutory girl, a suited, short-haired, bespectacled, fairly stocky specimen about twenty-three years old, who Murdo was. They were laughing loudly at the girl's expense. The girl was getting redder and redder. They must be telling her about the Damsel of the Month. Perhaps they were suggesting the girl should offer her services.

No way, Murdo thought. She was quite attractive, but totally the wrong outline. She was British Standard Pear Shape, not the deformed egg-timer – with all the sand in the top – which his readers required.

There were many nods in Murdo's direction, and glances of respect and amusement from the men but affronted disgust from the woman.

Eventually, Murdo decided to himself, she could take no more. She got up and walked over.

'Are you Murdo Sinclair?' she said.

Sinclair got to his feet, admitted he was, and asked her if she would join him.

'Join you?' she yelped. 'Join you? You, sir, are a

debaser of women and a defiler of bookshops. It's men like you who have kept women downtrodden all these centuries. How would you like your naked body exposed to a load of leering lechers?'

'Are you sure you won't join me? No? Very well, it's strange you should mention my body, because in my next project that is just what I intend to do. Expose myself, naked, to whomsoever wishes to leer, or just look. Imagine. In a year's time you'll be able to stand there, looking at me standing here, and the book in your hand will have pictures in it of me with no knickers on.'

The girl picked up the remains of his gin and was about to hurl when she remembered her dignity. She sniffed instead.

'Will you be here tomorrow?' said Murdo.

'What if I am?' said the girl.

'If you will have dinner with me, I'll be glad to discuss the issues you have raised. Possibly we might commission an article from you on the subject? I have to go now, but when you have made your decision, leave a message with the desk. If you agree, I'll see you in here at 7.30. Until tomorrow, I hope, Miss . . .?'

'Devonish. Ursula Devonish.'

'Good evening, Miss Devonish.'

Conditioned by ten thousand handshakes, the businesswoman was unable not to grasp the offered Murdo right. She felt the familiar firm male. He felt the familiar, hesitant wet lettuce of the female expecting her hand to be wrung off by a man who'd been on a course which told him to shake hands firmly and look 'em in the eye.

Murdo smiled quietly to himself as he walked to the lift. Dinner with Miss Devonish. Sounded like a play title. He had been planning to look up an old school friend of his tomorrow, who had gone to Manchester art college and become a sculptor. There was, Murdo was sure, the beginnings of a major article in this friend of his, who earned his beer money by teaching evening classes. His habit was to pick up one of the students at the beginning of the first term – the students were virtually all female – and move in with her. If that didn't last, he would move on and move in with another.

He was always successful, with young ones and older ones, and he didn't care which so long as they were good cooks and didn't mind him coming home pissed every other night from some lowlife south Manchester pub.

The secret of his success – impoverished, scruffy oik welcomed equally and sequentially into Miss Bankclerk's bedsit and Mrs Divorcee's centrally heated town house – was at the heart of the battle of the sexes. Murdo would discuss it with Miss Devonish and then stay an extra night to look up his old friend.

Upstairs in the broad acres of his room Murdo picked up the Yellow Pages. Under Escort Agencies the first entry was a large display advert: Pinnacle Escorts. Apparently the most glamorous girls in Manchester were available if one rang Angie, and to prove it there was a line drawing of a young woman with a large bosom, a careless hair-do and a direct look in her eyes.

Murdo rang the number. A very cultured female voice answered the phone. Pinnacle Escorts. How can we oblige?

'Ah, yes,' said Murdo, suddenly not quite so urbane as usual. 'I'm alone, here, in Manchester, at the, er, Piccadilly, actually, and I was wondering if you could send someone, I mean . . .'

'That will be no problem, sir. Will you be requiring the young lady for the whole evening?'

'Well, yes, I suppose, I thought we might, well, and, we could have dinner, and . . .'

'I see. And your first name is . . .?'

'Angus.'

'Yes. Angus. Age range, Angus?'

'I'm twenty-six.'

'I mean, Angus, what age would you like the young lady to be?'

'Oh, ah, yes, of course. I don't mind, really, well, I suppose I do, about twenty-three, I should think.'

'Early twenties. Tall, short? Hair colour? European or coloured?'

'Don't mind. Any. I'm tall, you see, quite tall myself, and I don't mind.'

Murdo spoke severely and silently to himself. He needed to get back his sanguine air of calm. OK. She must be expecting him to ask about price.

'And what will the fee be?' he said.

'£25.'

'£25? Is that all? What is that supposed to cover?'

'That is the agency fee, Angus. Anything else is negotiated with the young lady.'

'And roughly how much will the "anything else" be?'

'Most of our young ladies charge £100 minimum. But really, you must talk to one of them. I think I have the right girl in mind. Can I ask your room number?'

About five minutes later the phone rang.

'Hello, Angus? This is Donna. I understand you require secretarial services? The fee is as described by the bureau, is that alright?'

'Well, I . . .'

'I'll be with you in about half an hour. Bye.'

Murdo went to the minibar and pulled a couple of levers. With hand unaccustomedly unsteady he poured a small bottle of gin and a larger bottle of tonic into a tumbler, and drained the lot in one.

Donna had sounded straight out of Sloane Square. She'd sounded like the girls who applied for receptionist jobs on glamorous magazines.

He looked at his watch. She'll be here at about seven. Into shower, smoke cigarette while cooling and drying in large white dressing gown provided by hotel. Start to dress carefully, then stop and decide to remain in dressing gown. Put away clothes.

Leave door ajar. Arrange oneself on bed with another cigarette and another G&T.

Finish cig and drink. She's still not here. Arrange oneself again. Hear soft knock on the door. She comes in, closes the door, and walks the six steps necessary for her to come into Murdo's view. She's very nice, very pretty, about twenty-two or twenty-three, medium height, shortish rich black hair, pale face. She's obviously conscious of her rather old fashioned looks, because she wears the pronounced lipstick and deep kohl eye make up of the silent movie, flapper days, and her dress, he now sees as she takes her coat off, is short and simply cut in tunic fashion.

'Hello, Angus. I'm Donna.' She stood, confident, waiting.

Murdo got off the bed in a slight fluster.

'Donna. How nice. Can I get you a drink?'

'Thank you, I'll have a white wine. Mind if I smoke?'

'No, certainly, do. White wine, white wine, ah. Here we are.'

'I'm sorry about that secretarial business, but sometimes they listen in to calls. Not here, usually, nor at this time of day. Usually later. But you never know.'

'That's alright. I was a bit thrown.'

'Thank you.' She took a sip of the wine and a pull on her cigarette. 'I'm a hundred, in advance. I'll just tell you what I don't do, because that makes it easier. I don't do any anal, or punishment, or tying up. Is that OK?'

'I see. Yes. I rather thought we might go to dinner . . .'

'I do that too. No charge for that if it's extra and a good dinner. Fifty pounds for two hours if it's on its own, no sex, just dinner. Chip shop or Michelin 3-star, doesn't matter. Do you want sex before or after?'

'Oh. Before, I think, er, yes. And, er, after.'

'Let's say two hundred and I'll stay the night if you want.'

Murdo counted out ten twenty-pound notes and Donna placed them in her handbag which she snapped shut and left on the table. She turned to Murdo, sipped and drew, and smiled.

Murdo, remembering himself and his purpose, refilled his own glass, and hers, and lay on the bed, also with a cigarette.

'You look very nice,' he said. 'With your clothes on.'

'And even nicer with them off, you mean?'

Donna put her glass down and placed her cigarette in an ashtray.

She crossed her hands in front of her, reached for the hem of her dress, which was an oatmeal colour and probably silk, and with one simple movement pulled it off over her head. Now she was in lemon yellow court shoes, shining white stockings, and a white suspender belt. Over the suspenders, Murdo noticed, were her white lace briefs under which a darker region could be discerned. She also had lemon yellow pendant earrings and a matching necklace of opaque glass beads.

Her breasts stood out, not big but beautifully shaped. There were large brown nipples, over-large in proportion to the breasts but highly attractive.

She leaned her head slightly to take off her left earring, then the other way for her right. She bent down to take off her shoes and the necklace dangled like an oval frame through which the perfect little plums of breasts could be looked at.

'Would you like me to keep my stockings on, or take them off?'

'On, for the moment, I think.'

The briefs were on the chair back now, and she walked towards him, poised and self-possessed, dressed only in necklace, stockings and suspenders.

She knelt on the bed, took his cigarette from him and stubbed it out in the bedside ashtray, then took his glass. There was quite a bit left in it. She drank it, letting it spill from the side of her mouth. It ran down her chin and dripped onto her left breast. She offered the breast to Murdo's lips. He licked the gin and tonic rivulet from the white plum with the brown stalk.

Her hand went to his thigh and crept up underneath the dressing gown. When she reached his stiffened mainmast she pulled the dressing gown aside with the other hand and bent her head. With her mouth wide open she allowed the cock to enter. Her tongue gave it light caresses. She moved her head back and forth, her lips and tongue and the inside of her cheeks somehow making contact all the way around the hard column of meat, but only just.

It was a teasing, gentle, zephyr of a suck, so unlike the plunging, wrangling mangling which so many girls thought was the suck men wanted.

Murdo sighed. 'You,' he said, 'are an artist. Where did you learn to do that?'

She raised her head from her work and looked at him as if he were slightly potty.

'Where did I learn to suck cocks?' she said. 'I learned it sucking cocks.'

Murdo had never been confronted with such professionalism before. The matter-of-fact way she approached everything was a novelty to someone used to the prurient world of porno publishing and the coyness and secret excitement of sex for free. Donna had done it all before, of course, but more important than that, she took charge. While obviously willing to oblige him in any way short of her forbidden three activities, she would remain somehow in control.

The sweet titivation of her expert fellatio was making Murdo very disturbed. If he – or she – wasn't careful, his famous reputation for staying power would be blown. Ha ha, blown, he thought.

Donna looked up again. 'Do you want to come in my mouth? Or where?'

Her hand, no less skilful than her mouth, kept his prick at near boiling point. She bent a little lower and pushed her little plums together with his cock in between. Her giant nipples were rubbing up and down two sides of his throbbing, almost self-willed member. He watched them, two brown toadstools making magic massage on his cock.

'I have to tell you, Donna, that wherever you learned to suck cocks I have never met anyone so good at it. The result is that you have taken five minutes to do what normally takes half an hour. I think I shall accept your offer, please, if you wouldn't mind.'

Donna once more covered the first three inches of his curving horn with her silk and satin mouth. Deliciously she breathed and kissed, lifting the sensations from deep within him. Soon he felt the surge. She sensed it too and grasped his cock in both hands as she placed her mouth more firmly over the end ready for the spurts.

She rasped the knob hard now, and sucked hard too, and was rewarded with a succession of five or six generous spats of warm fluid which she swallowed eagerly and easily. This was not the girl to choke on it.

Donna kept sucking until the last drop was out and Murdo had stopped moaning. She drew back, admired her handiwork – a glistening, clean prick – and went to the bathroom with her handbag. Murdo heard her cleaning her teeth and gargling.

She walked back in – she really was a pretty girl, thought Murdo, and so nice to have a good round bum and smallish tits for a change – and lit another cigarette. She bent to the minibar, revealing a considerable amount of black tuft, and came to lie on the bed beside Murdo with a new G&T for him and a white wine for herself.

'Next time,' she said, taking a drink and a draw on her fag, 'you can come on my tits.'

Murdo took one of them in his hand. It was a darling bud, a perfect, pouting fruit with balance and shape. He fingered the nipple and felt it move at his touch.

'Next time,' said Murdo, 'it will be you who will come.'

'Listen to big boy! Hey, Angus, listen. I've been doing this job for two years. I've seen men come, felt them come, and seen them fail to come. I've had spunk in my mouth, my cunt, my nose, my ear, I've had it all over me. I've watched it spurt from a man's cock right the way up and over and past the top of his head.

'Every time the man has been satisfied with my work, even if he didn't actually manage the spurting. I know what men like. But I'll tell you this. Not one of them ever made me come. They've licked and fucked till the cows came home, but I never did.'

'Donna, Donna, of the sweet and peerless breast and fine round behind. There is a first time for everything.'

'OK, Angus MacDangle. You make me come, and I'll

give you half my money back. You fail, and you owe me another hundred. Fair enough?'

'What could be fairer, O fairest one? Now, let's get dressed and go eat.'

So far, Murdo was highly taken with his first find in his research expedition. She was capable, beautiful, young and would do almost anything for money. He was beginning to see the pictures – she the silent movie queen, he the dark stallion on whose prick she would ride away.

He became even more interested during the dinner they had at the Kwok Man, one of the oldest Chinese restaurants in Manchester and certainly a foundation stone of Chinatown as it now is, large and bustling. Donna was the first person he'd ever met who could eat Peking Duck entirely with chopsticks. She selected the pieces of meat, spring onion and cucumber and placed them on the pancake, picked up the little bowl of sauce and poured a drop or two on, then folded the pancake neatly into a cylindrical parcel – all with chopsticks.

If Murdo thought that picking up the bowl was just showing off, he was suitably impressed when Donna ate her parcel, without dribbling or dropping anything, with it firmly held in the accomplished, slim sticks.

She did full credit to everything else they ordered, drank China tea, and managed to converse lightly and interestingly right the way through the meal without giving anything away about herself – although she heard all about 'Angus'.

Angus told her about the family woollen mill in Peebles, the affair his brother had had with an aunt fourteen or fifteen years his senior, the other brother who became a crofter near Thurso, and everything else that Murdo could make up on the spur of the moment about the fictitious Scottish family of MacCrian of which he, Angus MacCrian of that Ilk, was newly the head, his father having been recently killed while out stalking deer.

Angus was in Manchester to discuss a possible documentary programme about the Highland clearances which the BBC wanted to shoot on his estate, and no, he wasn't married, but yes, he did have several regular girlfriends, mostly of the twin set and pearls variety. They were, nevertheless, some of them hot stuff once you got their twin sets off.

Back in the hotel room, Donna had a challenging, amused and not a little excited look in her eyes. Whether it was the thought of the challenge, the extra £100 or the possibility of an orgasm, Murdo didn't know.

She began by lying on the bed and saying he looked very nice with his clothes on. He took them off and stood in front of her, a handsome, hard, muscular figure with his cock searching for her like an anti-aircraft gun scanning the sky.

She wriggled her panties off, turned around to kneel, and hitched her dress up over her backside. Murdo was presented with a fine full moon with a dark patch in its centre, surrounded by a halo of oatmeal silk and traversed by white suspenders. He knelt behind her and pressed up close. He felt with his fingers for the treasure beneath the forest and soon ascertained it was moist enough and had a big enough clitty for him to bang against. The thought had occurred to him that her total lack of coming might be due to a small clit or one that hadn't popped out properly, but no, it was there.

He grasped a half moon in each hand and pushed his cock into the forest glade. Her hand came from underneath and guided him home.

For fully fifteen minutes he shagged that girl. He tried long strokes, short strokes, fast and slow strokes. He pulled his cock right out, then zoomed it right in. He tickled her clit with his finger while his prick slid past. She was happy enough, but not grunting and groaning like Auntie Sheila would have been by now.

Without pausing in his rhythm, Murdo pulled the girl's dress over her head and took off the earrings and necklace, she lifting arms or whatever was necessary to help him. He undid the buttons on the suspenders and rolled the stockings down.

For a moment he came out, pulled the suspender belt

off and the stockings off her feet, turned her onto her back, wrapped her legs around his waist and went into her from the front.

Now he could kiss those marvellously petite breasts and the miraculously grand nipples. He could kiss her mouth too – she was quite willing – and meanwhile he could roger deep and long. He decided that the best tactic was a regular thrust, something fairly steady like once a second. Eventually down in the forest something had to stir.

Ten minutes later, his mind on autopilot, Murdo was brought back suddenly to tonight in Manchester by a small, low, sigh from the lovely Donna. She was responding at last.

Murdo began thrusting a little deeper and a little faster. She sighed again. His hand reached down and found her joystick. He stroked it with his fingertip while thrusting all the harder.

He took a nipple in his mouth, then the other, then the first one again, and pushed and pushed. He felt her legs begin to grip him more tightly. He kept banging away, steady as she goes, increasing the tempo only a little every time he heard that sigh.

Her arms, previously held fairly loosely around his neck, went to his buttocks. Her fingernails scrabbled at his skin. Now she didn't sigh – she murmured something. What was it? There it was again. No, it wasn't words. She was murmuring random syllables. It sounded like a Red Indian war chant. Um. Bo. Ba. Du. Na. Pa. Gi. Ha.

He went faster. The chant kept up. One syllable for every thrust. He felt her gather herself for her first-ever paid orgasm. He knew it was on its way. He could sense her entire body readying itself.

The chant was a torrent as he went at her at full tilt. Nabogupitanawomofitubulosukanani!

Then she was crying, weeping, digging her fingers in until it hurt severely, gasping and pleading, pushing her body up against his, desperate for the last few thrusts which would take her over the top.

And here they came. Murdo was approaching his own

climax and decided he could let rip. Switching into overdrive he smashed his cock into her as rapidly as human muscle would allow, and as hard, and as deep. He fucked her with all his might, and as his own tide of sensation swept through him he felt her quim contract and vibrate, just as her mouth opened to emit a jabber of nonsense and her arms let go and flopped onto the bed.

With his final spurt placed as far into her as he could reach, Murdo looked down on this lovely young woman. Her face was wet with tears. Her bottom lip was bleeding slightly where she'd bitten it in her transported state. Her eyes were closed and her chest was heaving.

Murdo bent his head to her heavenly breasts and listened to her heart beat. If it wasn't doing over 130 he'd be Angus McCrian of that Ilk.

Donna put her arms around his head and hugged him to her chest.

'If you can do that again by morning,' she whispered, 'I'll give you the other hundred back and pay for the dinner.'

By morning, Donna had not only done her night's work for nothing and paid for a dinner. She actually owed Murdo a hundred. Murdo, of course, wouldn't hear of it, and instead turned the conversation around to the great project. Donna would be just fantastic as his editorial and modelling partner in *Like It Like That?*

'Darling,' said Donna, in her finest lead-crystal accent, made more breathy by her gratitude for three orgasms in one night. 'I think it would be super. Absolutely super. Problem is, darling, one simply can't do it because of Daddy. He'd die of shame.'

'I'm sorry, Donna, but what has Daddy to do with it? I mean, in your present calling, how can you be that bothered about what people might think?'

'Oh but I can, sweetie, and I am. I'll tell you something I've never told anyone else, and I know you'll keep it a secret. My name isn't Donna. It's Araminta.'

'Nice name. But I still don't see, Minty dear, what . . .'

'My other name is Ravensworth-Clerque.'

'Ah. Quite.'

'Daddy thinks I'm in Manchester living on a grant, doing a PhD in textile chemistry after I took my first class honours at Oxford. He's partly right. But you see, being like he is, you know, giving all his money away to good causes and whatnot, I simply have minimal sponduliks because he believes I should manage on the grant, which he tells me is enough to support fifty-five families in the Third World and so should be more than enough for one woman in Manchester.

'Well, it isn't, of course, so I fuck once a week for my supper. I'll stop when I've got my doctorate. I'll dye my hair blonde, and spend the rest of my life hoping I don't bump into an ex-client. But appearing naked on the end of your cock in W H Smith's? No can do, darling.'

Murdo understood. He could see that one public fuck, never mind fifty printed in full colour, might make things decidedly awkward for Daddy if Daddy happened to be Dr Sedbergum Ravensworth-Clerque, younger brother of the fourteenth Duke of Coniston and the current Archbishop of Canterbury.

Donna left at about six, with £300 in her handbag and a promise to look Murdo up next time she was in London. Murdo, being who he was, could not expect to receive an invitation for a weekend at the Ravensworth-Clerques.

After three hours' deep slumber, Murdo awoke feeling hungry. A swift shower was followed by a soft-collared shirt, cashmere sweater, cords and handmade brogues. He went down to the restaurant. Helping himself at the buffet he was amused to watch one of the Japanese from the bar last night, filling a bowl. First went muesli, then peaches and grapefruit, then bacon and a fried egg. Murdo decided he would have something similar, but in two separate courses.

After a day spent wandering around libraries and bookshops, checking on the sex-manual market, Murdo returned to the hotel in time for a nap before getting ready for his date with Miss Devonish – for there had indeed been a positive response left with the reception desk.

He sat in the bar, glad to note that Miss Devonish's colleagues were absent – so far, anyway. He was on his second large G&T by the time she turned up, looking a little flustered but very charming in what she obviously thought was the right thing to wear for an evening out with a top-shelf magazine editor.

Beneath the neat, economical hair and the fashionably over-large spectacles was the little black dress – lowish and tight across the bosom, where Murdo was pleased to note there was more than had previously met his eye – and very tight across the squarish, peasant buttocks.

Her legs were on the stocky side and perhaps she had been better advised to keep her skirt lengths longer. Still, Murdo got a very full display of underthigh when she sat on the low chair and crossed the pins in question. She would have a Scotch – a malt, please, and yes, a large one.

She was coming on strong, Murdo thought. Dressed as sexily as she knew how – because she didn't know a lot about how – and mixing that with a masculine drink like single malt, she was throwing out a challenge to him. Make any false assumptions based on the low neckline and exposed thigh, and she would be the winner.

There were more surprises for Murdo. He'd expected to get all the usual feminist autoresponses to his exploitation of the female form, but she talked very intelligently and rationally about how, though sexual equality legislation, political correctness and lesbian lib were all very well, women could never be made equal. They could only become equal through a fundamental change in male attitudes, which involved recognition of equality of value in the differences between men and women.

In a mortice and tenon joint, the mortice is as important as the tenon. This is where the lesbian libbers go wrong. They go around in hairy jumpers pretending that they've got tenons too, which only serves to perpetuate the current attitude of men which is that physical strength gives them superiority. They have nothing else left, now that women have proved that with the right training they can be just as good at car maintenance and lorry driving.

Physical strength is outdated in every field of human endeavour except sport and leisure. We don't need it for work any more, and the female's superiority at manual dexterity is now far more important than a man's ability to hump sacks of coal.

Murdo agreed with everything she said but differed on the eventual outcome. There will not be a change of attitude, he said, for the same reason as you can't get the male lion to do much of the hunting. For every man who flexes his muscles there's a woman who wants to stroke them, and for every opportunity for a woman to pose naked in front of men's eyes there are enough suitable applicants, and a great many more who are slightly less than suitable.

'And for every little boy,' replied Miss Devonish, 'there's a mummy prepared to indulge him and wait on him so he grows up the main man, expecting every woman to be his personal waitress. You see, Murdo, I'm not looking for a change in attitude in the male lion. I'm looking for one in the lioness. She has got to stop bringing up rugger buggers.'

By this time they were on the coffee and almond wafers at the tiny Italian restaurant they had both voted on after deciding to go to what looked like the best restaurant advertising in that day's *Manchester Evening News*. Murdo was impressed with Ursula Devonish. Ursula was clearly impressed with Murdo. Would anything else happen?

Ursula had displayed one weakness, and that was for substances alcoholic. She could drink, no doubt about that, and might possibly have watched Murdo slide under the table before her, had there been an equal contest. Murdo, however, had played unfair and under cover of her enthusiasm for argument and booze had managed to consume only half her total.

She was feeling playful. Back in the hotel bar she cocked her head on one side and asked him why he hadn't done the usual male thing and asked her to his room for a drink. Murdo decided to call her bluff.

'I wouldn't use such a diaphanous stratagem,' he said. 'Were I to think in such terms, I would not employ euphemisms.'

'What, you mean you'd ask me upstairs for a fuck?' she said, with bravado but also wondering if a coarse remark too far might have knackered the rest of the evening.

'No. I'd ask you upstairs for an orgasm in triplicate,' said Murdo, quietly, near her ear. 'You see, I'd like to put my tongue inside your cunt and lick you until you turn inside out. Then, when you were helpless and screaming for more, I'd drive my rock-hard cock right up you and fuck you until you blacked out from sheer ecstasy. Or would you like to sit here with another drink?'

In the lift Murdo took her in his arms and put his hands up her skirt at the back and down inside her tights and briefs. He kneaded the large, heavy, cool buttocks. They were built for work, he thought. This woman's ancestors carried water from the well and thrashed corn in the barn. He thought this as, his tongue halfway down her throat, she frantically pushed her pelvis against his hardening prick.

'Hurry up!' she implored him as he fumbled with his room key. Once inside she dashed for the loo. She came out fully dressed still, but Murdo was once again into his white towelling robe, courtesy of the management.

They repeated the lift position, tongues searching mouths, Murdo's hands this time finding no tights or briefs to hinder his grasp of her centre of gravity.

'I wet them,' she told his right ear.

His hands left their meaty groping to unzip the little black dress and unclasp the bra. She shrugged both off her shoulders and broke away for just long enough to get rid of them completely, and to place her glasses on a table. Then she was back in the clinch, thrusting her pubic bone against him.

Murdo's hands tried to caress whatever of her there was available, but she was only interested in deep, deep kissing and – her eager pushing told him – she wanted some cock as quickly as possible.

Murdo pushed her back towards the bed, like a ballroom dancer with an incompetent partner. She didn't know whether to follow him with her feet or keep her body crushed up against his, but once she felt the edge of the bed and had collapsed back onto it, she knew precisely what was what.

If his dressing gown had been silk she would have torn it open, so powerful was her desire. She threw the belt across the room, grabbed his cock in her hand and pulled him into her. Those working legs then circled his waist, her arms went around his neck, and Murdo was locked in.

Oblivious of any subtle strokes or rhythms that Murdo might have had in mind, she went at him like a mad thing. Her eyes were closed, her breathing was panic-stricken, her body was out of the control of her mind.

Within a minute she had come. Every inhibition had gone, every restraint was off. She was not any more the intelligent, educated businesswoman making a philosophical point. She was the frantic hot bitch consuming his prick as if it were the only thing that could save her from death and an eternity in hell. Just as quickly she recovered.

'Sorry about that,' she said. 'It's always like that, the first one. The problem is, with a lot of the older men who I have to fuck, after the first one you don't get any more.'

'Older men? Have to fuck?' Murdo was incredulous.

'Oh yes. You didn't believe any of that feminist crap, did you? Listen, Murdo, when all you've got is IQ – note, please, the small dangly tits, the fat square arse and the stubby legs – then you can't dilly dally with just a few of the very top executives. You can't keep the MD on a string while you fuck the Chairman. No. You've got to fuck every manager in the company.'

'Every manager?'

'Every manager who asks. It works. Already I'm senior to at least five of the bastards I fucked last year. And boy, have they got a surprise coming. But never mind that. I see your cock is still wondering what's going on. Where would you like me to put him? How about this?'

She nuzzled his marble pillar against her cheek while she sucked first one ball, then the other. Wanking him gently she then bent down and took both his testicles in her mouth at once. The warmth was very exciting for Murdo. He could feel the beginnings of his own orgasm stirring deep inside.

Ursula changed her attentions to the root of the pillar, and licked all around it, occasionally leaving off to give his balls another suck. Hearing him sigh with satisfaction she speeded up her wanking and sucked his balls a little harder. The sigh changed to a snort, which told her to be more careful. She knelt upright.

'This, Mr Sinclair, is how I got the move from assistant brand manager to product manager in charge of tinned vegetables.'

Her head dipped and her mouth opened. His cock disappeared inside her mouth, almost all of it. At first he couldn't work out how she'd done it, then he realised that the end had gone up outside her teeth into her cheek. The side of her face was bulging like a hamster's.

Her hands were on his balls, and her tongue reached down his shaft almost to the base. Slight movements of her head were all that was necessary to bring his come shooting up and into her cheek pouch – where, because of the way her mouth was, it couldn't collect. Spunk dripped from her teeth and lips, and thence from her chin back onto Murdo's dense black mat of curlies. She swallowed as much as she could with his cock quickly placed in a more normal fellating position, then bent to his pubic mound to lick up the rest.

When she'd finished, she looked up in triumph.

'That was fantastic,' she said. 'Thank you. Not only have we had a good fuck and a good suck, but I've won a hundred and forty quid in twenty pound bets and probably saved myself a lot of hard work. After all, once this gets around, how many senior marketing men will want to be compared with the great Murdo Sinclair?'

Murdo admired the chunky behind and the solid foundations of Miss Ursula Devonish as she walked away from the bed to where her clothes lay in a heap. She was a long way from Amanda in bodily proportions and a fair distance from Donna the Archbishop's daughter in general good looks. But she was pretty enough and, looked at from the point of view of a man with a few acres to plough and a few cows to milk, she would seem a good practical option.

What a pleasant surprise is in store, Murdo thought, for the stalwart yeoman when he first gets under the blanket with Goodwife Ursula.

Chapter Six

'Yes, it is tiring,' said the girl who was dressed only in a pair of French black lace camiknickers. 'It's alright now, at this time, early evening, but I might get a call at three a.m. I have to go. It's part of the deal. And then I have my classes during the day for my A-levels, and there's my little boy to look after . . .'

'Little boy?' asked Murdo, his arm around the girl sitting next to him on the bed edge, his fingers playing idly with her left nipple.

'Well, yes, it is difficult. But there's the babysitters, and the neighbours, and me, and between us we . . .'

Once again she stared into the distance. She had seemed so promising when she arrived, so smartly dressed, like a young lady of means off to a luncheon party, hat and gloves and the lot. This was obviously part of her act – the upmarket glass virgin who's actually a red-hot tart – but it was the only part of the act which was true.

Rather than a red-hot tart, she was a listless, boring little fart, thought Murdo. Maybe the rest of her clients were content to gaze at her, and rhapsodise about poking something so young and good-looking, but Murdo wanted action and participation. This girl just lay there and nothing Murdo could do would make her any livelier. She was clearly there for as little time as possible and became increasingly restless as Murdo's capacity for long-term shagging became more and more apparent.

Without paying any attention to the real requirements of the job, she tried a standard range of techniques to get him to come. She sucked him, wanked him with her hand, put his cock up her arse, sat on him – all for a few seconds each, and then burst into tears.

Murdo comforted her, gave her a drink and told her to put her clothes back on. She got only as far as her knickers when she started crying again, but it was a self-pitying sort of wailing and not the kind of heartfelt, tragic sobbing which might have induced pity with the financial consequences which Murdo guessed she was after.

He was now as anxious to get rid of her as she had been to get the job over with – but now she was unshiftable. Murdo, his better judgement giving way to expediency, put another twenty pounds in her hand and told her he had an appointment. And that was that.

Half an hour later Murdo was sitting in the Carvery of his hotel, the Birmingham Albion, staring with total lack of interest at a plate of fatless, flavourless roast pork. Why, he wondered, did modern Man insist on such stuff? The Carvery was only serving what the majority wanted, he knew. Boring, boring. Oh fuck. Is Birmingham always like this? Even the escort girls are boring. And as for the Brussels sprouts . . .

A waitress came past. She was big of bottom and large of tit, with not much space in between. A good sort, ideal for child rearing.

'This meat is boring,' said Murdo to her.

'Very well, sir,' said the waitress, switching on the smile she'd learned during training. 'Just let me take it away for you, and go and help yourself to whatever else you might like. Thank you.'

'But that will be boring too,' said Murdo helplessly.

'I'm sorry, sir. Can I get you anything else?'

'No, no, that's alright,' Murdo sighed, and went up to the Carvery counter. The chef, Murdo thought, looked like he'd spent a lot of time in the merchant navy. The chef thought that this suave, tall, dark, handsome man looked like he'd done everything and was fed up with it.

Murdo spoke. 'I'll have a couple of slices of the beef, please. And those crispy outside bits.'

He took his plate, added a substantial amount of horseradish, and retired to his corner, there to plough mournfully through the equally boring beef, made bearable by large and regular draughts of a quite reasonable Beaune.

His blank reverie was interrupted by a very smart-looking blonde in a suit. She sat beside him, legs to the side outside the table. They were nice legs. Her lapel badge said 'Miss Zoe Taylor, Assistant Manager'.

'Mr Sinclair,' she said. 'Room 259. I hear you think our meat is boring.'

She smiled at him, not at all in the way the waitress had. Life was looking less boring by the minute.

'Are you allowed to have a drink with me?' said Murdo, whose mind had switched decisively into another kind of meat and another kind of boring.

'I'm off duty. As of this minute. So I can do whatever I like,' said the girl, crossing her legs and proving they were nice all the way up.

'In that case, we'll have another bottle of this Côtes de Beaune,' he murmured, waving the empty bottle at the waitress with big tits, who nodded and sniffed in one movement, as if to say she knew what they were up to. Bottles of wine, indeed! Huh.

Miss Taylor undid her jacket and leaned forward. Where the open V-collar of the white blouse allowed, Murdo could just spy the beginnings of her breasts, hiding. The swell of them made his prick move.

Miss Taylor looked frankly and without embarrassment straight into his eyes. He looked back. Her eyes were big and brown, which made an odd combination with the blonde curls. Her face reminded him of one of the pictures on his office wall, the pastels portrait of Lillie Langtry. Miss Taylor had the same handsome, slightly cheeky look.

He hadn't noticed much about her figure. She'd been sitting before he'd seen her, but what he could now observe seemed very presentable.

Miss Taylor, call me Zoe, ran her index finger up and down the stem of her wine glass before taking a drink, looking over the glass rim at Murdo as she did.

'Perhaps there's some recompense I can make to you. For the meat being boring, I mean. Possibly there's excitement just around the corner which would make you forget all about Mavis's roast pork. Mavis is what we call the chef. He used to be a hairdresser before he joined the navy and learned to cook.'

The key fob on the table said 259. This, thought Murdo, which was two floors up in the lift and then about a hundred yards along a corridor, was a more likely location for excitement than 'just around the corner'. Thinking of her reputation in the hotel, Murdo suggested that she should bustle off and come up to his room in five minutes.

'Oh yes, I'll bustle off,' she said. 'But I'll be at your door in three minutes, not five. Don't drink all the wine while I'm away.'

Murdo was waiting with two filled glasses when Zoe breezed in through the open door. She shut it and stood with her hands behind her on the handle, easing each shoe off with the other toe and leaving the shoes where they fell.

The jacket was also tossed aside as she took a step towards him, followed by the skirt, the blouse, the tights and the briefs. She reached him totally naked, took the wine glass, and sat on the bed, her legs curled up beneath her so she looked not unlike the little mermaid of Copenhagen.

A fine pair of breasts – 36C, Murdo estimated to himself – hung together between her arms. Her left arm was held under her bosom and her right, her drinking arm, pressed in at the side so that all available space seemed filled with breast.

With his wine in his hand, Murdo stood and admired.

'Come on, Mr Sinclair, or shall I call you Sinkers? Get 'em off.' Zoe was anxious to start.

A moment later he moved towards her, glass in one hand, cigarette lit in the other, and a hard curving cock swinging and surveying the scene. She shuffled to the edge of the bed and put her glass down on the table. Both her hands curled around his prick. She stroked it upwards with her palms, feeling the warmth of it.

'Not exactly huge, is it?' she said. 'I mean, I've seen bigger.' She giggled.

Murdo pushed her on her back, persuaded her legs easily apart with his knees and hung there, expectantly, until she guided him home.

'It's what you do with it that counts, Miss Taylor,' said Murdo, slipping into his basic rhythm straight away. 'I think this is one piece of meat which will not induce ennui, disinterest, tedium or any other kind of boredom.'

She was already wet, he noticed, and within a matter of seconds she was making noises and thrusting her hips up towards him.

Her arms were around his neck and her legs were around his waist. She whispered in his ear. 'Fuck me. Harder. Fuck me. Harder. Harder. Harder! Yoweeeeeeee. Mmmmmm.'

Murdo felt a sharp little pain as her teeth nipped him in his neck. He waited until she had subsided, and then began his slow rhythm again. Not exactly huge, is it? I'll show you, Miss Taylor.

Zoe came four times before Murdo did. They collapsed together and zizzed for a few minutes, then Murdo was up and lighting a couple of cigarettes and pouring out the last of the wine.

'We need another bottle. Will you hide in the bathroom while I ring the porter?'

'No. And don't ring the porter. Ask the desk for Janice on reservations.'

'Reservations? They don't do wine.'

'No, but they can get it, and they do lots and lots of other things. Tell her I'm here. She'll know what to do.'

A few moments later Murdo was answering the door in his dressing gown. A tall, black-haired girl swept past him carrying two more bottles of Beaune and an extra glass.

'Zoe, darling,' she said. 'Lying there without a stitch on. You're a shameless hussy.'

She passed the bottles to Murdo for opening and began

undressing. Murdo paused, corkscrew halfway in, when the bra came off. They weren't big breasts, nothing like as big as Zoe's, but they were absolutely perfect in shape. They were stunningly beautiful, breathtakingly faultless, and Murdo felt his prick rise from its sleeping position at the thought of those nipples being coaxed into action by his experienced lips.

Janice walked across the carpet to the bed. While Murdo poured three glasses of wine, his cock standing stiff now, Janice put her head between Zoe's legs. Murdo could hear the sounds of rapid tonguework.

Janice swung her own legs up so that she could put one either side of Zoe's head. Zoe put her hands on Janice's bottom, hauled herself up so she could look over, and winked at Murdo before getting busy herself with her tongue.

Murdo, not wanted for the minute, drank his wine and poured another before Janice looked up.

'Aren't you going to join in?' she said. 'Plenty of room for a little one.'

'Not you as well,' said Murdo. 'All I can say is you must have seen some extraordinary cocks in your time. I'm not saying mine is the biggest in the world, but it certainly isn't small!'

'Shush, Janice,' said Zoe, wiping her mouth on the inside of Janice's thigh. 'They get very touchy about the size of their willies. Why don't you come on the bed, Mr Sinclair, and let Janice see your mighty prick at closer quarters? I mean, all we can see at the moment is the end sticking out of your dressing gown.'

Murdo did as he was told. Janice crawled off Zoe and took his cock in her hand. Smiling, she bent towards it and licked around the end, and then right down the shaft. She opened her mouth and took the first three inches in, lifting his balls in her other hand.

When she was satisfied that it could not get any harder, she pulled off it slowly, leaving it glistening wet, and then swung around to sit on it. She gave a sigh of pleasure as it sank into her, and closed her eyes in concentration as she began bumping, grinding and see-sawing her way to ecstasy.

Murdo watched her classically flawless breasts moving with her actions. They really were the artistic ideal. Zoe must have thought so too. She knelt astride his legs behind Janice and began fondling Janice's sweet tits.

The sight of Zoe's hands working the flesh made Murdo push up into Janice, and he pushed up even more as she reached a hand behind her, wetted a finger in Zoe's quim, then inserted it into his bumhole.

Janice came with a bang. She exploded, made a lot of noise, and then had had enough. She rolled off Murdo's body and made for the wine, turning when she got there to watch Zoe go down on him.

Zoe sucked hard, and plunged her head up and down. She pulled away and ran her hand up and down the rock-hard meat, admiring the way the skin covered and uncovered the purply-pink head. She bent again, and tickled the tip with the end of her tongue, then sucked it again.

Janice, her interest reawakened, got back on the bed and slid between Murdo's legs. She could get her tongue onto his crotch, to lick his balls and the root of his cock, while Zoe worked on the other end.

No man, not even Murdo, could stand this double stimulation for long, and soon Zoe was gobbling the spunk down as he shot into the back of her throat.

Janice watched, licking her lips, as her friend struggled to keep all of it in.

'Well, Mr Sinclair, I must return to my reservations desk. Zoe will doubtless keep you entertained. If you think you'll have any energy left at midnight, I'll call in. That's when I'm off duty.'

'I'm sure we'll be able to manage something,' said Murdo. 'A little something, perhaps.'

Janice was pulling her panties up. She turned and bent to pick up her bra, wiggling her bottom at Murdo.

'It looks the perfect size for some jobs,' she said.

Chapter Seven

It was the second week of Murdo being away from the office and the two deputy editors of *Sir Lancelot*, Anastasia 'Staz' Wrench-Burton and Camilla 'Frenchie' Tickell, had got quite used to it. Murdo was a masterly, and masterful, editor who had recruited two very classy assistants. They would never be satisfied until they had their own papers to run. Now, between them, they were half-and-halfway there.

Frenchie's first major change was to institute a new series called 'My First Time'. It was to be written by, or ghosted for, famous people. Frenchie was quite sure there would be no shortage of extravert actresses and so on who'd be only too glad of the publicity; the photograph too, if they wanted it. But to start the series off, the article was to be 'My First Time' by Camilla Tickell.

It was late evening. Everyone else on *Sir Lancelot* had gone home, but Frenchie smiled to herself as she tapped in 'Draft Feature, Issue 12' on the computer. The cursor blinked at her from the top left corner of the screen and immediately the memories came flooding back.

It might surprise you to know that I was a slow starter. Not only that, but I was a bookish, swottish sort of girl, rather cold and stern. Looking at my photographs of those days at the convent school, I can see that my glasses and my blonde hair, which I wore up and tightly knotted, gave me the appearance of a young research student, college librarian or apprentice Harley Street doctor's receptionist.

Also very noticeable are the large bumps beneath my school blouse. I always was rather forward in that way.

On the day I want to tell you about, we were on the school trip. It was one of those outdoor jobs. You know, huffing and puffing up vertical hills and sloshing through driving rain. Jolly spiffing fun, what?

We were in a hostel converted from a massive barn somewhere in north Wales. I can't remember exactly where. Was it Llan-something Fach, or was it Betwys-something Mawr?

Anyway, this barn had become a warren of little bedrooms which you could describe as functional, Spartan, or miserably sparse depending on your point of view. There were communal kitchens and shower rooms, and a place – a big place – for drying out sopping-wet boots and soaking-wet socks.

We all had our own little bedrooms, and my story begins with me standing in mine, in front of the mirror – the only luxury which the barn-converters had thought was necessary.

My hair was hanging down around my shoulders. It provided a lightly covering fringe for the nipples of my large breasts, and I took pleasure in watching them move in league with the brushing I was giving my hair.

I ran the brush across each nipple in turn. How they hardened up as I slowly drew the bristles over them, uniquely sensitive little turrets standing guard on top of high hills.

I put the brush down and rubbed myself with a perfumed oil I had bought on holiday in Sweden. It filled my senses with pine and birch and reminded me of sauna baths and the hiss of cold water on boiling hot stones.

The belly I stroked with the oil was flatly curved, just convex, with a focal point of fine white hair where my fingers were irresistibly drawn. I watched in the mirror as I began massaging myself with the index finger of both hands. My arms made my breasts press in together, the nipples looking even more desirable on the summits of tits which seemed to reach forward, eager for a hand to grasp them.

I remember I moaned as I spread my legs a little and put two fingers from each hand in my quim. I rubbed gently, savouring the rise of sensation and not wanting it to be over. I thrust my hips forward at the mirror and gazed, fascinated, as my fingers disappeared inside my own body, then reappeared, glistening with the hot dampness which marked my progress to point X.

Unable to resist any longer, I came, eyes closed, my head full of pictures of nameless boys and unidentified male torsos, with cocks I'd never seen pushing up at me.

You see, at this point in my life I had never been witness to a male erection. The only penises I had ever observed belonged to my father and my brother, and they were slack and dangling while being dried with a towel after a swim.

I had no idea what happened to them when they got stiff, apart from the notion given me by the line drawing in a biology textbook. This was not my textbook, I hasten to add. I'd been shown it by a girl from the High School in the town. The Girls' High School had a much more liberal view of biological studies than the convent did.

So, a prick with a hard-on in my fantasies was in black and white. It was a two dimensional section like the drawing, so you could see the various tubes and whatnot.

As I came by myself that day, standing in front of the mirror, the best my imagination could do was an amalgam of whichever hunks were in the Top Ten or on the movies at the time. They were naked, of course, and calling my name, and they had two-dimensional black and white plonkers sticking out of them at right angles.

There was a knock at the door. I shouted, 'Just a minute,' and put my clothes on at high speed. I must have looked flustered because Sarah, the girl who was at the door, gave me what my mother used to call an 'old fashioned look'.

'Miss Tanqueray wants to see you,' Sarah said. Miss Tanqueray, or Tank as she was known, was our petite PE mistress. In no way was she a Tank in build but she was very fit and sporty, and therefore the one who was always the leader on these character-forming school trips to wet mountains and freezing cold rivers.

'What about?' I said.

'Oh, you know,' said Sarah, smiling confidentially.

Well, I have to tell you that I didn't know, but I got a clue fairly quickly when we reached Tank's room. Tank was wearing a dressing gown. A short dressing gown. An open-at-the-front, short dressing gown.

She had a small, slimmish sort of body, neat and compact, most of which I could see. She sat on her bed and Sarah sat beside her. I stood and watched, my mouth open.

Tank began unbuttoning Sarah's blouse, while Sarah slipped her hand inside Tank's gown and massaged her small but beautifully formed tits.

Sarah, taking the dominant role, pushed Tank back on the bed and kissed her on the mouth, her hands roaming freely all over her body. They writhed in pleasure, and made sighing and mmmm-ing noises and I can tell you I was very soon as randy as buggery.

They stopped for a moment and looked at me. My right hand was feeling my left tit, quite unconsciously. I stopped as soon as they looked.

'That's all right, Millie,' said Tank.

Millie! That's what they called me in those days. Millie short for Camilla, rather than Frenchie short for tickler.

The two of them got off the bed and came towards

me. Sarah sidled up and put her hand on my right breast. She could feel the nipple standing up. She smiled up at me – I was a good deal taller and more statuesque than her – and then kissed my breast through my blouse.

They stripped me, making marvelling remarks about my gravity-defying tits and letting their small hands flit delicately over pale white skin which offered a warm smoothness to the touch. I did have good skin then. Still have, as a matter of fact.

I stayed where I was, relaxed and in the power of my newly favourite people. Naked I reflected warm tones where the light of the bare bulb beamed onto my ample curves, and I waited dreamily for the next stage in the tripartite seduction.

Sarah and Miss Tanqueray stripped each other, kissing and fondling gently as they did. Their bodies were quite different to mine, smaller, slimmer, less curvaceous but equally delicious. Perfect little plum tits stood out from lithe frames, and neat mats of hair, one black, one dark brown, marked the spot.

They stretched me out on the bed. One leg was resting on a pillow, the other had its foot on the floor. Sarah knelt beside my hips and began tongueing. At first she kept the tip of her tongue working around the entrance to my pleasure cave, but then began bolder incursions and was soon pushing the whole of her tongue right inside.

I sighed with enjoyment as Miss Tanqueray joined in, her tongue working over breasts and nipples then leaving these to fingers and palms as it traversed my long neck, found my lips and forced its way between them.

My arms held Miss Tanqueray tightly as we kissed, a fierce passion engulfing us. Sarah had her head squeezed between my Junoesque thighs as the kiss from our PE mistress awakened pure lust in me, gratified as it came by another girl's tongue inside my quim.

My hands searched Miss Tanqueray's body, found the way in, then pulled the smaller woman onto the bed. Miss Tanqueray found her knees being placed either side of my upturned face – I was a very quick learner – and soon she felt a wet and warm licking along the inside of her thigh. She adjusted her position so that I could get my tongue right in her hole. With Sarah's help I got two pillows under my bottom so she could better nibble at the edges of my quim.

Sarah sucked her index finger and then examined it, making certain there was plenty of spit anointing it. Then, with precision and care, she pushed her finger into my puckered bumhole! I squeaked. Then I sighed. This was heaven. While she became more and more urgent and active with her tongue, flicking the erect end of my clit and rubbing her rough tastebuds over the sensitive flesh, she was also shagging my arse. The finger moved slowly at first, then accelerated, taking its time from the tongue.

I could feel myself going. I was floating away, transported on a magic carpet of double sensation. I forgot to lick Miss Tanqueray as the approaching orgasm made me oblivious to everything else. Faster and faster went Sarah's elbow. Deeper, quicker and more noisily her tongue plunged in and out. My hips jerked madly up and up as I felt a rush and a tide of impulses take me over completely and I shouted at the top of my voice as my classmate and my teacher brought me to the very pinnacle of experience.

And may I tell you that my first time with a man, which happened about six months later, was nothing compared to 'My First Time'.

Things have got better since, of course!

Camilla keyed in the spelling checker, got up from her desk and went out into the main office and the coffee machine. Writing that article had made her randy. Strange, she thought, sipping her coffee. One would think that working here would inure one to sex and sexiness. But it didn't, not altogether anyway.

She put her coffee cup down on top of the filing cabinet and walked out of the office. On the floor below was a firm of solicitors, very upmarket solicitors, and one of them called Paul was an acquaintance of Camilla's. More than an acquaintance, really.

Camilla had just had an idea. As a supplementary to 'My First Time', perhaps done as an extended caption to the photograph, there would be a short summary of the writer's most recent bit of rumpy-pumpy, to contrast with the earliest virgin gropings.

What should she call it? 'Last Night on the Back Porch'? In any case, Camilla had decided to write her piece from real experience, and she was off now to do the fieldwork. She knew where midnight oil was burning. It was one floor down, and it would be easily bright enough to do her research by.

Within three minutes of Camilla's placing the coffee cup on the filing cabinet, a certain handsome, slightly grey-haired solicitor had something rather more scrumptious than a memo landing on his highly polished desk. It was the deliciously naked rear of Camilla, who was shaped rather like the fifties film star Jane Russell, she of the tight sweater and personally designed bra.

Camilla had been wearing a garment Jane Russell had never worn, and which nobody else in London was wearing or had worn for years. She walked into Paul's office and immediately wriggled out of her chamois leather hotpants – no room for knickers underneath – and sat engagingly with her back to him on the edge of the desk, her knees opening and closing in a casual way and her legs swinging as they might have done had she been sitting on the school railings waiting for the boy who carried her books home.

Paul got up, walked around to her and placed his hands on her truly magnificent pair. They were big. Very big indeed. After a judicious fondle to remind himself of a great natural phenomenon, Paul's hands went behind

Camilla and under her sweater, to find the clasp of her bra. Such a flimsy thing, he thought, to keep such weights in place.

With the clasp undone and the breasts released from their prison, Camilla raised her arms to allow the sweater and bra to be peeled off. While Paul amused himself on the slopes of two of his favourite mountains, Camilla's hands were busy too. They undid the genuine bone buttons of his fly, delved inside the blue worsted with the chalk stripe, found the gap in the silk and cotton mixture shorts and brought into the open Paul's stiff and pulsating cock.

Camilla opened her knees a little wider and shuffled forward on her bottom – a bottom which perfectly matched her outrageous tits. This was a bottom to be reckoned with, a big, round planet whose orbiting during a perfectly ordinary high-heeled walk could make men fall to the floor, gibbering.

She pulled Paul towards her by the cock. He pushed when she'd got his knob end in position, and sank home gratefully while keeping going his exploration of two of the best known of the Himalayas.

Leaning slightly back she wrapped her legs around his trousered backside. His hands went down to her buttocks. She leaned back further until she was on her elbows, lying across the desk top, watching in satisfied amusement as Paul, immaculate as ever in his suit, slowly pumped his way up the sacred river, through caverns measureless to man, down to the sunless sea.

Paul for his part loved feeling Camilla's arse, he loved looking at her astounding breasts, he loved watching her watching him, and he loved seeing his cock going in and out of her blonde-fringed jampot. He could take controlled, civilised enjoyment from all these factors with the added frisson that he, apart from one of the post boys, was the only man in the building, which was home to about ten firms of accountants, solicitors, stock brokers and, of course, publishers, whom the lovely Camilla graced with her favours.

The post boy got it because he had the biggest dick in the universe, as had been proved at last year's all-building Christmas party. He was Camilla's toy boy. Some toy. Some boy.

But with him, Paul, Camilla did it because she liked him. She liked his charm, his elegance, his greying temples and his unflappability. Not for the first time this was tested and found good when the post boy in question came barging in to the office unannounced, thinking that at this hour nobody would still be working.

'Sorry, guv,' said the lad, seeing the perfectly trousered rear of one of London's leading solicitors moving in and out to a well known tempo, with two naked legs wrapped around it.

Camilla gave him a wink over Paul's shoulder as he left the envelope on the desk beside her naked flesh. Paul merely said, 'Quite alright, old boy,' and kept thrusting.

As the door closed behind the lad, Paul increased the tempo. Camilla's smile became less urbane and more excited. She narrowed her eyes and concentrated on tightening her quim muscles as much as she could.

Paul was banging hard and fast, his cock ripping in and out like an engine. Once again he transferred his hands to her tits and squeezed as much as he could get into each palm, palpitating them in time with his cock pushing deep inside her.

Camilla, with a tiny cry, felt herself flood moments before the hot stream surged from Paul. After a few moments of contemplating each other, Paul withdrew, satisfied for the moment.

Camilla, feeling only that she'd just got going, picked up her clothes and, not bothering to put them on, swaggered her way up the stairs to her own private office where she knew the post boy would be waiting. Oh well. So it would be the post boy in issue 12, not the solicitor. Probably just as well. And she would be able to wax lyrical about the fantastic size of his cock.

Chapter Eight

Not five minutes after Zoe left him, Murdo was drifting off to sleep. He was beginning to lose heart about this project of his. He had thought it would be fairly easy to find the right partner for the manual, but everywhere there were difficulties.

Maybe he'd chosen the wrong method, looking among professional girls. Maybe he should have tried the amateurs. I mean, look at Zoe and Janice. And all those girls he'd had such fun with at house parties when he was a youth. Most of them were married now, of course, with children called Giles and Miles.

So, the great Murdo was being beaten at a game he thought he knew. Murdo Sinclair. Losing his touch. Losing his bottle. You'd think he was some wet-behind-the-ears boy, the way he'd carried on with these tarts. He'd got nowhere. He was useless. A failure. What to do, what to do? If only he could get to sleep . . .

It was a beautiful summer's day at the great country house and the daughter of the noble family, Janice, was playing tennis with her cousin Murdo. Janice was about eighteen years old but seemed so much more assured and worldly wise than Murdo, the twenty-six-year-old teenage boy.

He was far too good for her at tennis, though, and too powerful, but he let her make a game of it. His favourite shot that day was the forehand pass, not for any sporting reason but because this meant the ball would end up in a corner where the mower hadn't reached, and Janice would have to spend a few extra moments bending down looking for the ball.

She knew what she was doing and made certain that Murdo got an eyeful of her bum and white frilly knickers. Zoe, the parlourmaid, was watching the game while half busying herself with a tray of coffee. She sniffed disdainfully as she saw her mistress's shameful flirting.

The problem was, thought Janice, if yesterday and the day before were anything to go by, knicker-gazing was as far as Murdo would progress.

Janice had given him the eye and the eyeful, and over lunch she'd dropped hints so heavy she thought they would make a hole in the carpet, but the handsome Murdo, the athletic, clean cut, strapping youth of twenty-six going on sixteen, failed entirely to pick them up.

Janice was desperate and took desperate measures.

'Zoe,' she hissed as she was towelling herself at the courtside. 'I'm going to be indisposed.'

'What?' said Zoe.

'Ill. Sick. Unwell. Less than one hundred per cent. I'm going to go to my room and lie down. Your job is to get Murdo to come up there to visit me in my hour of need.'

'Bollocks to that. I'm not pimping for you. Not fucking likely.'

Zoe was a servant, but when it came to sex games and mutual fun, servant and mistress were more than equals. Zoe was thus well versed in the art of servant-mistress relationships.

'But Zoe!' pleaded Janice. 'How else am I going to get him in my bed? Look, I tell you what. You can go in the spyhole and watch.'

'And fifty pounds,' said Zoe.

'Fifty quid? Shit a brick. Alright. Zoe, you will go far.'

With the bargain fixed, Janice began feeling faint. Murdo was concerned but he stopped short of giving her his arm. Zoe eventually had to take over and usher her young mistress back to the house.

'After lunch, suggest he comes up and reads to me,' said Janice. 'And make sure he does it, or no fifty pounds.'

'And no live show for me to watch,' said Zoe.

Janice bathed, read a few magazines, and then as the time approached reviewed her wardrobe. There were one or two items in it which would have made her father raise an eyebrow and it was one of these she selected, a short frilly nightie.

Standing and looking in the mirror it came to about halfway down her thigh. The neck was high, tied with ribbon.

Lying down on the bed, on her tummy, on top of the bedclothes, if she wriggled down slightly, she could feel the hem of it rising. Just across the top of her legs was where she wanted it, covering her bunch of curly hairs by the barest fraction. Or, maybe, allowing a little bum cheek and just a few hairs to show.

She heard the door open, and Zoe's voice saying, 'Go on, go in. I've got to be off to see to the tea,' and the door closing, and the footsteps across the carpet which stopped short as Murdo caught sight of her.

Two more sounds followed – a loud gulp from the man/boy, and a very, very faint sliding sound as Zoe moved the spyhole cover back in the old priest-hole and began watching events.

Janice stirred in her pretended sleep, feeling the edge of her nightie rise a little further. Now the boy would be able to see some bottom, and the hairs, peeping out. Either he's going to turn and run, she thought, or he's got to come over here and do something.

She heard the footsteps. He wasn't going to run! She heard him breathing heavily. She stirred again, only a little, and opened her legs a tiny bit wider. Now he would be able to see the beginnings of her quim. Surely a hand would descend on her backside, or a finger trace a gentle path up the inside of her thigh.

Instead there were sounds she could easily recognise from those made by her own jodhpurs after riding. He was opening his flies. Janice heard the hand search inside and bring his cock out. Hell's bells, he's going to leap straight on and give me one from behind!

Instead she heard him wanking. She could hear his hand

sliding up and down and his breathing becoming more disjointed. This was no good, no good at all.

Janice turned in her 'sleep' onto her back, her legs apart, her nightie up around her waist. She opened her eyes and looked right at a stiff cock being masturbated.

'Murdo, darling,' she said. 'I didn't know you cared. Come here, my sweet, and let me do that for you.'

Murdo, struck dumb by the triple horror of a half-naked girl finding out he was looking at her, and of anyone finding out he wanked, and of a girl seeing his erect cock, could do nothing but obey.

He took the two necessary steps towards the bed. Janice swung herself round so she was sitting on the edge of the bed, her nightie primly covering her thighs down to her knees. She leaned forward. Murdo could see down the top of her nightie. He could see the swelling mounds of two perfect young breasts.

And then her hand was on his cock! Gently, slowly, she moved her hand, feeling the stiffness, enjoying the velvet feel of the warm skin. She gave him another heavy hint by pulling on his cock as if to bring him nearer. He didn't move, so she shuffled and bent her head towards the purple nut which, she noticed, looked liable to explode at any moment.

She opened her mouth to take it in, her hand sliding down to weigh his balls, and he came. The spunk hit her in the face, so she moved, her mouth open, and managed to collect some of it. She licked her lips and looked up at the red-faced boy.

'Always liable to play your drop shot too early, Murdo. Now, take your clothes off and come and lie down beside me.'

Murdo, now entirely in her power, did as he was told. She lay back on the pillows, revealing her thighs once again. Murdo crawled towards her across the bed like a dog, his pizzle swinging beneath him, already starting to grow again.

She took his hand and placed it on her thigh, and moved her legs apart. He pushed slowly up and tried to get a finger into her quim but didn't seem to have the technique.

'Never done this before, Murdo?'

He shook his head, unhappy, embarrassed.

'And you one of the over twenty-fives. Well, I never did. Watch me,' said Janice, showing him how to put his fingers in and how to massage the right parts. In less than a minute she made herself come, a small, private orgasm but the first of several, she hoped, some of which might be bigger.

Murdo's cock was standing stiff now. He knelt upright, his fingers busy trying to do what Janice wanted, while she played with his prick.

'Never fucked a girl either?' said Janice. He shook his head again.

'Very well. Now's your chance.'

She sat up and pulled her nightie over her head. For the first time in his life, Murdo saw a girl of fuckable maturity with no clothes on. His cock jumped in Janice's hand.

She opened her legs wide, pushed him down, and guided his cock into its hot, wet haven. He jerked like a fish on a gaff and came after half a dozen movements.

'Murdo!' she said, reproachfully. 'I can see this is going to be a long tutorial. Thank goodness you boys can get hard again so quickly. Now, while your little willy gets its strength back, we're going to have a lesson in cunt-eating.'

She took his head between her hands and steered him to the inside of her thigh. Her legs were wide apart, her knees pulled up, and everything was fully exposed to the pop-eyed stare of Murdo, who had seen nothing like this since he and his baby sister used to go in the bath together all those years before.

Then, of course, the difference between boys and girls was simply a matter of curiosity. Now it was a matter of instincts and wild urges which were to be channelled into controlled actions if Janice was to get any satisfaction that afternoon.

Holding him by the ears she placed his face near the junction of thigh with crotch.

'Kiss me,' she commanded. 'On the white skin near the freckles. That's it. Now, gently try and lick the freckles off. Good. Move up a little. Explore the fringes of my cunt. Use the end of your tongue, gently, gently, good boy. Now, push your tongue in the crack – aaah, nicely does it – and push it up to the top. There. Feel a little bit of a thing sticking up? That's called the clitoris. That, my dear heart, is what little girls are made of. Sugar and spice and a clit. Shortly you will be putting your puppy dog's tail in next to it, but for now I want you to act like a snail and crawl all over it with your slimy tongue.'

While Murdo gradually got the hang of strenuous licking and the proper use of the darting tongue, Janice lay back and enjoyed it. She saw her maid Zoe's wide eye against the spyhole and gave her a little wave.

'Murdo, the time has come for you to go deeper. Push, boy, push! That's it. Lick harder. Harder!'

Murdo, thoroughly enjoying himself at last, nuzzled his face into her quim enthusiastically and licked her inside and around and up and down. What he lacked in finesse he made up for with energy and attack.

Janice was approaching her first serious orgasm. The juices from her quim ran freely and soaked the man/boy's face. Life was becoming more and more noisy as Murdo slurped and slipped in the stream of fluids and Janice shouted and halloo'd with joy.

'Come on, Murdo, come on! That's it, that's it, yes, yes, again, in, in, stick it in, harder, harder, harderrrrroooo!'

Murdo, his nose bruised by the thrustings of Janice's pubic mound and his senses bounced out of their normal settings by her rapidly bucking buttocks, emerged from the fray wet and smiling.

'Did I do it properly?' he asked.

'Oooohhh yes, Murdo sweetie, you did it properly. How's your cock? I want a fuck.'

His cock was almost hard. She lay him on his back and went down, eagerly, pulling his cock up to full alert with her vacuuming lips. No sooner was it standing than she was on him, her hips gyrating in movements Murdo never knew existed.

Prone, he looked up at his lovely cousin Janice, leaning towards him, a hand either side of him on the bed, her titties dangling and swinging as, with eyes closed, she fucked herself on his prick.

Amazingly – to Murdo – she was there again in a very short time, and she was shouting again as she experienced a gigantic, quivering coming that soaked his own pubes and thighs with liquids.

Now in top gear, Janice realised that Murdo hadn't shot on this occasion so she leaped off him and took his cock in her mouth. She plunged and she reared, and she sucked like water going down a plug hole. Murdo flapped his hands helplessly as he felt the spunk rise and then flow into her throat.

She swallowed, and wiped her mouth like a very thirsty person finishing her first drink and watching as the glass is filled again.

Murdo's cock looked limp. Janice scratched his balls in a leisurely way and thought that perhaps the fun was over for the moment.

'What's your dirtiest thought, Murdo?' she asked, mischievously, stretching her body in a massive yawn and placing one of his hands on her tits.

'I don't know,' he said, plucking up the courage to massage and fondle. 'They're just general, of girls, with no clothes, or impossible ideas like my mother's friends asking me in for tea and then putting their hands in my trousers.'

'And whose hands are they that actually get into your trousers in reality?'

'Mine, usually. I mean, always.'

'Always, Murdo? Are you trying to tell me that of those nice pretty boys at your school, not one of them has ever had his fingers wrapped around your cock? Tell the truth, now.' To emphasise her point, Janice grabbed his slack penis in her fist as she would a branch she wanted to break off a tree.

'Well, I mean, they all . . . it's usually . . . yes, I suppose I have been . . .'

'Naughty little poofter woofter! Can't have this. Illegal, you know, even among the upper classes. Now, fuck off, there's a dear, because I have one or two things to attend to.'

'Can I come again and see you? Tomorrow? Tonight?'

'Not tonight,' said Janice, suddenly getting rather bored with her handsome learner-lover. 'I'm going out.'

'Out? Who with?'

'What's it got to do with you, who with?' said Janice, sharply. Murdo was good looking, but now she'd had his novice cock he didn't hold quite the attraction he'd had before.

'Well, I thought, I mean, you and me, us . . .' He tailed off, lamely, as he noticed the angry sparkle in her eye.

'Listen to me, Murdo Sinclair MacSinclair of that Ilk and Laird of My Arsehole. Just because you've had your noble cock up my fanny, and just because you have spilled your blue-blooded seed on my chin, it doesn't mean to say we're fucking engaged. Now, piss off.'

Zoe came into the room soon after Murdo had slunk away.

'You were a bit hard on him, weren't you, Miss Janice?' she said. 'And he had such a nice cock.'

'What knowest thou of cocks, thou fat tart?' said Janice. 'Here's your fifty quid. Now, you can piss off too.'

Immediately in the dream it was the next day. It rained so there was no tennis. Janice sat in her room, reading. Coffee was brought up, but instead of the maid it was Murdo with the tray.

'Just put it down there, will you?' she said, recrossing her legs so that he got a glimpse of thigh. 'Well? What do you want?'

It was fairly obvious what Murdo wanted. His trousers were bulging with it. However, he could find no words to express his desires and so his anxious bulge had to speak volumes for him.

Janice's hand crept casually to her neck and undid the buttons at the top of her summer dress. She slipped her hand inside and luxuriously felt her own tits.

'Stay where you are!' she told him, crisply, as he began a lurch towards her. 'And take your clothes off.'

Without a word he did as he was ordered, she feeling her tits the while.

'Now, wank it. No, I'm not going to wank it,' she said, as he again took a hopeful step towards her. 'I want you to come into the cream jug. Go on. Wank it. Imagine it's Smith Minor doing it behind the cycle sheds.'

His hand began to move faster as Janice eased herself into a new position on the chair which allowed her to pull her dress up and show him her knickers. In front of his eyes she pulled the gusset to one side and played with herself with both hands, pulling her quim lips wide and pushing several fingers in and out.

He dashed for the coffee tray with a groan and held the cream jug to his cock end. Janice watched as the stuff oozed out. She stood, her fingers to the last fastenings of her dress, obviously ready to take it off.

'Now, get yourself a nice creamy coffee,' she ordered, unbuttoning, but not lifting the dress right off until she had made him drink all his own spunk mixed with coffee and cream. By now his prick was hard again, the sight of a naked Janice – at least, naked except for a skimpy pair of panties – having the expected effect.

She turned away from him and bent over, pulling the thin material of the panties down as she did so. His hand went back to his cock as he watched her rounded buttocks revealed and the knickers fall to the ground. She kicked them to one side, spread her legs and then looked at him upside down, from between them.

'You're not allowed to touch. Only to wank,' she said, her fingers running up and down her thighs. She reached up and under and pulled her buttock cheeks apart so he could see her bumhole.

'Would you like to put your cock in there?' she said. 'Well, maybe one day. But not today. Today, you're going to have another wank. That's it. Faster. Bend your knees. Come on, faster, faster.'

She picked up her panties, stood upright, and walked towards him. She pulled his hand away from his cock and wrapped it in the knickers. Three or four pulls and she had him coming, his sperm seeping into the thin cloth.

That afternoon Janice kept to her room again and, of course, it wasn't long before the rampant Murdo was sniffing around. Janice had on a silk dressing gown fastened only at the waist with a simple tied belt. Most of both her tits were visible as she lay on the chaise longue, reading, her back on the raised end with cushions, and one knee raised to allow the silk to fall away and reveal her slim legs.

'Well, hello, if it isn't young Master Stiffcock,' said Janice, languidly scratching her quim as she turned a page with the other hand. 'Well, don't just stand there. Get your knickers off and we'll get down to business.'

With such a promise, the naive Murdo was stripped in a twinkling, and he walked towards Janice, hand on cock, almost with a swagger.

'Zoe!' called Janice. 'He's ready.'

The bathroom door opened and the parlourmaid entered, dressed in her uniform except, Murdo noticed, the skirt seemed a lot shorter and – crikey – there was no blouse under the pinafore top. Her tits kept showing themselves as she walked towards him.

Zoe the maid pushed Murdo backwards towards the chaise. Janice got up to allow her to lay him out on it, then stood behind her and thrust both hands from behind into her ample bosom beneath the starched top.

While Janice mauled Zoe's knockers, Zoe grasped Murdo's prick firmly and brought him off in a few swift and expert flicks of the wrist.

'See what I mean, Zoe?' said Janice. 'Such a disappointment, boys, aren't they? I think I'll stick to older men and other girls.'

The two of them fell to the floor and grappled and fumbled and pulled. Murdo found himself staring at two intertwined, writhing naked females and he gazed, fascinated, as they went into the sixty-nine position, tongues slurping each other's quims and bums, then they spun around so they could eat each other's nipples.

His cock, hopelessly hard again, demanded relief and he could not stop his hand going to it and moving the skin of it slowly up and down. How he wished he could stick it between Zoe's tits or, even more exciting, in that small hole of Janice's he'd been promised one day.

His hand was going faster now and he would have come had Janice not noticed and tapped Zoe on the shoulder.

'Come along, young master,' said the parlourmaid. 'Can't have you doing everything for yourself.'

She grabbed his cock in her right hand and slid her left down behind his balls and, winking her eye, pushed a finger up his arsehole.

Just a few more skilful flicks and he was coming again, this time all over Zoe's upper bosom. With each spurt she thrust her finger in harder so he groaned with pleasure and his knees buckled.

'Look at that mess he's made,' said Janice. 'You will have to be punished, you naughty boy. Zoe, go and clean yourself up and bring me the you-know-what.'

'Er, what's the you-know-what?' asked Murdo, nervously, as the naked Janice made him bend over the end of the chaise. She had some rough hairy string, the sort the farm used for hay-baling. She tied his ankles to two of the chaise's legs, and his left hand to the miniature balusters which supported the back. Only his right hand was free but, with him being bent over so, it wasn't much use.

'The you-know-what is a certain item which is kept ready for those special times when punishment must be meted out to those who deserve it. Like you. Ah, thank you, Zoe.'

Murdo tried to strain his head around to see but couldn't. He heard a swish through the air and then felt a stinging pain across his buttocks.

After years of public school training, he didn't utter a sound.

'Your turn, Zoe. And put your back into it.'

She certainly did, and her aim wasn't as good. The cane fell across the lower part of one buttock, the upper part of the opposite thigh, and just caught the tip of a ball. Murdo felt sick.

'Zoe,' said Janice. 'That won't do. Must keep to the target area. Can't be tampering with these – and here she lifted his bollocks with the cane – 'or there might never be another Mull of Kintyre, or whatever it is. If you can, confine your stripes to this area here. Swish. See?' Zoe did see.

'And the next one, Murdo,' continued Janice, 'is for being such a fucking little creeping Jesus. Good shot, Zoe. And this one, Murdo, which I'm going to give you, is for being a show-off on the tennis court. There. Oops, just a touch too hard, possibly. Zoe? Oh, cracking shot, Zoe. That was for prem jack, or almost coming in your trousers. And that, what a beauty, was for wanking in front of a lady.'

Between the two of them the girls gave poor Murdo twelve of the very best. He was sobbing with self pity by the time they'd finished.

Janice untied him and found that, despite his tears and his very sore backside, his cock was standing.

'Zoe, will you look at this?' said Janice, stroking it. 'Get your arse on that bearskin rug, my dear, and enjoy six inches of the best-bred Scottish beef you're ever likely to see.'

Zoe lay down as she was told, and a sobbing, shaking Murdo was coaxed on top of her, where her experienced hand had his tool in its appointed spot on the instant.

He didn't move very much, so Zoe grappled her legs around his waist while Janice reached for the cane. She gave his bottom a gentle touch.

'Feel that, Murdo, you snivelling wretch? You did? Good. Well, unless you start pumping your cock into my friend here with a bit more enthusiasm, I'm going to give you another six. Got me? So get moving!'

Murdo began thrusting, but it was pitiful to watch. Janice lost patience and gave him a swish across the back of the knees. This bucked him up no end and Zoe began to make a few noises of contentment.

Much to Janice's surprise he kept going for a full three minutes of solid shagging, which was enough to set Zoe off like a Chinese jumping cracker.

Recovered, she slipped out from underneath and went to stand beside Janice. She slipped a finger in Janice's quim while Janice put her arm around Zoe's neck and fondled a tit.

Murdo looked up from the floor at the two naked women playing with each other. Just two days before he would have said such a thing was impossible. Now he knew just how possible it was, and his backside was killing him.

'When are you going home, Murdo? Three days' time? Four?'

Murdo managed to squeak a weak, 'Four.'

'Good egg,' said Janice, brightly. 'I'm busy the next two days but that'll give you time to get your arse in better nick, and so you'll be able to crawl up here and beg for some more, won't you?'

Murdo nodded, dumbly.

'Is that all you can say? Is that all he can say, Zoe? Gosh, your tits are fantastic, let me give one of them a suck, mmmmmm. No, Murdo, I want more commitment.'

Murdo got to his knees, his head bowed, his arms dangling by his sides.

'Janice, and Zoe, I beg you to be allowed to enjoy your company again in three days' time. I promise to be a good boy, because I know that if I'm a bad boy, you will punish me.'

'That's better, Murdo. Now, fuck off, will you, there's a pet. Zoe and I have an unfinished trifle to trifle with.'

Murdo crawled out, his clothes wrapped carelessly around him, while Zoe and Janice disappeared into the bathroom. Janice had an enormous old bath with hugely ornate taps and while it was running the two girls kissed and fingered each other, taking it in turns to cover each other's breasts with lickspittle.

In the bath they could sit at either end and their feet only reached the other's knees. Janice slid under the water more, and reached for her parlourmaid friend's quim with her toes. She could get her big toe in, and Zoe responded by grasping Janice's foot and pushing the toes in as far as they would go, and scratching herself with them, rubbing the toes up and down in her crack.

At the same time she reached for Janice with her own foot, and so the both of them were masturbating themselves with the other one's toes. Water splashed over the sides as Zoe came, but Janice didn't so she stood up and placed a foot on either side of Zoe's neck. The maid looked up, tongue flicking out, as Janice lowered herself. Janice held on to the taps as Zoe licked her off from below, her tongue probing and her finger penetrating another entrance.

After only a few moments of this Janice went off bang, and the two girls collapsed, exhausted, into the enormous bath.

'Wow,' said Janice. 'Hurray for maids' afternoons off. When's your next afternoon off?'

'This isn't my afternoon off, Miss Janice. I'll have to serve tea.'

'Don't worry, Zoe. I'll get Murdo to do it. He'll look nice in your uniform. Serving tea and buns and everything. Cups of tea. Cups of tea . . .'

Murdo awoke. It was dark in his room. There was a figure beside his bed, a girl. She was whispering something.

'Murdo,' said Janice. 'It's six o'clock. I've brought you a cup of tea, but I go on duty in fifteen minutes. Which do you want? Tea, or me?'

Chapter Nine

Murdo returned to his apartment in London to try a new tack. He was going to place an advertisement in the *Evening Standard* jobs section. It said:

> Hey, good looking! Lovely girl wanted, aged 17–21, for unique, demanding modelling assignment. Very high rewards and world-wide exposure in return for complete commitment. Modelling experience not required. Living-life experience essential. Photo, statistics and a few words about yourself, please, to Box No. 15.

He expected about a dozen replies and got over eighty in the first post. There was no possibility of him handling all this administration on his own in rcasonablc timc, and hc didn't want the *Sir Lancelot* office involved, so he rang his Auntie Sheila and asked for help and some headed notepaper.

Sheila sent him the blushing receptionist, who arrived half expecting an immediate romp with Murdo Sinclair, randy editor, whom she thought of as a cross between Rudolph Valentino, Shakespeare and an Aberdeen Angus bull.

Instead she found a businesslike and busy man, dressed in shirt and slacks, chain-drinking coffee in a hyper-luxurious flat which was blue with Gitanes smoke.

'My man Broadhurst is on holiday,' Murdo explained. 'I gave him two months off while I got this project underway, and he won't be back for another thirty days.

Meanwhile, my sweet, I have one hundred and nineteen would-be stars' (he'd had the second post) 'and I've got to get them sorted out. Here are the pictures. I've put them into piles – Perfectly Good Looking, Good Looking, and Looking. The first job is to reject all the Perfects and all the Lookings.'

'Why are you rejecting the Perfects?' asked the receptionist, a Good Looking girl herself verging on the Perfect, of medium height, nice figure if slightly heavy on the buttocks, dark hair, and an eye-stoppingly pretty face, rather like Charlotte Rampling's, Murdo thought. 'By the way, I'm Christine.'

'Do you know what this project is about? Good. Well, I'm rejecting the Perfects, Christine, because our readers must be able to identify with the model in the pictures with me. I don't want a centrefold figure, and I don't want a *Vogue* cover face. She has to be the sort of standard which readers can feel is almost attainable given luck and a following wind, rather than unattainable and from another planet.

'So, get on the phone. Write them a short note on Sheila's paper when you can't get through. Meanwhile I'll go through the Good Lookings again and try and cut them down a bit.'

They took it in turns to make coffee and, four hours and a packet of Gitanes later, ninety-nine girls had been rejected and twenty photographs remained. The pictures varied from a *Tatler* type black-and-white studio portrait to a Kodak Brownie holiday snap of a girl with her bikini straps slipping.

The only thing they had in common was that Murdo fancied them. They were short and tall, blonde and brunette, big-breasted, small-chested and, from the picture or the measurements supplied, all more or less pear-shaped.

'Pick me ten to shortlist,' said Murdo. 'I've got some business calls to make on the other line, and then I'm going in the shower.'

Christine decided not to rely on the photograph for her

evidence. She would read and re-read the 'few words about yourself'. Her task, she thought, would be to find the ten most likely to be able to fuck like rabbits. Murdo had already selected them as sufficiently qualified in other ways. The first note was from Jenny, twenty-one, a secretary.

'I guess from the careful wording of your ad that this job is something that a lot of girls wouldn't do, so let me tell you there isn't much I won't do. I'm the secretary to an assistant manager of a building society, and when I get out of here of an evening I'm desperate for excitement.'

Christine read the next one, and the next. They were very similar, all trying to make themselves out to be sexy, amusing, go-for-it girls. Christine would have to look through the pictures after all.

This one had big knockers and a big bum. This other one had freckles. And this one had a squidgy nose, and this one the most amazing long legs. Good heavens, how was she to tell . . .?

Christine made her choice. She put the pictures face down on the carpet, shuffled them, and picked up ten. She telephoned them all with invitations to interview, sent written rejections to the others, and went over to the drinks table to pour herself a very substantial gin and tonic.

She was halfway through this when Murdo emerged from his bathroom in a loudly striped dressing gown. He got himself a large twelve-year-old Glen Morangie and sat on the couch to examine Christine's choice.

'I'm very pleased you've managed to do this,' he said. 'I was just about reduced to picking them out of a hat. I don't suppose you've thought of putting in an application yourself, Christine?'

The girl smiled as she refreshed her drink then walked across the room and curled up at Murdo's feet.

'I don't think so, Murdo,' she said, playfully stroking his right shin. 'Mummy wouldn't like it.'

'Fair enough,' said Murdo, shifting a little in his seat as he felt his prick stiffening. Christine had leaned her cheek against his knee. 'But would Christine like it?'

Christine put her drink on the carpet and turned so she was kneeling between Murdo's legs. She parted the two sides of his dressing gown and looked, contentedly, at the erect cock she thus exposed. She took it in both hands and gently caressed it.

'Oh yes,' she said. 'I would like it. Well, some of it. But dear old mummy would be mortified.'

Christine bent her head and took the top three inches of Murdo's weapon in her mouth. She savoured it, and then withdrew, leaving her tongue to linger on it a moment. Her hand moved up and down along the shaft, slowly.

'You see, Murdo, mummy is a frightful snob. She's the village vet's wife, which makes her equal to the doctor's wife and the vicar's wife, slightly below the retired colonel's wife who lives in the Hall, but above everyone else's wife. Mummy would never be able to show her face in the village again if her daughter was to cavort naked across the pages of a book, even if it was with a member of the Scottish nobility.'

She bent to her pleasure again, and placed her lips lovingly around the silk-covered iron bar, which became carbon-steel hard with her ministrations. Murdo sat back, sipped his whisky and even thought about a Gitanes. No, that would be too decadent. No, it wouldn't, sod it.

Murdo reached for his cigarettes, lit one, took another sip of whisky, and looked down at the top of a dark-haired bobbing head. How very, very delicious, he thought, to relax after a hard day's work with a drink, a smoke, and a lovely girl's mouth around your cock.

Christine must have thought so too because she kept going for the fifteen minutes it needed before Murdo got near to coming. He had attempted to lift her from the floor onto the couch, thinking she might prefer the cock inside her, but she had shaken her head in silent disagreement. Instead, she redoubled her efforts, taking his prick in as far as she could and tickling it delectably with the end of her tongue.

She could push the end into her throat, Murdo realised,

while her tongue flicked out and rasped along that part of the shaft still out in the open. If she'd had a longer tongue or a deeper throat, she might almost have reached his balls and licked them while taking his glans right back into her epiglottis.

Christine took one of his balls in each hand and squeezed them softly. She pulled her head back until just the tip of his cock was in her mouth, and then opened her lips slightly so that it was resting inside rather than being gripped. In this loosely held position she bobbed her head back and forth, breathing deep breaths so that Murdo felt the warm, damp air circulating all around his shaft.

The sensations were irresistible and his hips jerked towards her face. She let go of his balls and held his cock firmly. Taking her mouth from it she just left the end of her tongue to play with the most sensitive spot around the curve of the glans, and then laughed with delight as the come shot out of the end and landed on her left shoulder.

'That was nice,' she said. 'Can we do it again?'

'Well, yes, after a short respite,' said Murdo. 'Wouldn't you like me to do something for you instead?'

'Oh no, I can't, I promised mummy. I'm a virgin and I've got to stay that way until I'm married.'

'Are you serious?' said Murdo, utterly astonished.

'Absolutely. The only thing I ever do with boys is suck them off. I'm getting quite good at it, and they don't seem to mind.'

'And you never . . . what, not even what we used to call heavy petting?'

'Oh, they get their fingers in sometimes, but only a little way. I don't let them go right in.'

'Good Lord,' said Murdo. 'What about, er, well, the same thing you were doing to me but the other way around?'

'What? Do boys do that? I didn't know. Oh, I say. Please, be careful.'

Another buyer for the manual, thought Murdo, as he drew Christine to her feet and then, from where he was sitting, ran his hands up her legs underneath her skirt. He reached the elastic of her tights and pulled them down. Dreadful things. She stepped out of them, and the panties which had come down too.

He unbuckled the belt of the sensible tweed skirt and pulled the zip. She stepped out of that too, and stood in front of him dressed only in a white blouse with a suede waistcoat over and, presumably, thought Murdo, a bra under.

His hands went around to her bottom and squeezed. She sighed, and her knees bent a little. He massaged her arse cheeks while he kissed the tops of her thighs. She sighed again, and bent her legs more.

His lips wandered across her lower tummy, his tongue flicking out to caress her skin wherever it might. He nuzzled his face into her tight black curls and she almost collapsed on top of him.

'Just put one foot up on the couch, here. That's it.'

Now Murdo could get his face right into her crutch. She was wet, soaking wet, and her hands scrabbled madly at the back of his head as his tongue found its way into her entrance hall.

Her bottom juddered and jumped in his hands. Her sighs became moans, then loud groans, then she started to wail like a mullah calling the faithful to prayer.

She pulled his head into her and thrust her pelvis forward. Murdo, half drowning in her juices, kept going and then, in a frenzy of jerks and bucks, she shouted something incoherent and fell sideways onto the couch.

There she lay on her back, her bottom half naked, her top half fully clothed, breathing as heavily as if she'd just played squash for an hour.

Murdo stood, straightened up his dressing gown, wiped his mouth and nose with his monogrammed Egyptian cotton handkerchief, smiled, and went to pour some more drinks. The next step would be to get all her clothes off.

Chapter Ten

Jenny, the secretary in the building society, was a big girl. She had large breasts, a narrow waist, and a good weighty bottom to act as her centre of gravity. She was standing in Murdo's bedroom, scratching her head, looking at a mass of theatrical costumes spread out all over the room.

She, along with the other eight of the shortlist who had turned up for the interview, was trying to work out an erotic charade. When they arrived they'd had the job explained to them by Murdo, who then said he couldn't possibly give them any sort of individual test and so would they please devise something he could watch, with his assistant Christine?

Verve, lack of inhibition, sexual experience and skill and general 'oomph' were the qualities required, so if they'd like to go into the bedroom and sort through the costumes – he'd hired four dozen mixed theatrical costumes for the day – and work out what they wanted to do, he and Christine would be back after lunch.

Jenny teamed up with Maureen and Norma, both smaller, slimmer girls of about eighteen. From the pile of costumes they drew two Little Lord Fauntleroy outfits plus a large, forbidding-looking black dress from Victorian times. Also there were some props – a small notebook and pencil, a leather-bound book, and a length of thin cane.

It was Jenny's team to go first. While the rest argued and chattered in Murdo's bedroom, these three paraded in front of Murdo and Christine in the main room.

'Now, children,' Jenny began, addressing the two

smaller girls. 'As your new governess I feel it is vitally important to find out precisely the standard of your education and general knowledge, and I am going to start with poetry. I have here the complete works of John Keats and I'm going to test you. I shall sit here on the couch, and you shall stand in front of me.'

Maureen and Norma did as they were bid, standing with hands clasped behind backs and looking for all the world like naughty aristocratic boys who'd been caught stealing apples by the head gardener.

'Very well,' said Governess Jenny, opening her book. 'Maureen first. Maureen, which of Keats' poems begins with the words "Season of mists and mellow fruitfulness"? Mmm?'

'I don't know, Miss Jenny,' said Maureen.

'I see,' said Jenny. 'Lower your trousers, you wicked boy, and I shall show what happens when you don't know the answer to a simple question.'

Maureen pulled down her blue silk pantaloons, and her knickers. She turned her back to Jenny and bent over. Jenny admired the slim buttocks and noted the brown tuft which was just visible at the junction of buttocks with thighs. She raised the cane and gave three light but sharp blows, leaving thin red lines across the white globes.

Maureen pulled her clothes back up and said, 'Thank you, Miss Jenny.'

'Now, Norma. To which bird did Keats famously write an ode? Was it a nightingale, a robin, or a skylark?'

'I don't know, Miss Jenny,' said Norma, already wriggling her pantaloons and panties down and presenting her bum, neat and tidy like Maureen's but possibly slightly larger, to the eager gaze of the governess.

Jenny gave her three sharp taps too, and then said, 'Now. You may ask me a question about Keats.'

'Please, Miss,' said Maureen. 'How long was his prick?'

'Why, Maureen, such a question! How am I to know how long his prick was?'

Maureen grabbed the cane and began flexing it between

her two hands. Jenny pretended to hesitate in fear; then sighed, turned, bent and lifted up the rustling black taffeta of her floor-length dress. Beneath it she wore nothing, and she showed the girls a bottom which was far from being slim. This was a bottom to ogle at, a moon of two harvest halves, enough to provide limitless exploration for any pair of hands.

Or even two pairs, for Norma could not resist squeezing it as she pulled the dress up further, and Maureen could not resist stroking it as she chose precisely where to inflict the punishment. The two 'boys' smiled at each other and, while Norma began taking off her blue suit, Maureen gave the wonderful bottom a couple of light swishes with the cane.

Norma, now with just trousers on, her pert breasts swinging with the action, grabbed the cane and gave Jenny a couple of delicate lashes too.

Jenny stood and turned and, seeing Norma standing there with bare breasts, took her in her arms and kissed her mouth. Their tongues entwined and Jenny's hands pressed and searched Norma's delicious little tits.

Maureen was busy on the hooks and eyes at the top of the back of Jenny's dress. The rest of the fastening was less authentic, thank goodness, and the metal zip sped smoothly downwards.

Here was revealed the clasp which kept Jenny's bra together. Maureen undid it and thrust her hands inside. Jenny stood off Norma a little, to allow Maureen's hands to come round from behind and grapple with a truly great pair of breasts.

Jenny felt her nipples rising and wished that her dress could be magically removed without losing contact with either of the other girls. Instead, Norma broke away and, while Maureen laid her head sideways on Jenny's bare shoulders and massaged those tits which would have been Listed Grade One had they been buildings, she pulled the dress forwards over Jenny's arms, and then down to the ground.

The bra came too, and so there was now the Junoesque

Jenny in shoes and stockings only, being molested severely from behind by a fully dressed Maureen while Norma in pants only looked on.

Maureen showed no signs of giving up her mauling. She would never be tired of moulding those bosoms and exploring them by touch, so Norma walked around behind the two of them and began to undress her 'brother' Fauntleroy. The trousers were easy enough, but getting Maureen to let go enough to get the jacket off was a trying exercise for the impatient Norma.

At last she succeeded. Now a slim naked girl was embracing a fully rounded naked girl, and looking from behind Norma could see various outcrops of Jenny jutting beyond her partner's more modest silhouette.

Still there was no let-up, so Norma took off her trousers, walked around the front, and lay on the couch with her legs wide open. Jenny's eyes narrowed with lust. Dragging a half-willing Maureen with her, Jenny made her way to the couchside and placed a hand on the inside of Norma's thigh.

Fascinated, she caressed that small area of smooth white skin which is the softest of all. Now Jenny straddled her and lowered her big, juicy, black-haired quim over Norma's mouth while keeping up the tempo below with eager fingers.

Maureen, desperate to join in, stood on the couch and thrust her pelvis towards Jenny's face. Jenny licked as she could, but Maureen had to support her head to get in close.

Jenny's movements became too urgent for any extra activity. Maureen knelt and cradled a breast in two hands while Jenny sawed her quim back and forth over Norma's tongue. Maureen's two thumbs twirled a single nipple, and her two sets of fingers traced the contours of a hill unlike any other except the one next to it.

Jenny was shouting now, her head back, her mind totally blown by the expert lips and tongue of her younger, smaller partner, and after six or seven shivering spasms she collapsed sideways on to the couch, her eyes closed in bliss and her mouth curved in a smile of beatific satisfaction.

Maureen and Norma were not satisfied. Maureen put her legs astride Jenny's heaving chest and rested her quim on the left summit, a cream and white Cheviot with a reddish brown cairn marking the spot. She rubbed herself up and down on the hard nipple until Jenny showed signs of life, then transferred her already wet palace of pleasure to Jenny's searching tongue.

While Jenny pushed her face up into the hot, damp lining of Maureen's vagina, Norma looked on jealously. She wriggled backwards off the couch and stood, watching, her right hand making large, sweeping movements over her body, crushing her pretty little tits, pushing hard across her stomach, then back up to left breast, then right. Her other hand was busy at the same time, her fingers tickling an erect clit which was so enthusiastic for action that it was almost leaping out into the open air.

Norma could stand it no longer. She too would straddle the vibrating body of big Jenny which was then ministering unto the needs of Maureen with whom Norma was back to back.

She grabbed Jenny's two hands and thrust them both into her damp cavern. Jenny had two fingers from each at work, while Norma bent to drink at the fountain which, between Jenny's legs, was once more beginning to seep warm fluids.

Maureen, hands on the couch above and on either side of Jenny, was rocking herself to oblivion. All Jenny had to do was keep her tongue out and stiff. Norma was rocking the other way, and squirming onto Jenny's fingers which now numbered six altogether.

Norma's arms were wrapped around Jenny's thighs as she buried her head in the ample and fleshly secret place. All three were on the verge, and all three were heaving and thrusting, trying to get more and more of the other person inside them.

Maureen pushed down on Jenny's mouth like a broody

hen settling on her clutch of eggs. She rotated and reeled and yawed and felt it coming. Norma wriggled and squiggled with the pace and energy of someone pumping up a bicycle tyre who has had a puncture with just a few hundred yards to go to win the race.

Jenny, sucking and licking at Maureen, and jamming her fingers into Norma as if she were a rock climber stuck in a crack on which her life depended, was bouncing her pelvis up towards Norma's diligent mouth.

In one tremendous clashing climax they each went off like a firework, bang, bang, bang, and collapsed in triumph. After a few moments, each got up to take a bow. The applause was sincere from both Murdo and Christine, for an excellent performance.

Having gone first, they were entitled to watch the other acts. Naked, the three girls got themselves a drink and settled in chairs to watch what Kath and Nancy had in store.

Kath was another big girl, rather like Jenny in figure. Nancy also was ample, possibly one could even say plumpish, but she had that sexual aura which said 'plenty' and 'comfort' and 'warm' and 'come and get it', rather than 'podgy from eating too many chips'.

There was a great deal of mime in their act. The scene was a farm in East Anglia, the audience was told, and Nancy was the farmer's daughter. Kath's car had broken down and she was turning up at the door looking for assistance.

Kath, wearing a very dressy business suit with high heels, mimed the trudge up to the farmstead and across the yard, including a slip on something highly agricultural and a fall into a large puddle of it. Thinking aloud, she was hoping to use the phone. Maybe, she thought, she might even be allowed a swill down in the horse trough to get rid of some of this shit she'd landed in.

Nancy came to the door looking fresh faced, pneumatic, and wearing an old fashioned pinny over a raggedy cotton dress. She had no shoes or stockings on and her arms were bare too, allowing Kath to think aloud in an aside that here was a wench well used to pitching hay and carrying milk churns.

Nancy said the farmer, her father, was out at the bullock sales with her brother. She had no mum, her having gone and run off with an American airforce man. Yes, Kath could have a wash, but they had no bathroom.

'Thass oonly a shar in the barn,' said Nancy, doing a very passable imitation of a Norfolk accent. 'An' there hint noo phoone hair noither.'

When they'd walked around Murdo's sitting room a couple of times and reached the barn, Kath found the shower, or shar, to be a rudimentary affair. She exclaimed that it had no cabinet or curtain, just a concrete pad to stand on and a shower head which you worked by pulling a chain. Nancy got Kath a towel and left her to it.

At least, she appeared to. Kath, acting like a silent movie star, was fairly sure that the girl hadn't gone far. Probably she was spying from somewhere.

Kath knew all about her fantastic physique and the effect it had on men and women alike, and she knew all about how to make the most of it. As casually as she could she put her foot up on one of Murdo's antique footstools, now playing the part of a hay bale, and fiddled with the strap on her shoe. That shoe off, and the next, she undid her suit jacket and her blouse.

Leaving them to hang open, giving the onlooking girl a glimpse of wondrous hidden treasures as Kath turned and bent, next the skirt was removed, and the camiknickers.

Kath stood up, naked from the waist down except for a pair of silk stockings held up by garters, her swelling hips promising anything and everything to all comers. Casually she scratched at her black triangle then, turning around as she did to make sure Nancy got a good look, she took off her jacket, then the blouse, then the bra, very slowly.

Now she had nothing on but the stockings. Deciding where Nancy was, she bent her bottom towards her as she doubled over to take off the rolled-down stockings. She stood and fondled her magnificent bosom, yawning and stretching, before pulling the shower chain.

Wow! Nancy had never mentioned it was cold! Kath was not in there long, and she jumped about a bit while towelling herself dry and warm. But now what to do?

She didn't want to put her suit back on. There was cowmuck on the skirt. She'd have to cross the farmyard with just her towel.

Nancy will have gone back to the house by now. Very well, then let's see what will happen there. With much stepping over puddles and fiddling with slipping towels, Kath arrived back at the farmhouse.

Nancy was busy over the sink, rinsing out clothes, it would appear. She turned as Kath came in and couldn't stop her eyes from travelling down to the cleavage, across the towel, and down to the finely rounded naked legs of which almost all were visible. Kath smiled.

'Those shirts look about my size,' she said. 'Have you got a dry one I could borrow?'

'These hair are moi farther's,' said Nancy. 'That'll be alright if you do borrow one, I'll go to hell if that in't.'

Beckoning Kath to follow her, the girl mimed going through the kitchen door and up the stairs. There were just two bedrooms, Kath said in an aside. She wondered who slept with whom.

Nancy produced a shirt from behind the couch and held it out for Kath. Kath dropped her towel and allowed Nancy a few seconds of open-eyed astonishment at being so close to so much naked woman before pulling the shirt over her head.

It was roomy enough to contain all of Kath from neck to crutch. The tails just flapped perfectly over her pubic hairs. The sight of Kath with arms raised had been a little too much for Nancy and she was in a dither.

'Why, Nancy,' said Kath. 'Whatever is the matter? Here, you look quite flushed. Perhaps you need some air.'

Kath took the two steps towards her and undid the buttons at the top of her dress. Nancy stood, her eyes closed, willing Kath to go further but desperately frightened at what might happen if she did.

Kath reached behind and untied the pinny and slipped it

from the unresisting Nancy. The dress buttoned right down the front and then came off like a coat. Underneath was a vest, and that was all. Nancy was naked, her eyes still closed, her body stiff.

'What's the matter, Nancy?' said Kath, trying to get the girl to put her hand on the breast beneath her brother or father's shirt. 'Haven't you done this sort of thing before?'

'Noo, oi never,' said Nancy. 'And thass the truth. Oi hint never done noo sex, only with Seth and my dad.'

'Is Seth your brother?' said Kath, gently teasing at the nipple at the summit of Nancy's left tit.

'Thass roight. He done it to me and moi dad as well, they both done it, but I hint never done no sex with anybody strange before.'

'Well you just relax, and leave everything to me.'

Kath paused in her attentions to Nancy's plentiful breasts, perhaps a little overweight but firm with youthful tone. She pulled the shirt back over her head and pushed Nancy back on to the couch.

Kneading her breasts lightly at a distance with one hand, Kath kissed the farmgirl first on the tops of her feet, and then on the ankles, the calves, the knees, the plump thighs. Nancy gave an involuntary gasp as she felt Kath's lips brushing the softest skin on the inside of her thighs, and she parted her legs wide.

Kath smiled and gave another theatrical aside. Inexperienced the girl may be, but her instincts were working well.

Avoiding the crinkly, damp entrance to Nancy's virgin territory (virgin, that is, except for father and brother), Kath traversed the rounded belly with her butterfly lips, then got to work on the breasts. She watched the nipples rise and stand proud, and then she knelt upright. She swung a magnificent leg across Nancy's body, lowered her own majestic tits to meet the farmgirl's, then pressed their bodies together in a hot embrace.

Nancy wasn't too sure about the kissing at first, but soon warmed to it. Her hands began to take part also, wandering over Kath's back and down to her perfect buttocks. Kath rubbed herself hard against the smaller girl, and then swung around into the sixty-nine.

Grabbing a thigh in each hand she thrust her face into the open quim and licked and sucked vigorously. Taking her cue, Nancy did the same, making up for her lack of expertise with a new found enthusiasm.

As Kath's highly educated tongue found the little diddler which, no doubt at all, had been totally ignored by all Nancy's relatives, Nancy let out a splutter.

Then, she went berserk, her body jerking as if she were being electrocuted. Kath kept hold of her by the thighs and kept her tongue well in, forcing the orgasm from Nancy which rushed up on the poor girl like a spring tide across the marshes of The Wash.

'Ow, ow, ow, ow, ow, OWEEEEEEE!' she wailed, her whole person lost in a completely new experience. She collapsed, totally useless, on the couch.

Kath snorted a little snort to herself as she searched around to find a pair of trousers to go with her shirt. There were some wellies by the door downstairs, she'd noticed. She'd have the lot sent back tomorrow.

Meanwhile, she looked down on Nancy, no longer an emotional or spiritual virgin. She gave her a kiss.

'Doon't goo!' pleased Nancy. 'Oi want to do it again.'

'Then I suggest you get yourself down to the village dance and pick yourself up a nice boy.'

'But oi like you,' she moaned.

'Boys are excellent, too,' said Kath. 'It's just that the young ones get over excited. But they learn. And stay away from your father and brother. If they want some, let them go out and find it.'

Kath gave the plump tits a farewell squeeze and made her exit, stage left, to return for her curtain calls with Nancy.

Next, the growing audience was informed, they would see the aftermath of a parachute jump which had gone wrong. Two female pupils had landed well away from the target area and their instructor, who had also jumped, was looking for them. The fourth part in the play was to be a farm worker ('More farms?' thought Murdo. 'What is it about farms that's so sexy?').

The instructor and the farm worker were to be males played by two girls, Georgina and Angela. They would have certain equipment with them to make up for a lack in a particular department.

The play began with the two parachuting pupils, Nicola and Sylvie, spreading two double bedsheets, fixed together, over the carpet. They then crawled underneath and the audience began to understand why a parachute jump had been made the theme.

Panicking, the instructor arrived. This was Georgina in a man's army uniform.

Oh no! His pupils had landed on top of each other. They were hurt. One was wrapped up in her parachute and the other was on top suffocating her. He dived under the sheet, or chute.

In the centre of it he found the lump, and such a lump as no parachute instructor had ever discovered.

Nicola and Sylvie waited for him beneath the sheet, totally naked. They had stripped while under it. The audience could see this because the sheet kept slipping. The girls smiled and sat up as the snorting, anxious instructor crawled towards them as fast as he could.

'Hello, Sergeant,' said Nicola. 'I think we'd both like another jump.'

The sheet slipped off completely as Nicola took his head in her hands and explored his mouth with her tongue. Sylvie unlaced his boots, took them off, then the socks, trousers and shorts, and grasped his army rations firmly in her hands.

This was represented by a pink plastic vibrator which had been hidden in the uniform.

'What a nice big one,' she said. 'I just fancy an early lunch.'

Her hands worked 'his' quim as her delicate lips kissed the head of the vibrator. Georgina was on her back now, lifting herself occasionally from the ground to help Nicola get rid of the rest of the uniform. Sylvie's mouth was right over where a cock would have been, and the hot, wet slurps were loud and regular as she did some serious sucking on the pink plastic.

'Leave some for me, dear,' said Nicola, over her shoulder, as she rode her quim across the instructor's tongue and nose.

Angela, the young farmworker, entered and watched while leaning on a gate chewing a straw. Didn't dare join in, he murmured to himself. The women's voices were upper class, frightfully nice, and obviously far above his station. That man – well, the only sounds he made were grunts and groans, so the hired lad couldn't tell what sort of a man he was.

The farm lad's fingers crept across his britches, and very authentic looking they were in scuffed leather. Presumably they'd come from a production of *Seven Brides* or *Oklahoma*! Clumsily, Angela undid the stiff buttons, found a wooden dildo and sprung it out into the open. Angela wanked it with eyes goggling at the next episode inside the parachute.

Both girls were sitting on the man now. One was sitting on his head and the other on his thighs, presumably with his vibrator/cock inside her. The girls embraced as the man reached up and tried his best to do justice to the four tits which hung deliciously above him.

As Nicola and Sylvie accelerated their tempo together the farm lad wanked faster and faster. He could see them crouching on either side of the man. They each took a hand and pushed it up into them, and massaged themselves with it until they were both nearly there.

One of them swiftly jumped on the man's pink plastic prick and galloped a few short steps and then cried out. Then she got off and the other got on and did the same.

The farm lad wanked even faster as the two female figures inside the parachute bent their heads towards the crux of the man. He could hear sucking noises. The women were both beyond the wildest imaginings of a simple farm worker, and he mimed an enormous orgasm with spunk spurting everywhere as he saw Georgina arch her back and shoot too but 'he', lucky bugger, was coming into a woman's mouth and she was swallowing it.

Nicola and Sylvie suddenly noticed the farm lad and beckoned him over. Dumbly he went, dildo in hand. They stripped the clothes from him while Georgina went to the bathroom – 'Pretend it's my rucksack I was carrying when I jumped' – and came back with a jar of Vaseline. Lovingly they smoothed it on the dildo and the vibrator, then Georgina and Angela, the two 'men', bent over on their knees, their bottoms waving in the air and their legs slightly apart.

'It must be awful being a man,' said Sylvie. 'We girls have three places to put a cock, but men only have two.'

With that, Sylvie and Nicola slowly inserted the dildo and vibrator respectively in Georgina's and Angela's bumholes. Sylvie pushed the dildo gently in and out. Nicola switched on the vibrator, got up and left it. She returned with a double dildo. 'Just thought of this' she said. 'It was in my shoulder bag.'

She took the vibrator out, lay Angela flat on her stomach, put some Vaseline on one end of the dildo and pushed it home in Angela's backside. Nicola then swung a leg over and sat on the other end and began a regular riding motion.

Sylvie was jealous. She turned Georgina over, keeping the dildo up her arse, and sat on her face while leaning over to move the dildo in and out. Gradually the four of them got more and more excited until, with a chorus of wild cries, they fell in a heap of writhing, orgasming bodies.

The audience applauded madly. Murdo's cock was as stiff as a tree trunk in his trousers and he wanted to show Christine, so he asked the girls if they would mind getting dressed and tidied while he discussed the events of the afternoon with his assistant in the dining room.

So randy was he that as soon as he heard the dining room door close he lifted up Christine's skirt, pulled her panties down, and bent her forwards over a dining chair.

She cried out. 'What about my promise to mummy? I can't! Please don't! Oh, yes!'

With no ceremony whatever he dropped his pants and whammed his iron-hard cock straight up her bumhole. She squealed, and wriggled, and then settled into a pattern of sighs and low moans as Murdo thrust hard and fast.

Soon he was hitting one hundred and twenty rpm, then one hundred and fifty, and then he was shagging her arse at incredible speed as he felt the come well up inside him. With three or four final, extra-deep thrusts he spilled his hot cream into her bowels and sighed his satisfaction.

'Christine,' he said. 'Come and work for me. I'll give you a big rise. And you'll still be a virgin on your wedding day.'

When they did get round to discussing the candidates, it became apparent that they had no real way of making a decision. They were all good enough. Christine said he should just pick the two who made his cock go hardest, then take them to bed and choose the one.

Murdo could come up with no more logical suggestion, but doubted whether he could bring it straight down to two. Four was more likely.

So, they went back into the sitting room to tell the waiting girls that Jenny, Kath, Nicola and Sylvie were the shortlist. The others were each given £1000 for their trouble.

To reduce the list to two there was to be another little test. Pairing them off as Jenny and Nicola, Kath and Sylvie, a scenario was described to them and they were given an hour to come back with their own dramatic treatment of the same characters and circumstances.

Christine and Murdo went out to the pub for a drink and returned to find the girls ready. First on, by toss of the coin, were Jenny and Nicola.

There was an office type desk in one corner of the vast main room of Murdo's penthouse, with a PC and various bits of office gear on it. Jenny, dressed in a Russian army costume, came in to sit behind it and Nicola, looking somewhat dishevelled, perched on a chair in the nervous-interviewee position. Jenny delivered a monologue to the audience in a pantomime Russian accent, thus:

'It is 1969, I am Political Commissar in Omsk, and I am almost wetting myself with excitement at the thought of what I might do to this dirty, tired, upper-class English girl who has arrived in my office just.

'The authorities in the Union of Soviet Socialist Republics cannot of course believe her bull and cock story of how she got here by bus and train. Such things could not happen in the USSR. Now, what shall I do with the luscious little Nicola? She is totally in my power, for I am Comrade Ludmilla Jennevyevova, Commissar of Omsk!'

Nicola turned to the audience and explained: 'She does not get much excitement in her posting in Omsk. She much prefers being back in Moscow where there are plenty of eager young girls wanting promotion in the Service and willing to do anything for a senior officer like Comrade Ludmilla.

'Here, in the remotest of remote places, fuck-all ever happens. And then, one day, a lovely, slim English girl in a ragged dress comes into her office, dirty with the dust of travel, and says she is such and such and demands this and that. What a windfall!'

'My dear Miss Nicola,' said Comrade Ludmilla, 'I am afraid the British Consul is unobtainable to the moment. Meanwhile, let me suggest you become clean and newly attired. Come with me to my private quarters. You shall have everything.'

Nicola said, aside: 'I have no illusions about what this means, but if it helps me make contact with somebody who can get me home, I shall indeed have everything and do everything.'

Ludmilla ran the bath (the taps were on the end of the couch) and took off her uniform jacket. She was wearing an army shirt which was almost bursting with the breasts it contained. She ran a hand over Nicola's bottom and patted it gently.

'Why don't you get undressed, then I can scrub your back for you?'

Nicola obliged, making no special effort to be either coy or flaunting. There was no need. Comrade Ludmilla was clearly as hot as a drover's dog, as Murdo's father used to say.

Naked, Nicola stepped into the imaginary bath and sat down in the deep water. It was a large bath and the water came over her breasts. She took the soap offered by Ludmilla, the action bringing her pretty little tits into view. Ludmilla could hardly contain herself.

Slowly, Nicola rubbed her tits with soap, and then her shoulders, and then she offered the soap back to Ludmilla and leaned forward. Ludmilla rubbed her hands eagerly to get up a lather and then stroked it into Nicola's tired muscles.

She is quite good, actually, thought Nicola aloud. She does know a bit about massage.

Five minutes of work on her back produced a definite benefit, and when the hands began to stray beneath her armpits, and onto the edges of her tits, Nicola smiled blissfully, took Ludmilla's hands in hers, slipped back in the couch/bath and placed the hands one on each breast.

Ludmilla felt their perfect firmness and their sweet pear shapes. She caressed the nipples and murmured with pleasure as they stirred and grew erect. Her hands wandered further, then, down to the hairy tuft and the quim lips of this delicious girl, and were rewarded as Nicola brought her knees up and allowed Ludmilla free access.

After a few moments of fingering, Ludmilla spoke for the first time for quite a while.

'Please, Miss Nicola, no more of this bath. I shall dry you, yes, and take you to my bed?'

Nicola stood without answering. She brushed the excess imaginary water from her sweet young body, and Ludmilla's hands trembled as she towelled and then led Nicola out of the 'bathroom', once around the carpet, and then back to the couch which was now a bed.

Here Ludmilla held the naked girl in her arms, her slim

white body seeming frail against the army-shirted chest and the army-skirted hips and thighs of the Comrade Commissar.

Nicola's hand went to the army shirt and began unbuttoning. Ludmilla alllowed her room, and looked down at the small white hands as they pulled the shirt clear of the skirt waistband and exposed two massive tits encased in a formidable looking bra.

'We have no Marks and Spencer in the Soviet Union,' said Ludmilla. 'We cannot obtain nice underwear. But we are the same people underneath.'

'Not quite,' said Nicola, releasing the bra's substantial catch and allowing two of the biggest tits in the USSR to flow free. By her reactions she made it seem like an avalanche. Two tidal waves of weighty substance unfurled and headed for the centre of the earth, pulled there by gravity.

'In Russia, my darling English,' said Ludmilla, 'we know how to define a good woman. When the man goes to work in the morning, he slaps her on the behind, and if the behind is still wobbling when he gets home at night, he has a good woman.'

Ludmilla roared with laughter while Nicola giggled. Tentatively Nicola put her hands on the Russian mountain sides and tried to encompass their peaks with her palms. There was too much quantity as well as quality.

Ludmilla took off her shirt and undid the button and loop at her waistband. Never taking her eyes off Nicola she slid the stout material to the ground, stepped out of it and the cotton underskirt, and rolled her woollen stockings down.

She smiled and took Nicola by the hand and laid her gently on the couch. She placed her hand on Nicola's small, neat bush as she knelt and reached to kiss each of Nicola's sweet cherries.

Nicola squirmed in warm response and opened her legs a little. Ludmilla went down on her and was soon digging hard with her tongue, wrestling with Nicola's joystick and snuffling her nose into the crack.

Nicola's legs opened as wide as possible. Her knees were up as high as they could go, and her hands were on the back of Ludmilla's head, pushing her further into the hot, damp jungle of the rainforest.

Ludmilla was enjoying herself, but she stopped, raised her head, and told the audience that she had been with men – she could not have risen to the rank of Commissar without – but she preferred girls. In fact, if she'd agreed to go to bed with Colonel Asparov of the KGB when he asked her, drunk, that night at a party, she would almost certainly be in Moscow now and not in the blighted desert of Omsk.

But, that little blonde airforce Lieutenant with the perfect arse had let Ludmilla feel her tits in the women's room and that had been that. Never mind. Here was the English girl, and by the sounds she was making she was about to have one almighty orgasm.

Nicola, under the skilful ministrations of Ludmilla, was soon coming like a train. Her legs were waving in the air, her voice was raised and all her problems were forgotten in the irresistible surge.

She opened her eyes to find Ludmilla looking down at her, her gigantic pendula swinging. Nicola reached up and touched them. Ludmilla lowered them towards her, and she could suck the nipples and feel the mass of them.

Afraid perhaps of being suffocated, Nicola slid out from under and turned Ludmilla on her back. The tits immediately became peaceful and non-threatening as they spread out.

Nicola put her face between them and began working her way down, across the Russian steppes and into the harbour at Vladivostok. There she found a tender and receptive quim and a surprisingly small clit which, when tickled by Nicola's tongue grew larger and larger until it actually poked its little head right out. Nicola could easily get it between her lips and roll it there, to which Ludmilla responded with a blissful sigh. Heaven was here.

It was perhaps time to grow bolder. Nicola slipped a

thumb in Ludmilla's quim, kept licking the clit, and thrust her little finger into her arsehole. You would have thought a bomb had gone off. Ludmilla went into a kind of fit, gurgling and making rattling noises and thrashing her head from side to side. Nicola redoubled her efforts on the Soviet clit and soon Ludmilla, the formidable Commissar before whom all in Omsk trembled, was a jelly. Her white body glowed pink with exertion and pleasure.

Stopping Nicola for a moment, she told the audience that she had not had such an orgasm since those three student nurses on holiday by the Black Sea. Nicola saw the moment and seized it with both hands.

'Comrade Ludmilla,' she said, sitting astride the Russian, bare, and rubbing her quim against the spilling tits. 'Would you like me to do that again later?'

'I should very much like that, Nicola my little beetroot. But first we have some vodka.'

'No, but first we have some talking. My story is true. You must promise to send me home on the first available Aeroflot. If you do this, I will lick your Sovietski Soyuz until it shouts "Long Live the Revolution". OK, d'you think?'

'OK. Now, get off my fucking tits, as you say in English, and pass me the vodka bottle.'

The applause was tremendous, and Kath and Sylvie, who had been watching through the bedroom door, also walked in applauding.

'We can't top that,' said Kath. 'We give in.'

Chapter Eleven

I have to disclose to you that my latest Work Experience has to be the most memorable yet.

Anastasia Wrench-Burton was writing up her notes about the week she'd spent at the Blue Dog Club in Manchester. Looking through her pages of shorthand, she'd decided to concentrate on one particular afternoon. More than enough had happened to fill the 3000 words (she'd allotted herself an extra 1000 now she was in co-charge).

I'm going to tell you all about the events of a certain Wednesday afternoon, in a certain establishment whose name I cannot reveal – but I will tell you it's in Manchester.

The set-up there is very luxurious. There's a small cinema – every seat's a double – and a bar and restaurant, and half a dozen selectively furnished retiring rooms.

We hostesses sit at the bar – where else? – and wait to be approached, or to get a phone call from a restaurant table or drinking booth, or it might be the buzzer.

The buzzer is in the arm of every seat in the cinema. If a client gets excited watching a film, he can buzz and whoever is on buzzer duty goes and sees to his needs.

This Wednesday afternoon I was first on the buzzer. It went even before the film started!

In the small, darkened room there was only one

client, so that was no problem. I went and sat beside him and, as we usually did, put my hand on his crutch. There was a serious bump there, alright, but he didn't want me to touch it yet. He took my hand away and held it like an old-fashioned cinema romantic, and we had to watch the film.

I'll repeat the film story here but I'm telling you that I don't like it and we don't approve of it on *Sir Lancelot*. It's in to show you what's available when you've got the money, even in this day and age of the New Man, political correctness, lesbian rights and all.

So, there I was, holding this man's hand and the film started to roll. First up was a young woman with the looks of Jane Fonda. She was talking on the phone, and from what she was saying it was clear she didn't like men. The voice on the other end asked her if she was sure that this wasn't psuedo-lesbianism, or a suppressed desire to be dominated by a male hero figure.

Our heroine, called Karen, laughed. 'What do you think I am?' she said. 'A frustrated concubine? You think I just need a good poking to make me see the error of my ways?'

Cut to bedroom scene. Karen was being seduced and stripped naked by a well endowed, red-headed girl who then suggested a jacuzzi. Karen followed her, not into the bathroom as she expected but into a large lounge-type room where she was grabbed by three semi-naked men, partly dressed as Roman legionares. Her nude body, pale and slim, was draped along a gymnasium vaulting horse. Her arms and legs hung down on either side.

One of the legionares smacked her on the bottom. He was a big guy, a Channel swimmer type and a deep ebony black. He shouted at her. 'Now would you like a bellyful of red hot cock, you fucking bitch?'

'Noooo,' she wailed.

'OK, bitch, get this instead!'

He hit her with a whip, which fell with stinging

power across her behind. She jerked her whole body, only the ropes which connected her wrists and ankles underneath the horse keeping her on.

'Look, bitch, look!' the black man screamed. She turned her head to see the big, stiff cock he was holding out to her from between the hanging leather straps which made up his kilt, all he was wearing apart from a black leather executioner's helmet. He waved his cock at her, mockingly.

'You fucking lesbian tart!' he shouted. 'What are you?'

'I'm . . . I'm . . . don't want . . . you can't make me . . .'

'I'm not going to make you do it,' retorted the man. 'I'm going to make you ask for it, beg for it, plead for it. You are going to weep for cock. You are going to want cock so much that you'd die for it. But you're not ready yet. Are you?' He gave her another slashing blow with the lash.

'Now!' he cried. 'You're a fucking lesbian tart, a cunt licker, a clit sucker. Your fingers are your best friend. But what you really want is cock, isn't it? You want some of this, don't you? Look at me when I'm talking to you!'

Karen turned her head again. She wasn't a very good actress. She made as if to blink the tears from her eyes but there weren't any. Either the whip wasn't really hitting her, or she was finding it a lot of fun.

The man had taken his little kilt off. He stood before her, hips and thighs bare, with a long, stiff, bobbing cock sticking out of his mass of pubic hair. She stared at its purplish head. The camera went right in to see a tiny clear droplet ooze from its eye.

Karen's voice came over the picture. It was her thoughts. The cock was crying, too. It was weeping for her and with her. Perhaps she would have it after all.

'Lesbian bitch,' the man shouted, tapping her

buttocks warningly with the lash while slowly wanking himself with the other hand. 'What are you?'

'Lesbian bitch,' she moaned. 'Fucking lesbian bitch. Cunt licker. Lesbian bitch.'

The man untied her hands and put one of them on his cock. She wanked it for him. Her voice explained her thoughts. She was feeling the wiry hairs as her hand came down and wondering at the heat and the hardness of it.

He pushed it towards her lips. She instinctively resisted but a warning tap on the bottom from the lash opened her mouth like magic. In went the cock, pushing to the back of her throat, making her gag. The man put her hand beneath his balls. She cradled them, feeling their heaviness. Satisfied, he withdrew.

'You've been a good girl. Now, you get your reward.'

Voice-over again. The man had disappeared from Karen's view and she sensed him climbing up on the leather horse behind her. She felt his hands at her crotch, feeling her quim lips and noting, she was sure, the wetness on the leather where she had already spilled her juices several times. Then there was a different sensation, of something trying to enter her. It was his cock. This was it. This was cock. The first time she'd ever had it. She'd had dildos, and girl's fingers and tongues, and a candle once, but never a cock before. Never a man's cock.

In it came. Oooooff! She felt it slide, searching her vagina, finding the entrance to her womb, stroking that tiny organ near the front of her slit which responded so well to her friends' tongues and fingers.

She felt two hands scrabbling under her chest. She lifted herself slightly and looked down and watched as the two large hands, black on the backs and warm browny pink inside, felt for and found her small breasts. The breasts disappeared inside the hands. She liked the feeling.

The cock in her was moving faster now. She could

feel sensations similar to others she had felt before, but these were better, stronger, louder, more real. The black man's prick surged back and forth and his hands moulded her tits. She felt her nipples touching the warm central skin of his palms. She felt his cock rasping in and out.

And here it was! With a voice-over commentary rather as if we were watching a BBC wildlife programme, we were told that her vagina went into an uncontrollable sequence of spasms as it tried to suck sperm from the cock end and convey it up and ever up into her womb. Just as she started to come she felt him making his final thrusts and then there was a gush of hot liquor, a river bursting through a rockfall to fill an underground cave.

She cried out. Then all was peace. After a few moments, the black man whispered in her ear.

'You know what? I'm gonna fuck you again.'

So there you are. That's the kind of thing now showing at a cinema near you.

The next film was rather better. There was a very stagey shot of a jumbo jet flying through blue sky, with the name on its side of 'Basmati Airways'. Cut to inside, see two rather nice youngish, white girls, about seventeen years old, lounging in the first class. Cut to girls' point of view of Indian stewardess' arse wiggling up the aisle.

Cut to general view of first class; see one other passenger, an ancient, wrinkled old chap with a turban, a long white beard and straggly white hair, dressed in traditional Indian style.

Close shot of one of the white girls. She's trying to get the other one – her sister, presumably – to look at the Indian stewardess's bum.

'Charlotte,' she hissed. 'Charlotte!' But Charlotte was asleep, so the other one eased herself from her seat and followed the stewardess to the first-class galley.

The stewardess was clearly a year or two older, but

the English girl was taller than the dark-eyed Indian, and slimmer.

As she closed the door behind her and stood with her back to it, her hands on the handle, she said, 'Hi,' somewhat lamely. 'My name's Caroline. How long until we land?'

'How long do you require, Miss?' said the stewardess, her bronze face shining with amusement, her teeth gleaming, her lips glowing. 'I am Ghita Badewar, at your service.'

Caroline put a hand on the girl's neck and ran her fingers up and down the prominent muscle. The girl just stood, quietly agreeing to whatever she might want.

Caroline's finger traced the jaw line and then lightly touched the lips. Basmati Airways Stewardess Ghita Badewar opened them slightly and kissed the finger, and the finger moved away to be replaced by Caroline's eager mouth, pressing down on the Indian woman's and searching between her lips with a questing tongue.

The stewardess's hands were busy undoing her uniform jacket. She took Caroline's hand and placed it on her blouse front, an expanse of pure white cotton swollen full of well developed breast. Caroline massaged it enthusiastically while Ghita's hands found their way to Caroline's own blouse and pulled it up and free of her skirt waistband.

Caroline had no bra on, the stewardess quickly found, and her small, white tits fitted easily into her palms. The stewardess's bosom was much bigger, and provided ample opportunity for lengthy exploration by Caroline's fingers and mouth. While Caroline kissed each nipple alternately, and felt the weight and gorgeous curves of her superb pair, the stewardess pulled off the rest of her uniform. Blouse fell to the ground and skirt was wriggled down to ankles.

She stepped out of it, and then stepped back a little, to let Caroline see her. Naked to the waist, her glistening brown breasts swung gently in the bright white light of the galley. She pulled her panties down and offered herself in suspender belt and stockings to the hungry gaze of Caroline, who never took her eyes off her new friend as she herself got rid of her clothes.

With nothing on at all, Caroline pressed her slim, lithe body against the sweating generosity of the Indian stewardess. She felt tits pressing against tits and pubic mound against pubic mound. She reached down and took two handfuls of buttock and pressed them, pulling the girl more into her.

The Indian did the same as they embraced again, their kisses making loud suction noises as their hands groped for flesh, any flesh.

Caroline knelt before the stewardess and pulled her hairy mons towards her mouth. Her tongue was out, searching, and the girl opened her legs slightly to allow Caroline in. Caroline felt hands on the back of her head. She withdrew one hand from around the girl's hips and thrust it up between her thighs instead, finding first her weeping quim and then the tighter, drier hole just behind.

The stewardess groaned and moved her hips back and forth automatically. Caroline pushed her finger in and out and tongued with all her energy. The stewardess wobbled helplessly as she approached her moment, and cried out plaintively as her orgasm overwhelmed her.

Getting to her feet Caroline feasted her eyes on this lovely body, but as the stewardess came round the aeroplane's engine note changed and she began a breathless race to get her clothes back on.

'My sister and I are staying at the Imperial,' said Caroline, also dressing. 'Why don't you pop round this evening?'

Back in the first class seats, Charlotte was sitting next to the old man, chatting vivaciously.

'Caroline darling,' she said to her sister. 'Do you know what this wonderful old gentleman has told me? He says that after fifty years of dedication to his religion, he can make his cock change shape before your very eyes. I've invited him round to the Imperial this evening to show us.'

Cut to Room 63, Imperial Hotel, Bombay. See clock saying seven-thirty, then see, lying naked on his back on the huge double bed, the old man. His thin body was pale almost to white, and his muscles hard and well defined.

Hardest of all was his cock which at that moment was slowly changing from being a squat, fat cylinder 'about the size of a tin of Brasso' as Charlotte so eloquently put it, to a long, thin, pointed sword which would, the old man said, be totally unlike the metal polish container but rather more the size of the bayonets the British soldiers had used to put down the Indian Mutiny.

Watching this transformation, their eyes wide, were three beautiful naked girls. Charlotte knelt, idly fondling her own breasts. Caroline sat with her legs beneath her, her hand outstretched on the coverlet so that her friend Ghita could place her large and fruity bottom on it and Caroline's fingers could find their way into hot and sweaty crevices.

The old man's eyes opened and his face relaxed, the change complete. His cock stood out vertically from his body, a tremendous pillar of rock. Caroline pushed her hand into Ghita's quim and encouraged her to lift herself towards the cock. Ghita knelt forward and, with Caroline's fingers in her backside, took hold of the cock in both hands and ran her tongue up and down it.

Charlotte wanted some too. The old man had told her that holding back his ejaculation was another feat he and his fellow mystics could perform, so she got a hand to it and ran her tongue up and down the other side.

She met Ghita's lips at the top. They kissed, and then resumed their licking. Despite his religious discipline the old man's cock was aquiver with the attention of two tongues, and when one girl sat back to hold his balls and pump his cock with her hand, while the other placed her mouth entirely over the end of it, he came at last.

Great masses of sperm shot up the antique bayonet and filled Ghita's mouth. Gesturing wildly, she managed to indicate to Charlotte that she had to take over. Some spunk shot in the air as they changed, but Charlotte managed to catch most of the rest. Neither of them swallowed. What to do with it all?

Simultaneously they turned to Caroline, put their lips to her nipples, and squeezed come from their cheeks all over her delicious little tits. She rubbed it in, her attention suddenly drawn from the tops of the girls' heads to another change taking place in the old guru's cock.

Now it was bending like a rainbow. It arched from its roots in his crutch in a curve which reached his navel. The old man said a few words, which Ghita translated as meaning he needed to replenish his energies and wanted Caroline to lie on top of him.

She did, and the old boy began to lick her breasts. Painstakingly he ate up every drop of his own spunk, and the more he ate the harder he thrust his cock into Caroline's arse, a place into which it had been guided by Ghita's loving hand.

While Caroline bounced and bounded on the stiff meat rainbow, Ghita diddled Charlotte, and Charlotte diddled Ghita. Their turn would come to sample the old man's chameleon cock. Meanwhile their bodies, one brown and full of curves, one white and lean, entwined in luscious all-girl pleasure.

The End. My cinematic companion put my hand on his bulge now the second film was over. I got his cock out, then he pushed my head down to it. It only took a couple of slurps and it was dribbling come. I'd just had lunch so I was glad there wasn't much.

The man gave me a tip – twenty pounds, every little helps – and went. I went back to the bar and was immediately summoned to one of the bedrooms.

As you know I'm a tall girl. For this work I was dressed in a short dress, a skimpy little thin silk tunic, and I did look stunning (see photograph if you don't believe me). I went into this room and there, relaxing with a few beers, were the four members of a world-famous pop group who were appearing that week in – oops! – did I say Manchester? No, must have been somewhere else. I'll give them all false names so you won't be able to identify them – unless you know them as well as I do now.

They all snapped to attention when my appearance was the result of their shouting 'come in' to the knock on the door.

I strolled across the room like a model on a high-class catwalk, making straight for Jock.

'Mr Jock,' I said, cooing in a deep voice redolent with sex and summer nights. 'The newspapers have been telling lies about you. They say you don't like girls. Do you like me, Mr Jock, or not?'

Mr Jock certainly did. He was on his feet in an instant and showing me the way to the next door bedroom.

Jock only had on a pair of canvas shorts. They were off halfway across the room, and he dived naked onto the bed and spun around, lying propped up on the pillows, to watch me.

My hair was pinned up and I stood, a knee slightly forward, and took my time about unpinning it and shaking it loose. The river of hair fell beyond my shoulders, contrasting sharply with the white of my skin and the pale green of the thin silk, through which Jock must have been able to discern the dark circles of my nipples.

I kicked off my sandals and wriggled my panties down, then slowly undid the ribbon which tied my dress at the neck. I smiled and pulled the dress over my head – slowly. Jock, his prick in his hand, was beside himself with desire. I walked, a naked goddess, towards him. His hand moved twice, and the come seeped out of the end of his cock.

Still smiling (true professional) I picked up a tissue from the dressing table and wiped the creamy yellow slime from his belly and pubic hairs. I watched as his cock shrank from its former hard pride to a shrivelled little cone of pink skin, smaller than anything I'd seen since me and my little brother went in the sea at Southend when we were at infant school.

My hand tried to revive it. No response. I pulled it, tweaked it, sucked it, wiggled it, and got nowhere. It remained a pathetic excuse for a cock, something you might mistake for a rubber thimble.

In walked the rest of the group – Mick the bass, Baz the lead guitar and singer, Tadger the rhythm guitar and second singer.

'Come with us, my darling,' said Baz. 'And I'll tell you what. We can fuck better than he can.'

My tall, luscious body uncoiled itself from Jock's bed and went to meet the majority of one of the most famous pop groups in the world. I was taller than any of them – a foot taller than little Tadger – but, as Tadger muttered to himself as he watched my enormous breasts go past his eyes, they're all the same size lying down.

But where would I lie down? I decided on the green door, which led, it now transpired, to Tadger's room. This, he announced, gave him the right to go first. I stretched myself out on his bed, one leg raised, my head resting on my clasped hands. My whole body was exposed to the goggle eyes of the group, and Tadger's hand shot out to restrain Baz as he stepped forward.

'Oy, Baz,' said Tadger. 'My fucking room. My fucking fuck.'

'OK, Tadge,' said Baz. 'Yes. I must remember that line. My fucking fuck.'

Tadger, not caring about the standard he might reach in the Queen's English, was pulling off his shirt and dropping his pants as fast as he could. When he stood up again, a hairy chested short-arse with the muscles of a small gorilla, I did manage a smile. He might be short, he might be higgorant, he might be hairy, but old Tadger had a bloody enormous cock, above average in length and far, far above average in girth.

Tadger smiled too as he swaggered towards me, holding his prick as if it were a great torchlight and he was searching the sky for enemy aircraft.

His usual technique with girls involved little subtlety. To get results he relied on size and the curious appeal a hairy dwarf has for bigger women, and I was just as susceptible to Tadge's gifts as all the other big girls.

I welcomed his gigantic offering between my thighs and wrapped my legs around his hairy arse. I hugged his hairy back, and enjoyed the feel of his long hooked nose burrowing in my warm, spreading and fully endowed bosom.

The little bugger went at it straight away. There was no starting with slow strokes, teasing, withdrawing, plunging back in, gradually speeding up. No. If you wanted a lot of messing about, you didn't go to Tadge. He was a no-messing-about kind of a bloke, and he drove his very large and impressive nail home with his well muscled and totally hirsute hammer with a rapid-fire rhythm that had obviously never changed and probably never would.

In exactly two minutes and fifteen seconds of fucking, thrusting at the average rate of two strokes a second, Tadger suddenly bucked and jerked as his cream went home.

I had enjoyed it, but I hadn't come yet.

'Thank you, Tadger, that was very nice,' I said. 'Now, which of you boys is next?'

'Leave the best til last,' said Baz, pushing Mike forward. Baz stood, slowly masturbating, as Mike the bass tried to look nonchalant on his way to the beautiful Venus de Milo, except I had bigger tits and both my arms.

Mike had an exceptionally long but rather thin prick. It curved up and stretched, and was slightly ribbed, and it reminded the imaginative me of a very long piece of rigatoni.

Still feeling warm from the width and strength of Tadger, I felt quite strange as I received Mike's cock. It slipped in without me noticing, but then it kept on slipping until I thought it was going to come out of my mouth.

Mike noticed my wide eyes as he pushed the last two inches in and felt the end of his knob touch the neck of my womb.

'It's body building I need,' he said. 'If only I could build up my muscle, I could win prizes with my cock.'

'Like the girl from Devizes,' said I, coughing slightly as Mike's ten inches began moving in and out.

'What girl from Devizes?' said Tadger, who, in his own words, didn't know noffink, and was then sitting in an armchair lighting a fag and taking the top off a bottle of Bass with his teeth.

'There was a young girl from Devizes,' I gasped, my breath having to find spaces between the regular feeling of being pierced to the heart by Mike's cock.

> 'Who had breasts of different sizes. Ah.
> One was so umph, ah, small
> It was nothing at all, ah,
> But the other was large and won prizes.

Shit, Mike, give me a rest will you? Just use the first six inches for a few minutes.'

'Here, I know one of them limmerthingies,' said the Tadge, drawing on his fag, supping on his beer, then burping. 'Pardon.'

'There once was a Bishop of Birmingham,
Who buggered young girls while confirming 'em.
As they knelt seeking God
He excited his rod
And pumped his episcopal sperm in 'em.'

Baz stopped wanking for a moment to turn to his mate. 'Tadger,' he said. 'How come you know a word like "episcopal"? You've never used a word like "episcopal" in your life.'

'I heard it, didn't I? Then the woman wrote it down – she was a toff, one of them women at that Royal Variety do, a countess or something. She loved it. Liked me to come in her face. Dirty bitch. Anyway, she told me the poem and wrote it down and said I had to look that word up in a dictionary. Only I haven't got a dictionary. So I can say it but I don't know what it means.'

There was a loud giggle from me, which was quickly silenced as Mike began thrusting his full length, and at full throttle. I was drumming my heels on the small of his back as he went into the final phase, and was crying out for help from the heavenly host as his hot come spilled into my deepest recesses.

'Wow. Thank you, Mike. Come along, Baz, stop playing with your willy. Come over here and put it to some use.'

I had got off the bed and was washing myself at the sink. I turned, smiling, towelling, and ushered Baz on to the bed with a gesture. He lay on his back while I straddled him and guided his cock in. I then began to gyrate my hips and lift my bum up and down, slowly and thoroughly, so that the whole of his cock felt the benefit.

He looked up at my great dangling tits and raised a

hand to each. He felt their weight and marvellous ponderousness.

'What did you do before you worked in this place?'

'I was a secretary,' I lied, convincingly.

'What, is the money better here, then?'

'Something like that,' I said, moving my bottom deliciously.

'Why don't you leave this spot and come to work for the group? You could be the secretary of secretaries. Name your salary, you can have it, ooooahhh,' said Baz, as I did a quick series of short sharp pumps.

'I'll think about it,' I said, leaning forward so that my breasts were in kissing range for the eager Baz.

'Here, Baz,' said Mike, like Tadger lighting up and drinking from a bottle. 'Listen to this.

'An elderly man of Dumfries
Was feeling the thigh of his niece.
He cried, "No insertion!"
But by sheer exertion
He managed a breach of the piece.'

'Good, eh? I've just made it up. What do you think?'

'Tremendous, Mike. Tremendous. Oooh. Aaaah. Cor. Aaaaaaaah.'

Baz came as I leaned back, my fingers busy inside myself, and bounced our combined way to orgasm.

Baz got me a beer and a smoke and I was ready to relax – then there was a knock on the door. It was Jock. I felt sorry for him.

'Jock, give us your cock,' I said.

While the others watched, smoking, breathing heavily, drawing hard on their cigarettes I, my mouth-drooling figure totally exposed, put Jock's semi-erect prick between my soft lips.

Soon it was rigid. Almost as soon, it came. I swallowed, not a lot, and reached out my hand for a bottle of beer. The sight of Jock being sucked made Tadger get excited again. His stocky member reared up and asked for attention. I looked around. The others were still droopy.

'Come on, then, little Tadger. I'll lie flat on the bed, here, like this, and you stand there on the carpet and lob it at me. If I open my mouth at the right moment I might just catch some of it.'

Tadger, hands on hips, pushed his cock forward. I, lying with my head on the side, took the first three inches in. It had a massive bulk, this prick, and I had to struggle to get it in, but once it was there Tadger could push in and out gently and I could massage it with my tongue and cheeks.

'You know what?' he said.

I made a noise as if I was trying to reply to the dentist who was busy on my tooth at the time.

'Sorry. Of course. What I was going to say was, this is my idea of heaven, being sucked off by a beautiful tall bint with stupendous knockers – hear that, Bazzer? Stupendous? That's another word I got off the countess. Would you like me to come in your eye?'

I shook my head as Tadger gave me rather too much to cope with, thrusting harder and faster and then coming in a flood. I swallowed as fast as I could but a fair bit escaped. I wiped it from my chin with a corner of the sheet.

'I don't think I'll want any tea today,' I said.

'Full of protein, spunk is,' said Baz. 'I read that somewhere. And Vitamin A. Or was it B?'

'Darling Baz, look at your willy. I do believe you want to go out of turn.' I passed my hand along Baz's length and cradled his balls. He was ready. Mike waved him on. He was happy with another beer for the minute.

I got on the bed on all fours this time, my magnificent arse in the air, my melon-sized breasts hanging down, and Baz climbed up behind me. Pushing into my quim from behind gave him a newly heightened feeling, and he felt his cock stiffen as he began pushing his pubis up against my soft white flesh.

Leaning forward he could just get a hand on each tit, and he laid his head on my back as he enjoyed the best fuck of his life.

I began to push against him as I felt my own arousal becoming more insistent. I took a hand off the bed and took Baz's, and first made him grapple harder at my tits, and then showed him where to put his finger so that he could stimulate my clit while he shagged me.

We were sweating, and going for it flat out. I was grunting in time with Baz's pushes, and Baz was shouting Yeah! Yeah! Mike, watching, looked down at his cigarette. It had two inches of ash on it. He hadn't moved for several minutes, but he did now. He stubbed the fag out and got on the bed.

I now know that he and Baz had been having an affair, on and off, ever since the group started. The other two lads didn't know, but the sight of Baz banging into me from behind was too much.

He knelt behind Baz, gave his cock a quick dab of spit, and whammed it in.

Chapter Twelve

Murdo Sinclair had had enough of searching for a star. He needed a break. For a moment he considered going back to the office and spending a couple of weeks on his beloved magazine, on the principle that a change is as good as a rest. A chance look out of a taxi window decided him otherwise.

They were crossing the canal at Little Venice and he saw a man, dressed only in shorts and blue canvas yachting shoes, lounging in a folding chair with a cold beer. This man had not a care in the world, at least for that amount of time spent on the deck of his boat. Murdo was inspired. This is what he would do.

He rang a friend of his when he got home. Yes, he could borrow the cruiser for a week. It was moored near Marlow, on the Thames, but its engine was out of commission. This didn't matter at all, since Murdo wasn't going anywhere.

Next evening found the laird of the top shelf doing exactly what the man in Little Venice had been doing, except that Murdo had added his one anti-social habit, which he reasoned was OK out of doors on a river – his pipe. It contained a rare Balkan mixture which, a girl-friend once said after scenting it, was reminiscent of goat hair being burnt in a kippering shed.

While Murdo relaxed with his cool bottled beer, his pipe, no book, no newspaper and no radio, with the evening sun giving everything around him a golden glow, a short distance away in a very nice flat in Marlow two girls were getting ready for a night out.

Becky and Clarissa were twin sisters, born of Sir Ranald Dalton-Thwayte, bart., and Lady Amelia just over eighteen years before. They, like Murdo at that instant, had not a care in the world. They had money, they were – as the newspaper ads for Girl Fridays used to put it – super girls with lots of personality. And they were gorgeous to look at.

Not unnaturally, they liked to enjoy themselves and this usually involved a great deal of sex. The boys on the society circuit had become boring to them, and so tonight they were after something different. They were going hunting for a surprise. Tonight, the surprise was waiting for them, unknowingly, on the deck of a Thames cruiser.

Becky chose a bottle-green dress with a moderately low neckline and a short, floaty skirt. As she moved, her perky little breasts bobbled beneath the thin material and her hips slid deliciously under their deep green covering. She looked totally feminine, soft and yielding – which was right, because that is how she felt tonight.

Clarissa was feeling a bit more bouncy and assertive than her younger sister (younger by three minutes, that is, but no less important for that). From her wardrobe she selected a thin, tight-fitting red sweater which, with no bra underneath, outlined her neat tits in perfect detail. With it went an extremely tight pair of trousers, black silk, soft and clinging. The sight of her finely shaped legs going all the way up to her bum was enough to raise both eyebrows and the contents of any pair of flannel trousers.

Thus dressed to kill they trawled the pubs in Marlow and found nothing. Thinking that perhaps their evening was one of those fated not to come to fruition, they decided on a riverbank walk in the twilight and then they would get a taxi and go to a club in High Wycombe.

Murdo was settling down with his fourth bottle of beer, his pipe lit and his body relaxed in a hammock which he had slung between the mast and the cabin rail, when he saw two slim figures come into view, a good hundred yards away up on the towpath.

They were both female, young, and nicely made. That

much he could tell from the way they walked. One had on a lightweight, swaying, lilting sort of little dress that allowed a man a good peep at her thighs. There was much revealing and covering up as she walked, with a skip and a flit which made it all the more engaging.

Beside the first girl walked another. At first he thought she had nothing on below her sweater. Then he registered the trousers and, as she got closer and walked into a pool of light from another boat, he saw how close fitting they were. He could even make out something of the contours of her quim lips. These two were the answer to a sailor's prayer, had he been a sailor and in praying mood.

When they came abreast of him they stopped and looked down. He gave them a wave. They waved back.

'What a super boat,' one of them said. 'Is she yours?'

'Come down and have a look,' said Murdo. 'I've only got beer, I'm afraid.'

'Are you sure that's all you've got for us?' asked the second girl, the one in the trousers, giggling. 'I wouldn't mind something a bit stiffer.'

Maybe Murdo was imagining things, or maybe two girls had just happened to call on him who were hotter than a jam tart just out of the oven.

They were absolute crackers, he saw, as they came on deck. About eighteen or nineteen years old, not over curvy but with enough to satisfy, and red hair. He liked red hair. It reminded him of that girl from Stornoway.

'Hello,' said the one in the floaty green dress, holding out her hand. 'I'm Becky Dalton-Thwayte, and this is my sister Clarissa.'

They sounded like a couple of debutantes.

'Hello yersen,' said Murdo in as coarse a Highland accent as he could manage. 'I'm Rory McCall, from Wester Ross.'

'What's the beer?' asked Jennifer. 'Is that from Wester Ross too?'

'No, it's fucking Watney's, begging your pardon, I mean, it's Watney's.'

'Don't you worry, Rory, old mate. We don't mind "fucking", do we, sis?'

Becky put her foot on a coil of rope. The breeze flipped her dress and 'Rory' briefly saw a flash of white thigh and something darker, possibly bottle green underclothes.

Clarissa thrust her thumbs into her waistband, pushed her pelvis forward, and swaggered towards Rory as he wrestled with bottles and an opener.

'No, we don't mind fucking at all, Rory baby. What about you?'

Clarissa took the proffered bottle, put it to her lips and swung her head back. She noticed a prominent bulge in Rory's shorts as he returned from his short journey to Becky and back.

'It's a jolly warm night, don't you think, Rory?' said Clarissa. 'Do you mind?'

She put the beer bottle down and her hands went to the hem of her sweater. She hesitated, briefly, holding the thin red wool in her hands long enough to make Rory lick his lips, then she pulled it over her head.

'Sorry,' said Clarissa. 'A bit pissed. Didn't mean to shock you. Here. I'll put it back on.'

'No, that's alright,' said Rory, feeling his cock putting untoward strain on the old stitching of his veteran shorts. He took a swig of beer.

Clarissa came over to him and put a hand on his shoulder. She belched, as Rory first gazed at her luscious little tits, then almost put his hand on them.

'*Pardonnez-moi*,' said Clarissa. 'Frightfully rude. Sorry. Here, let me make up for it.'

And with that she took his tanned, muscular hand and placed it for him. He gently squeezed her perfectly white, perfectly soft little tit.

That manoeuvre completed, she put her own hand on his bulge.

'I say, sister Becky. He's got a super big chopper.'

Well, thought Rory/Murdo. Either she's just trying to be extra nice, or she hasn't seen many big pricks. Maybe the sort of boyfriend bedded by a Dalton-Thwayte only has a little one. Not that mine's terribly little, he told himself. It's just not vastly enormous.

Clarissa giggled again. 'Have you ever done it standing up in a hammock? Isn't that supposed to be the most difficult?'

Her hands were at her pants now and within seconds she was stepping out of them totally naked. She walked across to the hammock, her tight buttocks swaying.

With some skill she climbed in, lay on her back, brought her knees up and placed her hands on them.

'Come on, then, Barnacle Bill. Get your mainbrace out and give me a good splicing.'

Naked and on her back in a hammock, Clarissa opened and closed her legs and crossed her hands over her knees like some insane Charleston dancer. She was feeling high from too many Camparis and she was very much looking forward to being pleasured by the determined nautical cock which Rory was showing her over the edge of the hammock.

To Clarissa it looked like the sausage roll to others' frankfurter sausages. Murdo's private thoughts had been right. She'd seen a lot of cock, but not much good quality. Clarissa grabbed it and gave it an enthusiastic rub.

Rory, with an athleticism Clarissa hadn't expected, leaped into the hammock, pulled his shorts down around his ankles, unceremoniously pulled her knees apart, and began pushing his cock in.

It wouldn't go at first. Clarissa tried to make more room, Rory badgered and rammed, but between them they were getting nowhere. Sister Becky came to the rescue. Digging in her Gucci handbag she found a small jar of Nivea cream. Daintily collecting a smudge on the ends of two fingers she walked over to the swinging hammock, inveigled her hand between the two grunting bodies, and anointed the end of Murdo/Rory's belaying pin.

Clarissa had the weapon in both hands and her legs were over Rory's shoulders. Becky slapped him on the arse and he automatically thrust forwards – and in it went, to the breathless delight of Clarissa.

'Screw me in the scuppers with a hosepipe,' she quoted.

'What shall we do with the drunken Clarissa?' Becky muttered to herself, looking about the countryside and the riverside path, half expecting a policeman to come charging up in response to the mayhem occurring in the hammock.

Becky had never heard Clarissa make such a racket. Rory was banging away in orthodox fashion, but his prick was obviously something special because Clarissa was making more noise than an American football team and the cheerleaders put together.

She was hugging him round the neck now, her legs about his waist, and with every thrust there was a new cry of approval from the totally entranced Clarissa. Whatever it is this guy has got, Becky thought, I hope it lasts a long time.

Rory speeded up and the hammock swung violently. Clarissa was helpless, transported, her arms and legs flailing in the air, her voice a series of wails and eerie moans. If there was a policeman in the area he probably wouldn't come now, thinking there were ancient watery spirits and deep-river ghosts abroad.

There were big grunts from the man too, oompha, oompha, oompha, and faster and faster he went. Clarissa couldn't take any more and fainted. Rory went into his final phase with a charge of lightning thrusts and, as he came the rope between hammock and mast snapped and the two of them hit the deck.

An unconscious Clarissa was rudely awakened by a simultaneous blow in her back from hard boards, and a thrust beyond thrusts as the cock crashed into her vitals, propelled beyond its previous record depth by the weight of Rory falling from a height of two feet.

Becky, concerned for her sister, skipped across to her side. She needn't have worried. She'd gone again, sure, but with a wide smile on her face.

Rory picked himself out of the wreckage and staggered over to the beer crate, his shorts still around his ankles, his knob flopping between his thighs.

'Sucking your cock must be like trying to drink beer out of the other end of the bottle,' said Becky, taking a swig herself.

'Aharr, Jim lad!' replied Rory, slightly drunk and a bit lost for words.

There was a big beach-type towel on the deck. Becky pulled it over Clarissa's sleeping form, stepped to the mahogany door with brass fittings which proclaimed itself as the way to the sleeping quarters, and with a knowing look at Rory, went through.

She heard him crash to the deck again as he fell over his shorts. Then they were off, the door was open, there were feet on the ladder, and Becky was treated to the sight of a hairy white bottom.

His prick was already standing as he turned to look for Becky. She was sitting on the edge of a bunk, her feet swinging, her hands by her sides. He came over and stood in front. Her eyes were on his cock and its fierce red end.

She slipped from the bunk and knelt in front of her sailor boy, smoothly caressing the prick with both hands and her tongue. She was working up the courage to try and get the end in her mouth.

Here goes, she thought, and opened her mouth as wide as she could. She had a small, pretty mouth and the result of her efforts was not a large opening. He pushed gently forward. Her head went back. She knelt up a little taller so she could bear down on it more. He pushed again. It wouldn't go past her teeth. She looked up.

'I'm frightfully sorry, Rory old bean, but I've already eaten tonight. Leg of lamb, actually. The only way I'm going to get this one in my mouth is if we carve something off it first.'

She stood, pulled her knickers down and off, lifted her dress up, and placed a leg on his hip. He got the message and put his arms around her and heaved.

With her arms around his neck and her legs resting on his hip bones, he lowered her onto the end of his cock.

Wet with her saliva it began its journey into her gaping

quim. She gulped and grimaced. Never had she felt anything so big going up her before.

He swung his hips forwards and allowed her to drop a little.

'Fucking hell, Rory,' whispered Becky in his ear. 'You should be doing this for money.'

'Oh, I do,' replied Rory with a chortle. 'And they take pictures of me doing it. At least, they will when I get back to my work.'

Becky thought he was joking, of course. She was moving slowly up and down his mainmast, her sweet petite bottom doing wriggles and rhumbas as she began to feel at home with his cock.

'I'll leave you my card,' said Becky, breathlessly. 'Come to my flat on Friday at three p.m. and we'll do this in my circular bed. I'll pay you. Cash. Lots.'

Amused by the thought of a girl, seven or eight years younger than him, paying him for a jump he played hard to get.

'I'm not leaving my boat,' said Rory. 'Not for any amount of money in my sporran.'

'If you do what I say, you'll be able to have crates of beer sent to you from Wester Wotsit and you won't have to drink any . . . more . . . omygod . . . any . . . more . . . WATNEEEEEEEEEES!'

It was Friday afternoon and there was a coolish breeze along the quiet Marlow street at third-floor level, which was where Becky was standing on her balcony. Below her she could see a sunlit pavement and road, empty apart from a couple of parked cars and a pigeon or two.

Becky was feeling frisky and was wearing a short, semi-transparent dress like the ones Greek slave-girls wear on the movies.

It was blowing in the wind now, and anyone looking up would see right to the tops of Becky's very fine legs, which was what Murdo did as he rounded the corner and saw this beautiful girl leaning on a wrought iron balcony rail.

It was as if they were strangers and there was no

appointment. He was a casual passer-by, and she seemed to be inviting him, the way she stood, letting her dress fly up.

He turned into the building's open door and mounted two long flights of stairs and turned for the third. There was a doorway at the top, open, lit by the sun from behind. Standing there was the girl, sideways on, her body outlined in perfect clarity beneath the flimsy garment she was wearing. Murdo could see long slim legs, promisingly curved buttocks, a slim waist, cheekily proud tits . . .

He felt his cock stir as the girl turned and disappeared. He ran up the steps two at a time. When he got to the top she was gone. He went through the open door, across the drawing room and through another door. This was the bedroom. The curtains were half drawn and a shaft of sunlight, full of dancing, sparkling motes, shone on the girl, a beautiful girl with red hair which spilled over her shoulders. She was sitting with her legs curled beneath her. Her head was held high and slightly back and she looked at him frankly and open-eyed, as if to say she knew what he wanted and of course he could have it, but he had better be up to scratch.

One shoulder strap of her dress was down, so that the neckline of the dress fell away a little and Murdo could see the top of her breast. He watched her eyes go from his face to his groin, and a light smile appeared as she saw the growing bump in his jeans.

'Well, Mr Rory MacGurgle or whatever your name is, you had better get that strapped up properly, or let it out. It looks most uncomfortable as it is.'

Murdo walked to the edge of the bed and undid the buckle of his belt. He pushed down his jeans, kicked off his sandals and stepped out of the blue denim. Now he had on only a cotton shirt of a plain, faded pink, and a pair of loose-fitting boxer shorts.

The girl put her hand out as a seated duchess might to a standing young man who was being introduced. Murdo was standing in every sense of the word, and the girl's hand felt the hot meat and pronounced it good.

Shifting her position so that her breasts were more visible to Murdo and she was also able to pull down his shorts with both hands, the girl spoke again.

'How do you do, Mr MacGurgle's cock. I'm Becky, and I'm going to give you a big kiss.'

Becky was as good as her word and briefly slurped her lips and tongue along the shaft. 'Take your shirt off,' said Becky, 'and lie back on the bed. Watch.'

She reached beneath her sweet little tits and undid the belt of her dress. Then grasped the hem of the skirt and pulled it up and over her head, moving her body this way and that as she did so. Murdo felt his cock twitch and rise even farther.

Becky was dressed now only in a pair of panties, white silk, through which Murdo could see a darkened patch. She wriggled these down her magnificent legs and Murdo felt his cock positively jump at the sight of her triangular red welcome mat.

'Now, Mr MacGurgle . . .'

'Please don't call me that. My name is Murdo.'

'Murdo? Not Rory MacGurgle? OK, Murdo.'

Becky swung her leg over the prostrate Murdo and guided his cock into the hot spot. She sighed in satisfied pleasure as it slid smoothly into her. Placing a hand on the bed on either side of his shoulders, she began a long and complicated series of writhings, plungings, circling movements and rapid rises and descents.

Murdo looked up into her lovely face, her eyes closed in concentration as she was motoring along. The pace increased. She cut out the complex twirls and swirls and just kept to the rises and falls. She was fucking him hard and fast, and her breath was coming in gasps.

Her head went back as she fucked him even harder and even faster, and she cried out, something like 'Yarr-roooo!' Murdo thought, as he felt her vagina go into a rapid, involuntary spasm of muscle jerks and her fluids flow warmly down his shaft.

Becky, for the moment over the hill and far away, fell on top of her lover and flopped. He was still as stiff as ever, his cock demanding more.

He pushed up, gently probing Becky with his cock, not wanting to overwhelm her but having to obey the urgent commands issuing from his rigid member. Becky groaned and awoke.

'So, Murdo wants more, does he? Well, OK, but you can do the work this time.'

Becky rolled off his body and lay next to him, legs in the air. She looked at him with a coquettish eye, and smiled happily as he rolled over too and placed himself between her eagerly waving thighs.

In the dick went, up to the curlies, as far as it would go. Out it came, withdrawing like a scimitar from a curved silk scabbard. In it went, thrusting home with determination.

Murdo's cock felt as hard as a Glasgow policeman's mahogany truncheon. In and out it went, without mercy, without restraint. He was fucking like a steam engine, a remorseless, relentless engine which chuffed and whistled and ground its way up the hill.

He felt Becky stir beneath him. She was starting to respond again. He went a bit faster. She murmured her appreciation. He grabbed her legs in the crooks of his arms and pushed her further over. Her quim could not have been more accessible, and into it he thrust with all his might.

Becky whimpered. And again. He was getting to her. The great Murdo's cock was transporting her from normal life to something altogether more blissful. In he rammed, out he pulled, in he rammed again.

Becky's arms were round him, willing him closer and deeper. Her legs grappled at him, her pubic mound pushed up ever harder towards him. More, more, she wanted more.

Murdo felt his own climax approaching and went for it. He fucked as fast and as hard as he could and the woman beneath him gurgled and jibbered and bucked as his hot stream shot into her passage, which opened and closed in its frantic attempts to convey his precious seed upwards to its eternal destination.

'Phew,' was all he could say a few moments later.

'And fuck me pink,' said Becky.

He rolled off her and lay on his back, noting with pride that his cock was still hard and at full stretch.

'Aha,' said Becky. 'My difficulty now is that I have to leave you. I have places to go and people to see. You, I see, still have some energy left. This is fortunate as I have taken the liberty of arranging a second appointment for you. My old school chum Veronica is waiting in Clarissa's room – Clarissa, incidentally, couldn't be with us this afternoon owing to a hangover from last night. She's had to go to the health club. Anyway, you just stay there and I'll send Veronica in. Vron, by the way, can be a bit strange. Don't worry if she seems peculiar. It's only her way.'

She gave his cock a little goodbye suck, slipped her dress over her head, crumpled her panties up in her hand and swayed from the room, leaving Murdo with a lovely vision of a neat little arse covered in gauze.

Murdo fingered his cock thoughtfully. It was certainly as hard as ever. He moved his hand up and down the familiar shaft. He felt sleepy. Maybe he'd have forty winks before this other girl arrived.

'Let me do that for you,' said a soft, upper-class English voice. 'Or would you rather I did something else?'

His hand suddenly stilled in mid-stroke, Murdo opened his eyes and saw two upper thighs, a black triangle of hair, a gently swelling tummy and a narrow waist. These components of the body beautiful were swaying like a Hawaiian dancer as their owner pulled her dress over her head, now revealing a very big pair of breasts with large brown nipples sticking out.

The face was smiling and surrounded by flowing black hair. She had lovely teeth. Her eyes were luminous but dark at the centre, the pupils slightly dilated, and she looked at him openly.

'My name is Veronica and I am here to satisfy you. Tell me, sir, would you prefer I gave you relief with my hand, or would you like to come in my mouth? There are other options available, of course, all free and part of the inclusive service provided for you by the Veronica Fly-me All-in Holiday.'

'All-in sounds a good idea,' said Murdo, wishing she were a bit less professional. She reminded him of a waitress.

The gorgeous-looking girl bent over his cock and placed her lips around the end of it. Her right hand went to his balls and stroked them lightly. Her left hand played with his cockshaft, tickling it at the base, wanking it, stroking the big vein.

Her mouth went up and down on the purple club end and her tongue licked divinely at the most sensitive parts. Murdo watched her, and looked at her marvellous tits shaking with the activity, and gazed in fascination as his cock slid in and out of the mouth of a young naked woman beautiful enough to be Miss Great Britain.

She certainly knew what she was doing. Now she had a ball in each hand and was bending harder over his cock, and taking more of it in. She seemed to be able to take an ever increasing amount.

She squeezed his balls gently as, taking a deep breath, she plunged down on him and encased the entire length of his prick.

Murdo realised she was one of these people who have learned how not to gag, like sword swallowers and people who can drink pints of beer in two seconds. His whole cock was in her mouth, the first three inches of it down her throat.

He reached for her tits as he felt the come welling up inside him, and he kneaded their ample meat as he shot straight down into her stomach.

When she was sure he'd finished, she pulled slowly off him. Murdo expected a noise like a cork coming out of a wine bottle, so tight was the feeling. In fact she smiled, swallowed a little, raised her hand to her mouth and burped.

'Sorry,' she giggled. 'Pardon. It always does that. Like a bicycle pump, your organ, and the air has to get out somehow. Was that satisfactory, sir? Oh! Oh, I say! Will there be anything else?'

Veronica had noticed with surprise that Murdo's prick was still standing. Normally when she'd administered the V-special deep throat job, cocks flopped, drained of life. But here was something different, something new – and Veronica knew for a fact he'd already been with Becky, so he must have come at least once with her. How very odd.

Veronica stood beside the bed and raised her arms above her head, clasping her hands together. She turned, slowly and luxuriantly, to allow Murdo a complete inspection of her statuesque body, with its jutting tits so large and youthfully solid, her sharply indented waist, her swelling hips and superbly rounded bottom, her soft and cushiony thighs, her small black forest with the brownish, curling lips just discernible within.

Murdo's hand was on his cock again.

'It all looks very nice,' he said. 'What would you recommend? Which is the dish of the day?'

'Well, sir, you've already had the dish of the day. I think it might have to be something very special for dessert.'

She stood in front of him and put her fingers in her quim. Closing her eyes she frigged herself for a few moments and then did something else down there, Murdo couldn't quite make out what.

He realised when she got on the bed. Facing away from him she swung her leg high over him. He saw her quim gaping, and he saw a trail of dampness from the forest glade to the clearing in which her puckered little bumhole hid.

Reaching behind her for his cock she guided it to the lubricated spot and sat back. The quim juices transferred to the tight entrance by her clever fingers had done the trick. He slid into her arsehole without any bother.

She leaned forward and grasped his feet, rubbing her tits from side to side across his legs as she rotated her big round arse.

'This, sir, is the V-special double extra with side orders. I hope you like it.'

Murdo did indeed like it. He liked the feeling of the nipples brushing across his legs, and he liked the sensation of the full weight of her breasts when she pushed them against him.

Particularly he liked looking at the shaft of his cock disappearing into her arse, and the big white cheeks moving up and down and round and round, and the gloriously all-round feeling of his prick shaft in that confined sheath.

The skin of his cock, a lurid, deep red by now, seemed utterly decadent as it disappeared and reappeared between two pure white and unblemished buttocks. How those shining moons orbited the pillar of his world, how they worked at massaging the nerve ends in the blood-filled organ. He began slapping her arse cheeks playfully.

Veronica gripped his feet tighter and thrust faster down onto Murdo's prick. She bounced and bounded, her white flesh wobbling with the effort. She was sweating. This was hard work. Faster and faster she went as his slaps became more insistent.

Every time her bottom rose, he slapped it hard, twice, a crisp blow on each cheek. If she stayed in the air too long she got more slaps. There was a distinct rhythm to it. She couldn't go any faster. Please let him come.

Her prayer was answered. She sat down hard as she felt the first shot of hot spunk, and Murdo played a drum roll with his hands on her back as he jerked his cock into her with each spurt.

When it was all over, it was a very tired Miss Great Britain who dismounted from the highland stag. Her eyes were half closed as she reached for her dress.

The sun had moved round since Murdo had first entered the room and seen Becky on the bed, but there was still enough illumination where he lay to show up his cock, and to cast a long dark shadow from it.

There was a picture of it on the wall, a silhouette, a shadow cast by the golden glow of heaven of a cock at last collapsing from its rigidity. Veronica fell to her knees and held the softening prick upright.

'Truly,' she said to the shadow on the wall, 'the Lord has blessed you. Blessed be the long, the hard and the stiff.'

'Quite so,' said Murdo, reaching out for one of her magnificent melons.

'And blessed be the fruit which groweth past all understanding. And if you keep doing that' – she was sucking his cock again – 'we'll never get home tonight.'

Chapter Thirteen

Camilla 'Frenchie' Tickell, temporary co-editor in charge of *Sir Lancelot*, was a happy rabbit. Her idea for a feature series, based on the first sexual experiences of well-known people, had been a roaring success.

After her own story had begun the series the magazine had received all kinds of enquiries, some of them genuine. The next month they carried the story of Fennella Lambert, the actress, who had just been 'killed' after eight years in a long-running soap.

After her riveting piece of sexual history appeared in *Sir Lancelot*, detailing her seduction as a virgin by a member of the clergy, she landed a big part in a Hollywood movie – much to the delight of the tabloid press.

Sir Lancelot slipped effortlessly past the other men's magazines and took up the top spot, and the office was inundated with offers from slightly has-been showbiz stars who wanted to relaunch their careers.

This next instalment was going to be a cracker, thought Frenchie. She was going to give it double space and a subtitle:

> 'My First Time', or should we say 'Their First Time'?
>
> *The chart-topping singing duo, The Imogen Sisters, tell their story of how they seduced two male virgins in one night!*

It had needed a lot of rewriting. Chart-topping singing duos, particularly ones who hadn't topped the charts for donkeys' years, were obviously not as good at literary matters as they were at things harmonic. Anyway, Frenchie was reasonably pleased with it at last.

We were on tour in India and decided to see the countryside for a day or two. We got out of the smog and sounds of the city and were bowling along a dusty road when – bang! Our car broke down.

A few minutes later, carrying a small suitcase each, we began the trudge down the long, hot, straight and narrow road which would lead eventually to somewhere – we hoped.

Inside half an hour we had overtaken a bullock cart. It was going more slowly than we were, but that was a small price to pay in return for having the load taken off our feet.

The man in charge, or rather boy, made no attempt at conversation, nor did he remark on the interesting fact of two stunning (if we say so ourselves) white women with auburn hair beneath our wide straw hats, dressed in thin cotton frocks which would have been considered unforgivably immodest had any of his own sisters worn them, hitching a lift on his cart.

He was on his way to the nearest town where there was a market. He had a few chickens in cages and some rapidly wilting vegetables. What he hoped to get in exchange, we couldn't even guess.

There were about four miles to go to the town. It took us two hours and it was late morning when we got there. The first priority was a drink. Stalls at the market offered milk of an uncertain vintage but we had been hoping for something more adjacent to a gin and tonic, perhaps preceded by two gallons of ice cold lemonade.

On the corner we spied the Connaught Hotel or, more accurately, the Con–aug–t Hote–. Its shutters needed painting, its doorway awning needed mending, but it had a certain faded grandeur and just possibly there might be the vestiges of civilisation within.

At the desk was an extremly handsome young man whose reactions at the sight of the famous Imogen Sisters were altogether more in line with what we generally expected from such persons. Not for this lad the indifference to the impossible of the philosophical bullock cart boy. No. This lad had felt his cock tweak and was dreaming it might not tweak in vain.

He explained politely that his name was Amerjit, and that certain drinks were indeed available but only to residents. Lunch would be served shortly. Partaking of lunch would count as residency – in fact, so would the overt intention of partaking. If we were to express such an intention, he could serve us immediately with limitless iced lemonade, and gin and tonic for as long as his small store of tonics lasted.

On the off chance, Ingrid asked him if he had a car.

'Yes, indeed, Miss. We have a truly excellent motor car. Today unfortunately it is having an operation performed upon its cooling system which, in the way of such things, has become counter-productive in its operation.'

'Will the car be available tomorrow?' asked Ingrid.

'Yes, indeed, it will be available. Yes, indeed. For the use of residents,' he added. We looked at each other.

'Amerjit,' said Ingrid. 'Bring a large jug of lemonade onto that verandah there, where we can sit in the shade and sip. Take our bags upstairs to your very best twin room and expect us for lunch, dinner and breakfast. That is, assuming that you have arrangements installed for the washing of dirt and dust from the persons of tired visitors, I mean residents?'

'Oh, yes, indeed,' said Amerjit, his eyes brightening at the thought of us washing ourselves. 'We have the bath and the shower and, on certain of the holy days, they both work.'

After a refreshing lemonade we would try the bathing facilities. We mounted a fairly grand staircase, led by Amerjit, and were shown into a room big enough to sleep fifty.

'Through there is the bathroom,' said Amerjit. 'Oh.' His face fell. 'I am very sorry. The maid has forgotten to change the towels. I shall bring you some clean ones. These are from the last guest, a Russian engineer of grubby habits. I am sorry. Please, excuse.'

And this is what happened next . . .

Flustered, Amerjit disappeared with the old towels. By the time he got back, Imelda was in the bath and Ingrid was in her silk dressing gown. Ingrid sat by the window in a cane chair, legs crossed, the silk casually open at neck and thigh and the light from the window silhouetting a lovely breast through the gossamer material. Amerjit coughed. Ingrid waved him towards the bathroom.

'Take the towels in, Amerjit, then come and talk to me.'

Amerjit almost had a fit when he walked into the bathroom and found the naked Imelda staring frankly back at him, with breasts above water level and a patch of red-brown hair visible at the junction of two fine thighs just below the surface.

'The bath's working today, Amerjit,' said Imelda. 'But not the shower. You'll have to come up and fix the shower if I want one, won't you?'

Amerjit left the towels and backed out of the room, his eyes trying to look everywhere except at Imelda's bosom but failing to see anything else.

Ingrid was smoking a cigarette in a holder and sipping at a gin. Amerjit stood alongside as instructed.

'Now, Amerjit,' she began. 'Have you any girl-friends?'

'No, indeed, Miss. All day I work here at the hotel, and at night I study. I am going to be a lawyer. I have no time for girls.'

'That is a pity,' said the languid Ingrid, uncrossing her legs and crossing them the other way, making sure that a long expanse of soft thigh skin was flashed upwards to Amerjit's goggling gaze. 'Because it seems such a waste of a nice young man like you. How old are you, Amerjit?'

'I am seventeen and a half, Miss.'

Ingrid shifted her position and accidentally, as it were, brushed the back of the hand with the cigarette across the bulge in Amerjit's trousers. He jumped.

'I'm so sorry,' Ingrid said, getting quickly to her feet. 'Have I burned you?'

She bent to look, and stroked the bulge as if to make sure that no cigarette ash had attached itself to his trousers. Amerjit made noises like a drowning frog.

Ingrid pushed her body against him, her thigh pressing his erect but restrained cock.

'Don't you like me?' she asked, innocently, as Amerjit jumped again.

'Oh, yes, indeed, Miss. It's just that . . .'

'That you're not used to girls, isn't that it?'

He nodded, unable to speak, as Ingrid ran her hand up and down his thigh, pausing long and tenderly on the bulge which now threatened to prise the seams of his trousers apart.

'Tell you what,' said Ingrid, fiddling with the buttons on his fly. 'Let's get him out in the open air and see what the problem is, shall we?'

Her cool hand went inside, grasped the hard, hot brown shaft and brought it into the light. She skinned it slowly back and forth, her fingers pressing and slipping as she experimented with its hardness and movability.

'Do you know what to do next?' asked Ingrid, an eyebrow raised in a slightly mocking way.

Amerjit nodded his head but mouthed a 'no' with his lips.

Ingrid backed towards the bed, still holding onto

the prick which got ever harder in her hand. She lay back, undid the silk sash of her dressing gown and pulled the material to one side. Amerjit beheld a white tummy, slightly swelling, with a tuft of hair at its base. There, two creamy white thighs parted to offer him a stairway to heaven. She made another pull at the gown and two perfect breasts were revealed, not large but with a shape defined by the god of breasts as that to which every woman should aspire and every man should want to hold.

Groaning with incredulous delight Amerjit was manoeuvred on top of this bird of paradise and he felt his cock slide into her warm, wet crevice.

This was the first time such a thing had ever happened to him. He had an older sister who had told him about matters of procreation, and she had shown him her tits and her quim, and her bum, and had massaged his cock until white fluid seeped from the end. But she wouldn't go any further.

Ingrid, realising that Amerjit didn't even know to move in and out, began some small movements of her own. She expected him to come any instant, and so he did, his eyes wide, his mouth open and gargling a few words in the local dialect.

Ingrid pushed him off and got up, wrapping herself in her silk.

'Well, Amerjit, I'm sure that was nice for you but it did nothing for me. I can see you are going to need some serious tuition, and we only have today. And possibly tonight, if you can bear to leave your studies for that long. Ah, I see it's time for your first lesson.'

Imelda had come in with just a towel wrapped around her.

'Meldi, darling. Little Amerjit here doesn't know much about girls. Now, why don't you show him a thing or two while I have a quick bath. Then, we'll give him a Mistress Class together.'

'Well, Amerjit,' said Imelda, 'the first thing you have to learn is good manners. Now, it is the most appalling manners, you know, for a chap to be hanging around with lots of clothes on, while a girl hasn't, shall we say, much on at all? So, first lesson is, get 'em off.'

She took off his sandals while he struggled to get his trousers and underpants off. As she bent forward to help with the shirt, her towel fell away. She stood, towel held to waist, her breasts exposed in all their glory. She made a half attempt to pull the towel up but managed to hide only one breast. The other, with its rosebud nipple, peeped over the top of the white cotton.

Amerjit was now lying naked on the bed, a hand over his genitals, his eyes glued to Imelda.

'Oh, come, come, Amerjit. Are we shy? I'll tell you what. You show me yours and I'll show you mine.'

Amerjit's hand moved away, revealing a long, slim, semi-slack prick lying across his brown thigh.

'Quite a good flop, as I believe they say in the army, Amerjit,' said Imelda, holding her towel to her with one hand but coming close enough to get hold of his cock with the other. She felt it leap in her palm.

'Gosh. I think it wants to play. But I've just been in the bath and you've just been in my sister. Come over here.'

She took him to the wash stand where there was a jug of water and a bowl. She washed his cock and balls for him, then took the towel from her body to dry them.

Amerjit's prick stood up immediately. It positively heaved itself upright.

Imelda turned and put her back to him. She reached between her thighs and pulled his prick through, and pressed her buttocks against him. She wanked his cock as if it were her own, Amerjit pushing hard to give her enough meat to massage. She got the shaft of it nestled into her quim and squeezed it there, while rubbing the nut between finger and thumb. Amerjit, beginning to feel braver, put his hands under her armpits and tentatively felt her breasts.

'That's my boy,' sighed Imelda under her breath. She paused in her wanking to gather some spittle on the end of her index finger, which she then transferred to the glans of his prick. She rubbed that with just the fingerprint pad of the one finger and was rewarded almost straight away with a jet of spunk which shot across the room and landed on the faded carpet at a distance of five or six feet.

'Very good, Amerjit,' said Imelda. 'Now, do you think you'll be able to control yourself for ten minutes? Because that's how long my sister and I are going to be, showing you what can be done to a woman with just a tongue. Sit in that chair.'

He sat, nodding, dumb, as Imelda Imogen, pop star and nympho, walked across to the bed, placing one foot precisely in front of the other to get maximum movement in her tasty little bum. She lay across the bed, one leg casually raised by bringing the foot up beside the other knee. Her hand strayed to that knee and idly scratched it, lightly, with just one fingernail.

She allowed the hand to move onto her thigh, then lay back with a sigh as her fingers moved up the inside, past the freckles, and found the browny pink lips of her tunnel.

As she massaged the furrow of contentment she said Mmmmm, and Aaaah, and then: 'Amerjit, do you know the word "cunt"?' You do? Do you know where it comes from? No, not from the British army, from one of your chaps. A goddess, minor of course, called Kunti. Also from a Greek of the same name, well, nearly. Kunthus, actually. Then there's the Kundalini, a spirit supposedly based in your spine. Mmmm. Just there, I think.'

'Here, darling sis, let me.'

Ingrid was in the doorway, her thin dressing gown clinging to her damp body. Every curve, every inlet and outcrop were revealed and hidden at the same time as she walked across the room. Amerjit, staring, hypnotised, felt his prick move again.

Ingrid bent her head to the hairy place between Imelda's thighs. Keeping herself open to Amerjit's view, she protruded her tongue and gently licked the spot. Imelda made some more satisfied noises as the tongue worked deeper and harder. Ingrid added two fingers, and rubbed the roof of Imelda's cave while tonguing the walls and floor. Imelda, after a sudden rise in the tenor of her groans, came with a bang. Her legs jiggled and flapped and her arms pulled at the back of her sister's head as Ingrid forced the tongue in as deep as it would go.

'Ah, that's better,' said Imelda, recovered. 'That's the way to do it. Now, Amerjit, do you think you could manage something like that? Come over here and try.'

Ingrid lay back on the bed as the hesitant Amerjit approached, licking his lips nervously. Ingrid shuffled well across, so that Amerjit had to climb on and kneel beside her on all fours. Imelda, keeping close, thrust her hand between his legs from behind and cradled his balls.

'Now, Amerjit. Get busy. And just in case you go slack at the job, I have the very encouragement you'll need.'

She gave his balls a squeeze, not too hard, but enough. His head went down to the little coco mat and, as Ingrid's legs opened wide, he began to lick a quim for the first time in his life.

The taste was curious, a sort of musty, slightly bitter flavour. There were many folds and pockets, small secret places which he didn't know the name of – if they had names. Much of his exploration was like wandering lost in the woods – he went round in circles, backtracked, went over the same ground a number of times, but gradually from Ingrid's reactions he began to understand which pathways were the most fruitful to tread.

In particular he learned about the little stiff bit. There was a small, knobby part near the top towards the front of this fresh pothole into which he was diving, a stalactite which vibrated when touched and whose vibrations obviously sent important messages to the rest of the system. He found that by concentrating on this odd little object he could elicit the kind of responses from Ingrid that she had been getting from Imelda.

Ingrid began to bounce beneath him. Her legs tried to wrap around his head but the angle was wrong. Her hands pressed him down, further and harder. He was vaguely conscious of Imelda doing something to his balls and cock but he wasn't sure what, as Ingrid's impending climax took him over completely. He was her slave. His job was to make her come. It was an unpaid job. There was nothing in it for him except the distinct possibility of asphyxiating, but he stuck to his task.

His tongue was weary and aching. His jaw felt as if he'd been to the dentist. But Ingrid was insistent, and was making umphing noises, and was pushing her body into his face while at the same time pressing his face into her body.

He darted his tongue sharply across the little stiff object, rasping it with his taste buds, back and forth as fast as he could.

With a succession of squeaks and umphs, Ingrid rose towards her goal. She was almost there. A few more licks, come on, Amerjit, again, again, again, AGAIN!!! Wow.

Her legs fell back onto the bed and her hands released the pressure on his head. He emerged, blinking, into the light, to realise that Imelda was at him with both hands, one from behind holding his balls, and one in front sliding up and down his cock, which was hard and curved and ready for action.

Emboldened and with an air of new sophistication, Amerjit turned and lay down on his back beside the prostrate Ingrid. Imelda, still holding his cock in the air, got closer. She wanked him slowly, looking with amusement into his eyes and seeing the awakening of India's Great Lover after just thirty minutes of combat with the Imogen Sisters.

She bent her beautiful head towards his prick and opened her lips. Amerjit's eyes stared, wide, at this entirely new possibility, and then closed in bliss as the softest, sweetest mouth took his apprentice's cock into its warm and velvety time-served depths.

Amerjit had entertained thoughts of Imelda straddling him. He had heard of such things, of the woman making love while on top of the man, and hoped to try it one day. But the brilliant, luxurious sensation of being sucked put all such antics from his mind. This was the ultimate. This was what a woman was meant to do for a man.

It took Imelda, an expert, whose hands were manipulating his balls and scratching at his cock root, about one minute and twenty seconds of mouthwork to bring the come surging up his shaft. She kept sucking as it came – and how Amerjit shouted in his delight – and didn't stop until it was all out and his cock was as clean as a whistle.

She sat up and smiled, her tits looking heavenly, her hand just straying to her lips to wipe a tiny escaped drop away.

'Well,' Amerjit,' she said. 'That was first course. I had soup and you had fish. I think it's time you went down to the kitchen and got us something more substantial. Will half an hour be OK?'

Amerjit dressed and, with a spring in his step, went off to cook some lunch. This would be special, for his new friends, the two princesses from England. This would be a royal lunch. There would be Murghi Massala, there would be a Biryani with almonds and golden sultanas and candlenuts and silver leaf. He would cook the lightest Puri bread and the most fragrant vegetable Bhajia with pineapple and mango. This would be some lunch.

We dressed too and went for a short walk around the town. We created a stir, of course, wherever we went in our flimsy cotton dresses with our long bare legs giving every man all kinds of ideas, but we're used to it. The lustings of a few locals weren't going to upset us.

After lunch, which was truly wonderful, we went back to our room and slept all afternoon, in separate beds. Then we bathed again before going down for an early evening drink in the hotel bar. The barman wasn't Amerjit! It was another handsome young man, about Amerjit's age, seventeen or eighteen, and his name was Ramiz and he seemed very on edge.

His hand shook as he poured the gin and tonic. He made a terrible hash of getting the ice out of the ancient metal tray it had been made in, with ice cubes crumbling into pieces and flying across the bar almost as frequently as the apologies.

Realising what must have happened, we smiled to ourselves and looked forward to a night with a little more variety than Amerjit's cock alone could provide. How much, we wondered, had Ramiz been told?

First, dinner. There were barbecued things from the tandoori oven, kebabs of meat, some of it whole, some of it minced, with a hot-tasting yellow sauce which seemed to be yoghurt, mint and various spices.

Then there was a selection of rich dishes, something deep red-coloured with tomatoes and paprika, something dark brown with fish in it which was so hot we could hardly eat it.

Everything had a full quantity of garlic, and by the end we were sweating profusely – which of course is the idea of spicy food in hot countries, we told ourselves.

The barman was still in a state of high agitation so we decided it was time for a little peace and quiet on the verandah, if Ramiz would be so kind as to bring us an iced dry sherry, seeing as there wasn't any malt whisky. The night was close, sultry, and both of us lay back in our cane armchairs and put our feet up on little stools.

We wafted ourselves with the fans provided and made sure that the skirts of our dresses were riding high up our thighs, ready to make Ramiz almost drop his tray of drinks. And this is what happened next.

When he'd gone, Ingrid asked Imelda if there was anything to notice about him.

'He's changed his trousers,' Imelda said. 'They were black before. Now they're brown.'

'Problem is, sister dear, do you think he's done something involuntary at the back or the front?'

They giggled, and then suppressed it as Amerjit appeared in an apron, asking if they'd enjoyed their meal.

'Terrific, Amerjit. Loved the little balls on sticks. Perhaps the fish curry was a trifle on the nuclear-powered side for two amateur curry eaters like us. But what we want to know is, what have you been telling poor little Ramiz? He's like a cat on hot bricks.'

'Please, memsahibs, Ramiz is my cousin. He works behind the bar. He is excited by seeing two such beautiful memsahibs. I have told him nothing more, I promise.'

'Amerjit,' said Imelda, 'you're a rotten liar. That poor boy has already had one accident in his trousers, and that's not just from seeing a flash of memsahib's leg. What time does the bar close?'

'It closes when you no longer require it, Miss. No one else will be a customer tonight.'

Imelda got up and walked back into the bar room. Ramiz was polishing the same glass he had already polished twenty times. Imelda swung her hips as she walked towards him, making sure the hem of her skirt floated out and allowed the boy a glimpse of perfect leg well above the knee.

He cleared his throat and squawked a rough approximation to, 'Yes please, Miss?'

'Ramiz,' said Imelda. 'I think you're a very naughty boy. I've a good mind to spank you. Now, put a couple of your very coldest bottles of beer on a tray, and bring them up to my room, with a packet of English cigarettes. OK?'

She swung out through the door with a coquettish glance over her shoulder. Ramiz got busy with the order, fumbling with bottles and glasses and almost dropping the lot.

He thought he had better tell Amerjit what was happening so he went out onto the verandah. There he found Ingrid on all fours behind the armchairs, with Amerjit kneeling behind her. Her dress was thrown up over her back and Amerjit was fucking her.

Ramiz stuttered. Amerjit told him with his eyes to clear off. What could Ramiz do? He went and picked up his tray and headed upstairs, knees trembling, hands trembling, everything trembling.

He was like Amerjit had been earlier that day, a virgin. He had never even seen a girl naked, much less a memsahib like Amerjit had, sitting in the bath and lying on a bed. Knocking on the door with nervous knuckles, he heard a crisp voice commanding him to come in.

How the tray stayed in his hands he would never know. Imelda was by the window, leaning casually against the side of it with her head resting on the long drapes. She was wearing a garment completely unfamiliar to Ramiz.

It seemed to be made of lace and froth. It was pink

and white, a kind of sleeveless jacket which was tied at the neck and then went out at an angle and was very short. Ramiz could see the beginnings of Imelda's buttocks where her legs met the hem of this strange garment, and it appeared that this was all she had on until she turned towards him. The movement revealed that there was another item of clothing under the first one, a pair of lace-trimmed panties. It also revealed for an instant the central portions of a pair of white breasts.

The only point where the jacket was tied was at the neck. It was open all the way down the front and only stayed in place when the wearer was still. When she was moving, as she was now, across the room towards him, the jacket floated open and closed and portions of breast and, once, a nipple peeked at him. He groaned.

'What's the matter, Ramiz? Don't you like my outfit? Doesn't your girlfriend have anything like this?'

Ramiz shook his head, quite unable to speak.

'Well, you must get her some. They're called baby-doll pyjamas and they're all the rage in England. An actress called Carrol Baker wore them in a film.'

She took his tray from his shaking hands and placed it down on a table. Then she took both his hands in hers and guided them under her pyjama jacket to those priceless peeping jewels.

Ramiz, still speechless, felt his knees knocking. Then, he heard his knees knocking. Imelda, trying not to laugh, asked him to be careful not to trap anything between his kneecaps.

She helped him get a little bolder, showing how to caress her tits and how to stroke the nipples. When he was able to do this for himself, she undid the bit of pink ribbon at her neck and let the jacket fall completely open. Then she placed a hand on his bulge and was pleasantly surprised to find a ridge of hard meat of considerably greater length than she'd allowed herself to hope.

'Well, Ramiz,' she sighed in admiration. 'Quite the elephant's trunk, what? Or is it a poisonous pet snake you keep down your trousers? Let's have a look, shall we?'

Ramiz's hands froze on her tits as she put both her own hands to the job of unbottoning his trousers. She burrowed inside, past shirt tails, through shorts, and found what she wanted. She yanked it out into the open, a great, long, hard cylinder of cock, straighter than most, a very potent weapon.

'Ramiz! What a beauty! Come over here and show me what you can do with it.'

Alas, they didn't get as far as the bed. As Imelda marched him across the room, pulling him behind her by his length, she felt a sudden seeping of fluid on her wrist and looked back and down to see him coming.

'I thought this might happen, Ramiz. That's why I wanted the beer and cigarettes. Now, I suggest you go into the bathroom, take your clothes off, have a nice bath with lots of smelly crystals and scented soaps of which you will see endless supplies, and come back in here when fully refreshed. Then, I'll show you what to do next. Go on. Run along.'

Imelda retied her ribbon while Ramiz shambled to the bathroom, half putting his cock away, half taking his shirt off, totally confused by the first sex he'd ever had not involving just himself.

Imelda had finished the first beer and was well into the second by the time he emerged, dressed rather endearingly in Ingrid's dressing gown. It just reached below his crutch. Were he to get a hard on, thought Imelda . . . just a minute, what was that? Yes. She could see the end of his cock hanging down. Bloody hell. It must be just as long when it's slack as it is when it's . . .

Imelda was lying on the bed, propped up by the pillows. Her jacket fell open near her waist. Ramiz could see an expanse of white skin, most of a tummy and just the very beginnings of the underneath of a breast.

'Ramiz, darling,' said Imelda. 'Do come over here and take that silly dressing gown off. That's better. Now, I want to show you what to do with that mighty weapon of yours. Come along. Bring it here. There. That's a good boy.'

Imelda turned on the bed towards the mute, naked youth standing at her side. Exhaling smoke as she stubbed out her cigarette, she watched the long cock twitch at the thought of what might be coming. The cigarette out, her hand went to another object similarly shaped but many, many times the size. As she lazily stroked it she felt its power begin to return. She pulled him by it towards her, so that she could get the end of it to her lips without stirring from her pillowed position.

The boy was half-kneeling on the edge of the bed, looking down in amazement at the end of his prick, his long, hard prick, which had previously known no comfort but his own right hand, disappearing inside the mouth of the memsahib.

She seemed to relish it. She took it out and looked at it. She tried it for hardness; not quite satisfactory yet. Her tongue tip touched it on its very end, and then on the curved ridge of its glans, and her hand moved all the way up and down the shaft.

If it gets any harder, he thought, it will break.

She looked up into his eyes and smiled. Leaving go of his cock she swiftly undid the ribbon and took off her jacket. Then, more slowly, she placed her thumbs inside the elastic of her panties and wriggled them off her hips, showing to Ramiz first her browny-red tuft, then the outward signs of her quim, and making sure her thighs moved with agonising temptation as the wisp of lace worked its way down her legs.

She lifted her feet towards her so she could whip the knickers over and off. She threw them across the room, then lowered her legs to the bed. They lay there, flat and together.

Then she reached for his cock again and gave it a few quick wanks and, with one hand on the shaft and the other round his tight, muscular behind, she eased him onto the bed on top of her. Her legs opened. The long, long cock was presented to the appointed place.

A remarkable cock of startling dimensions, which had never seen full service before, was waiting to find its way into a delicious memsahib's quim which, still young and juicy, had seen service long and often.

Imelda's hand made certain that the knob end was perfectly positioned, then put both her hands on his backside. She gripped a buttock with each fist, fiercely, and pushed her body hard against his. He pressed home and in it went.

Hell. It felt as if it were a yard long. She wanted it right in. She got a leg out from under him and wrapped it around his back. She got the other leg out and it found its way over his shoulder. She could not be more exposed.

Ramiz shifted his position slightly and pushed home more. His cock touched the neck of her womb and she shuddered with pleasure. He pulled out a little, then thrust back.

Imelda closed her eyes and moved her left leg slightly so it reached as high as possible over his shoulder. Now to enjoy being penetrated to the very core.

Ramiz got the idea. The memsahib wanted his cock in as far as possible. His cock was hard. It had never been harder, even when he had found that magazine in the waste bin of the American's bedroom in the hotel. There had been pictures of girls in that magazine, girls with huge melons instead of breasts and no hair down below. He had taken his cock out there and then and pumped it furiously, but even on that day it had not been as hard as now.

Imelda stirred beneath him as if in luxurious sleep.

'Mmmmmm,' she said. 'More,' she said.

He began to thrust and withdraw, slowly. It seemed to take an age for the whole of his length to come out of Imelda. On and on it went, more and more inches until at last the glans reached the rim of her quim. Then, slowly, he pushed it back in, on and on, up to the very hilt. He felt his balls pressing against her. He couldn't go in any further.

She took a hand off his backside and found one of his hands. She showed his finger where the clit was. He tickled it as he moved in and out of her.

The combination was too much for Imelda. She began jerking. Her hips were moving too fast for Ramiz. He couldn't go in and out as fast as that. He couldn't keep time, but that didn't matter to Imelda. She came with a wallop, her own knowledgeable finger displacing Ramiz' novice one as she speared herself on his shaft.

Having brought herself to such a climax, all she wanted was his cock fully in. She wanted to lie there, her legs all over the place, with the world's longest cock stuck right up her. But Ramiz wanted to come too. Imelda couldn't take any more. She tried to push him off but he was well in control.

He moved his full length in and out. Imelda shouted no, no, but he shouted yes, yes, and went faster, still using the entire dimensions of the serpent beast.

Imelda began saying a strange word. Wuff. Wuff. Wuff. Every time his cock plunged in, she said wuff. She wasn't fighting him now. She was just taking it. He gained confidence. He went faster. She stopped saying wuff and started shouting yes.

'Yes! Yes! Yes!' she cried, as he drilled his great machine into her tunnel with all his force. Bang, bang, bang, he went, the long shaft boring to the very rockface, as far as it could go, there to unleash its torrent of spunk to the groans and sighs of Ramiz and Imelda together.

He collapsed, exhausted. She didn't care about anything any more. She'd been fully fucked, far better than she'd had any right to expect from such a learner. But what a cock. What. A. Cock.

Imelda snoozed, then dropped off into a deep sleep. She was wakened by her sister. Her sister had no clothes on. Her sister was on the floor beside the bed, sitting astride Ramiz who was on his back on the carpet. Ingrid was shouting and screaming and making whooping noises.

She too had discovered the pleasures of being impaled on the longest piece of meat she'd ever seen. With enormous enthusiasm she was plunging herself down onto it after raising herself up until the tip almost popped out of her. Then whoosh, down again, with the careless rapture of someone swooping downhill on the big dipper ride.

Imelda watched, her hand automatically going to her own pleasure channel. She played with her clit as Ingrid went at it hammer and tongs, then she felt a hand on her breast. She'd completely forgotten about Amerjit, and here he was on the bed with her, turning her on her stomach, her head to one side so she could still watch her sister, but her legs splayed so her quim was in full view. She offered no resistance as Amerjit pushed his cock into her, but she couldn't concentrate so long as her sister was bouncing up and down like a mad thing in front of her.

At last Ingrid reached her climax. At last, the noise stopped. Imelda kept looking, because Ingrid had realised something was wrong. Ramiz hadn't come yet. Either he was learning self-control, or he'd used up so much spunk that night he had none left.

Ingrid slowly dismounted, like someone whose muscles are stiff and tired after a long hard day with the hunt. She bent her head to Ramiz's cock and began a plunging, sucking routine which, coupled with both her hands working on the shaft, soon had his lips murmuring sweet Indian nothings.

As she felt the first surge of come rushing up his cock she took her mouth away and held the cock at arm's length, watching the creamy tribute flow from its end and marvelling that such a thing could be all got inside her.

Imelda was now reminded that she had a cock too, not such a big one but a cock nevertheless. It was pumping steadily but not awakening her. She needed something extra. She needed the equivalent of a pickled onion with a piece of bland cheese, or the mustard on a ham sandwich.

'Ingrid, darling,' she whispered, throatily. 'Stop admiring that fucking cock and come over here. I want you to teach Amerjit something else. Get hold of his cock and show him what arse-banditry is all about. Mmmmmm. Thank you.'

Chapter Fourteen

Much refreshed by his short holiday, Murdo renewed his quest. Somewhere, somehow, he had to decide who was the perfect woman with whom to have sex – in front of a camera, for the enlightenment of the young and inexperienced members of the sexually active public.

There were now just the two candidates remaining: Jenny, the curvaceous secretary, and Nicola, the slimmer, lither one. He had to choose between them, and there was only one way to do it.

Jenny would be first but before Murdo took her to bed he had to check that she would be good in front of the all-seeing lens and so arranged a photo session after hours in the *Sir Lancelot* studio. Jenny was already at work when Murdo got there, going through a few conventional nude poses with the staff photographer, who had already had a hard day and wasn't exactly putting the whole of his bubbling personality into the job.

'OK, Mike,' said Murdo. 'I'll work the camera. You get your trousers off and give her one.'

'What? Give her one? Now?'

'Yes, now. Don't you want to?'

'Well, I . . .'

Mike's confusion was sorted out immediately by the resourceful Jenny, who could see that here was another opportunity for impressing Murdo. She nuzzled up to Mike, her left arm around his neck, her right hand clamped securely on his genitals. As she massaged his collection she brushed his lips with hers, and made sweet murmuring noises.

Mike's knees gave way and he slid to the floor. Jenny got busy with his belt and his zip, then remembered about the shoes and socks, but still had him naked from the waist down in a minute.

She looked up at Murdo who popped his head out from behind the camera to give her a wink and a thumbs up, whereupon she bent her mouth to the task of stiffening Mike's member. It had grown, but it hadn't recovered fully yet from the sudden shock of being commissioned for unexpected action.

The wet, slurping administration of tongue and lips produced the desired effect and Jenny arranged herself with a knee on either side of the prone Mike before lowering herself onto his cock. He pushed up inside her, raising his hips from the carpet. She circled and see-sawed, bending down to offer her mighty tits for play-mates.

Murdo managed to get a roll of film off before Mike, grunting, shot his load upwards into the gyrating Jenny. She hadn't come, so she looked up at Murdo again. He signalled that what she'd done was enough for the moment so she swaggered off to the models' dressing rooms, trailing a robe behind her with one hand.

She certainly had a magnificent arse, thought Murdo, his prick twitching at the thought of what was in store for him shortly. Mike, embarrassed, was tidying himself up.

'When the other one arrives tomorrow, Mike,' said Murdo, 'get the two maintenance men to give you a hand. You can shoot the pictures and they can do the modelling.'

Three-quarters of an hour later, Murdo and Jenny were walking into his penthouse suite with a take-away Chinese. This wasn't any ordinary take-away, of course. This was no Meal A for two from the Yeung Chow Fan on the corner. This was a nine-course Pekinese from the most expensive Gerrard Street restaurant, a meal for two gourmets.

'I'll just put these dishes in the oven for a few minutes. Get yourself a drink. I won't be long.'

Jenny had already had two large vodka and limes while they waited for their food. She was a bit giggly.

Before pouring herself a drink she took all her clothes off, and when Murdo walked in she was looking out of a window with a vodka on one side of her on the sill, and a malt whisky on the other. She leant forward on her elbows, chin cupped in hands, looking out of the window at the city lights spread out below in a seemingly unending and ever-varied pattern.

Murdo walked into the room and stopped. The magnificent arse he'd already admired was pointing at him, its ample cheeks giving him a wiggling welcome, the legs well apart. Jenny looked round to see what effect she was having, and saw Murdo fiddling with some urgency with his trouser fastenings.

While she waited, Jenny had a draw at her vodka. It burned her throat. The next sensation she had was of a stiff cock searching for a way into her pussy. She reached behind and underneath her fanny and found the questing knob end. With a slight adjustment of her stance she guided Murdo home.

While Murdo got into his stride she had another pull at the vodka. Murdo asked her if she was trying to impress him with her versatility – being able to do more than one thing at the same time – and then began thrusting in earnest.

She put her drink down, braced her feet more firmly and wider apart, put her left hand down on the window sill and reached behind her again with the other. She found his balls and held them lightly while his prick surged in and out.

Murdo reached for one of her superb breasts, and slid his other hand across her tummy to the hairy junction where the traffic was just now approaching the rush hour. His finger found her little joystick and stimulated it, while he palped the marvellous breast and rogered her with his sliding cock at ever-increasing speed.

His pubic mound thumped and walloped against the plentiful white flesh of her bottom. She was on the verge, he could tell, and so he went into his final sprint, a last streak of all-out effort as he made for the tape, hoping that she would cross the line with him at precisely the same moment.

His hot jelly flowed as Jenny felt her passage flex and twitch and a wave of peerless sensation swept her from toe to top. He pushed in as far as he could for his last spurt, and then relaxed, leaning against her plentiful body.

'Hey, Murdo,' she said, draining the last of her vodka. 'You're just as good as you say you are. Do I have to wait until after dinner for my next test?'

Indeed she did, and after the food, and the whisky, Murdo nodded off lying on the bed with her beside him – but not for long. His snooze turned to doze as her hair brushed his thighs and stomach. Doze became wakefulness as lips closed around his cock which was fully up but not stiff. A tongue was working up and down, along, across and round, the tip of it finding his most sensitive spot.

Jenny pulled back to admire the slippery, shiny almost-adamant cock. She bent down and took both his balls in her mouth as she worked his cock with her hand. Now it was really stiffening. Murdo was hard and fully prepared. Jenny wondered if she should wait a bit longer. Perhaps he might want to try some warming up on her. Or, should she just go for it? She decided that this was a time for the girl to make all the running, so she threw her leg across his stiff and curving prick and sat on it.

Leaning forward with her hands on either side of Murdo's head, she lowered her massive tits until she could touch him with them. She swung herself from side to side so her tits swayed across his face. He reached up with his tongue, trying to catch a taste of her nipples as they zoomed past.

His prick grew even harder inside her and she began to shag him in earnest. The tits were moving more wildly, not in such perfect swings but rather more at random.

Her big arse bumped and ground with weight and enthusiasm, and all Murdo had to do was lie back and enjoy it. She went faster, at full tilt, banging like a good 'un.

He watched her tits jiggling and swaying as, eyes closed, she made her final push for goal. Suddenly, she was there, her eyes looking into some far distant place as her buttocks thrust down on him, trying to get every last millimetre of cock inside her quim.

After a few moments she noticed he hadn't come yet. With a sigh like the fell runner who finds, as he breasts the hill, that what he thought was the top is not the last summit after all, she began bumping and grinding again.

Murdo, without indicating what he intended to do, slid his hand down to his cock. As she lifted he withdrew and placed the knob at her second entrance. She sat on it willingly and gurgled her contentment as his well lubricated one-man submarine slipped silently into the dark, forbidden harbour.

Awakening to the potential of what she had had inserted and where, she began moving again, a more restrained version of the bumps and grinds this time, while Murdo began to feel his own spring welling up. He thrust upwards with his hips. She moved faster. He shot, five, six, seven times, and without speaking they fell back.

After a rest, Murdo got them some more drinks. Returning, he fell to chatting about the project.

'You see,' he said, 'the normal sex manual doesn't take any account of the situations young lovers find themselves in. For example, the pictures in manuals show people in their early twenties having it away in complete privacy, in a bed. Most of the couples who really need advice are younger than that. And, if they do have it in a bed, they will be nothing like so relaxed. They'll be trying to fuck quietly on a single divan, hoping they're not making the springs creak and worried in case the castors betray them and the bed starts migrating across the floorboards, with the girl's father listening underneath while he watches the football.

'Or, they'll be in the back seat of a car, or lying on the grass hoping nobody's going to go past, or they're on the settee hoping parents aren't going to come home from the pub just yet.'

'Is that what we'll be doing, then, if I get the job? Poking in mum's front room?' Jenny sounded quite excited by the prospect.

'Certainly. And we'll describe what it's like. It won't be all, "First you do this, then you do that." It'll be more "I really liked it when you did such and such" – you know, in the first person. But in context, the kind of context our young readers will recognise.'

'You mean like babysitting?'

'Exactly. Having the boyfriend or girlfriend in while you're babysitting your baby brother.'

'Or what to do when the father takes the babysitter home.'

'Right again. A lot of girls have their first proper sexual relationship with the father of the baby they sit for.'

'That's what happened to me.'

Jenny took a sip of her drink, adjusted her magnificent tits so they leaned more comfortably against Murdo, and told him the story.

'I could see he wanted me, and I was at that age when I wanted anybody, but I didn't know how to get it started, or how to let him know he could feel free. Anyway . . . do you want to hear this? It might make a story for your magazine.'

'I'd love to hear it, Jenny. Just get me another whisky before you get going.' She got the whisky and settled again, nestling up to Murdo.

'Well, this man, you see, he was taking me home. He and his wife had been out for a meal or something, and she was having a bath and going to bed while he drove me back to my parents' place. Thing was, my folks were away. I'd be alone in the house once we got there. If only I could get him to come in.

'I let my skirt ride up while we were driving. I saw him steal a look. I stroked my thigh as if I wasn't thinking about it. He shifted in his seat. As we pulled up outside the door, I asked him if he'd like a coffee. By this time my skirt was almost round my arse.

'When I'd got the coffee we sat and looked at each other. He needed more of a come-on. He wasn't going to risk getting charged with raping a teenager. I had a brilliant idea and went and got a video my dad had taken when we were on holiday in Minorca. We'd had a fairly private beach connected with our hotel, and me and my mum had gone topless.

'My mum's got a good pair of tits like me and she likes to show that they're still great. So, I asked him if he'd like to see our holiday video. He didn't seem all that keen but his attitude changed when the first shot of my mum came up, running down the beach after a ball with her bloody great melons joggling. Then I came on the screen, rubbing suntan lotion into my tits. I thought the camera was on me a long time. I wondered from that moment about my dad.

'Anyway, there I was, massaging my bare tits on the telly, and my babysitting father gave a groan. "It's alright," I said. "They didn't burn. I put lots of stuff on. Of course, the tan's a bit worn now. Look." And I lifted my sweater up, just enough for him to see up as far as the bottom of my bra.

'His eyes were fairly popping by now. "Were you brown all over, then?" he said. "Definitely," I said. "Would you like to see?" Not surprisingly, he said he would.

'I pulled my sweater over my head and undid my bra, and let the straps fall over my shoulders and down my arms. I made the most of my cleavage, I can tell you. He groaned again. "You can touch them if you like," I said. He had nice hands, soft and gentle, and my tits liked them. Maybe I groaned a bit too, because before long he had my knickers off and we were fucking in front of the fire. I hadn't really thought it through, what I was doing, and I wasn't sure I wanted him fucking me and coming inside. I tried to stop him. He told me to shut up and stop being a stinking lousy prick teaser, so I thought what the hell and tried to enjoy it.

'I can't say I did, much, not the first couple of times. Then, before long, they seemed to be going out nearly every night, and nearly every night I was having my knickers pulled down in the back of his car. I really got to like it then. He was very good. He showed me what he could do with his mouth on me, and told me how to suck his cock properly.

'We used to have games, eventually. We got so good with each other, even in the car seat, that we could bring each other right to the point quite quickly, and then we'd keep each other dangling. The first one to come was the winner, because that meant the other one had been too impatient in bringing the person off.

'It was great, and then he asked if he could borrow the video to show a friend. I didn't see why not. I liked the idea of a stranger seeing my tits.

'What he did was to get it copied. The friend owned a television shop, and they threatened to cut bits of me and mum into their video demo tape. We'd both be shown, bare titted, on fifty TV screens all at once in his shop on a Saturday morning.'

'Unless?' said Murdo, getting up to fill the glasses again.

'Unless me and my mum went with my babysat lover and his TV friend on a dirty weekend. Everything paid for. All we had to do was go. So mum told dad we were going on a shopping trip, spent all week doing secret shopping and changing the carrier bags and throwing away the price tags, and then off we went.

'It was to a sort of self-contained holiday resort, like a small holiday camp built around an old mansion. There was a show at night, and dancing, and plenty of you know what. Me and mum were both fucked three times each by both men on the Friday. On Saturday night we thought we'd save time and all be in the same room together.

'Anyway, we went to see the Saturday night show, and half way through they announced a wet T-shirt competition. Well, mum looked at me, and I looked at her. We were both a bit pissed.

'Up we went on the stage and we were issued with our T-shirts, just plain white they were, and we had to go in the wings and put them on with no bra underneath.

'The compere came in the wings with us to check, he said, while somebody was singing a song on stage. I could tell he really liked my mum, and she was being a bit shameless.

'So, on we went, and the compere produced this big garden sprayer and sprayed all our chests. Me and mum were easy winners, with another girl third, but they said they couldn't decide who was first and second, me or mum.

'The compere said something to mum, and she nodded, and then whipped her T-shirt off! So I thought, bollocks to this, and whipped mine off. The applause was deafening. We were declared equal first, and I put my shirt back on and went like that, dripping, with my tits showing through, back to the table.

'After a while, when the men had finished laughing and feeling my tits, we noticed that mum wasn't there. Straight away we guessed where she was, so we went round the back of the stage. There was this noise – uh, uh, uh, uh – and it was my mum's voice. And there she was, against the wall, her T-shirt half off and covering her face. The compere had his head in her tits and his cock up her fanny, his trousers round his ankles.

'We just stayed and watched. When he'd finished and pulled out, he ran off as soon as he saw us. But mum just said, "Oh, hello dears," and went back to our table. So that was how I started in serious sex. With a man I babysat for, his friend the TV shopkeeper, and my mum.'

Next day Murdo mooched around the flat, played some music, went for a walk for a couple of beers at the pub, and generally got himself recovered and in relaxed mood for Nicola, his second candidate.

She rang the bell on the dot of eight and walked through the doorway dressed entirely in black leather. It was very thin, very soft leather and it clung to every crevice and every pinnacle. Nicola looked stunning.

Murdo was planning on grilling them a fillet steak for

supper, but first he sat her down in an armchair with a drink. She downed it in one and pulled him towards her, her hand on his zip while his first mouthful of malt was hardly swallowed. She pulled his prick from inside his trousers, examined it carefully, breathed hot air on it, then gobbled it with enormous care and tenderness.

Murdo had the self-control only to take two more sips of whisky before she had him pushing himself further into her mouth. Her head was going like a fiddler's elbow and in no time at all he was pumping spunk between her lips. She sucked the last drop from him, tucked his cock back in his trousers, and zipped him up.

'There,' she said. 'I always like a little suck for starters. Can I have another glass of wine, please?'

After supper she went into his bedroom and stripped naked. He came in and she stripped him too, then laid him on the bed. Facing his feet she lowered her sweet quim onto his mouth and then leant forward. Her pert little tits squashed against his chest and her mouth once again closed over his cock.

What Murdo hadn't realised was that she had in her hands a length of sticking plaster and, by reaching as far as she could, she got it round his ankles. He was hobbled.

His brief protest was wasted as she pushed her muff harder into his face. She picked up his hands and pushed them onto her tits. While they gripped and squeezed she reached somewhere and got another length of plaster and, with a sudden movement, taped his wrists together.

She ducked under his joined hands, turned, and pushed his arms back over his head. She kissed him hard on the mouth and rubbed her body against his, writhing and scraping every part of her against every part of him.

With him unawares again, she managed to get him to shift so she could loop his arms over one of the knobs on the bedhead, and with more tape she had him secured.

She slipped off the bed, went out of the room, and returned with a short riding crop. Murdo began to say something but a little flicker with the whip shut him up. He opened his mouth again and she stuffed her knickers in it. Then, she lifted his balls with the end of the whip, resting them on the leather tab. She pushed the end into his crevices, searching for a way in. If he didn't co-operate, he got another flicker of the whip.

Nicola pushed his semi-limp cock about with the stem of the riding crop, expecting it to harden. It didn't.

'So, Mr Sinclair is being a naughty little boy. Backsliding. Not doing what his mistress wants. Well, we'll have to see about that.'

She pushed the whip under his balls and lifted. He had to move too, and she turned him over like a cook turns a steak in the pan. Carefully she measured her stroke and then cracked him a couple of sharp shots across the buttocks. He made some unidentifiable sounds, so she hit him again.

Murdo, very angry by now, spun himself round again onto his back. She, blissfully ignorant, went down on his cock with her mouth. He jerked himself free of the bedpost and put his joined hands to her neck in a garrotte. He pulled, not very hard.

Nicola, not realising that something had gone wrong, reached behind her and pulled her knickers from his mouth. What would be the next stage of the game, she wondered?

'Untape my feet,' said Murdo crisply. She did what she was told. They scrambled off the bed, Murdo still holding her by the neck.

He shoved her across the room to a small chair and bent her over it. She stayed there, without him holding her. He grabbed the whip in both hands and lashed her a mighty swipe right across the arse cheeks. A red weal appeared almost instantly. She shrieked.

Murdo found some scissors in a drawer and gave them to her. She cut him free, then dropped the scissors on the carpet as he gave her another good crack across the bottom with the whip.

'You made an error, Nicola. I went to an English public school. I associate beatings with injustice from incompetent perverts, not fun and games.'

'But I thought . . .'

'I'm sorry. You thought wrongly. Now I must apologise for losing my temper and hitting you. You are in pain. I'm very sorry.'

'That's alright. No, honestly. Oh hell.'

She burst into tears and Murdo took her in his arms and held her until she stopped. She looked up at him, red faced, and tried a smile.

'I suppose this means that Jenny's got it?'

'I suppose it does,' said Murdo. 'But we could add a special section. What can a boy do with two girls?'

Chapter Fifteen

Sitting in chairs in front of his desk were two sisters. Was this going to be Murdo's first double date for 'Damsel of the Month'?

Before starting work full time on his sex manual, Murdo had to spend a couple of weeks in the office, in restaurants and in bed, building up several months' worth of Damsels. Frenchie and Staz could handle the rest of the magazine, but only Murdo could do the Damsels.

The younger of the two girls sitting in front of him was utterly beautiful. She had long, long black hair and a fine face with great big eyes. Beneath her clothes – crisp white shirt with wide revers, faded leather waistcoat, jeans and boots – she appeared to have all the essentials for centrefold work.

Her sister was almost as good looking but, regrettably, Murdo had to say to himself, too old for the magazine. She must be twenty-four at least.

'Thank you for coming to see me,' said Murdo. 'I had only expected . . .'

'Yes,' said the older one. 'My name is Rachel. It's May here you want. But the thing is, she's only sixteen. It's the other aspects of the job, your article . . .'

'You know the rules, Rachel,' said Murdo. 'That has always been the deal and always will be the deal. This is a matter which cannot be discussed.'

'Would you say that May would be perfect for the Damsel pictures?'

'Having seen her here in her clothes, and the audition pictures you sent with no clothes, I would say so. But I need to look at her nude in the flesh also.'

'Fine. Now, as her mother . . .'

Murdo had a coughing fit.

'Yes, I'm her mother,' the woman continued. 'She's sixteen. I'm thirty-one. I had her, shall we say, fairly early in life. What I was going to say was, that as her mother I'm concerned that she won't be able, through a total lack of experience, to cope with the, er, rest of the Damsel day and, er, night. So I'll do that bit, and you can write about it as if it were May.'

'Intriguing,' said Murdo pensively, recovering from his surprise at finding that May's sister was her mother, only to be given another shock when May, the sweet, innocent May, secretly gave him the biggest and most suggestive wink he'd ever seen.

Murdo reached for his telecom and summoned the Nordic iceberg he called secretary.

'Take Rachel to the visitors' room and give her some coffee. May is going to have a picture test for "Damsel".'

Lights and set were already in position. May was sent off to dress up in a kind of outdoor rambler's outfit with full waterproofs. When she came back she was to strip in front of the camera.

Murdo explained that he wasn't especially testing her modelling imagination, although her contributions would be appreciated. He was just wanting to see how she would turn out when the full professional works were applied. Mike's Hasselblad with its saucer-size lens and two-and-a-quarter-inch negatives would see her rather differently from the amateur job she'd had on her audition pictures.

May posed in the set with a backdrop of lakes and mountains. Slowly she undid the Velcro fastening on her ankle-length, blue plastic cagoul and peeled it off, revealing nothing more sexy than a hip-length hairy brown sweater, grey flannel plus-two climbing trousers, big red socks and boots like single-decker buses. Her smile, however, would have had every rock climber on the mountain falling off his overhang.

So far so good. She bent away from the camera and

stuffed the cagoul in her rucksack, taking the opportunity to show the keen professional eyes of Mike and Murdo that not even a pair of grey flannel trousers could hide the perfection of her bottom.

She turned back, faced the camera square on, and pulled her jumper over her head, taking care to grasp the hem of her T-shirt and pull it up with the big woolly, just part of the way, so that the bare midriff and the promising swellings of her bra-less breasts were glimpsed.

Once again she turned to the rucksack and stuffed the garment inside, wiggling her bottom in the most outrageously camp way.

Already Mike and Murdo both had erections. Here was a Damsel who would have every *Sir Lancelot* reader wanking his prick off.

May undid the buttons on the waistband and fly of the trousers, and pushed her hand inside. They saw a pair of red knickers, briefly, and a flash of black pubic hair. She stood, one thumb hooked in the open trousers, and pushed her other hand up underneath her T-shirt. She felt her own nipples in turn, and groped herself thoroughly, before putting both hands to the job of removing her shirt.

This she did slowly, raising it like a theatre curtain, inch by inch. Gradually her superb bosom was revealed. First the luscious underswelling, then the bottom edge of an aureole, then the other, then a nipple, then the other.

She pulled off the shirt entirely and gave herself a little shake. The photographer and Murdo the hardened Damsel devourer gazed open-mouthed at the finest pair of tits either of them had ever seen. They were big, very big, but firm and proud. They were every man's dream.

Now she bent to see to her boots. Her tits changed shape as they dangled but they were still gorgeous, and when she sat on the ground to pull the boots off, leaning forward, her tits crushing against her raised knees, the most seasoned of girlie pro's would have admitted to getting a hard on.

She stood to lower the trousers, turning her back to show the watching men what her bottom was like when covered only by a skimpy layer of red silk. She leaned against one of the cardboard mountains to pull off her socks, and then turned towards them dressed only in her little panties.

She slid both hands inside them and rubbed herself with her fingers. Her eyes closed as she swayed, and she pulled her breasts together with the insides of her arms as her hands worked beneath the flimsy red stuff.

When she judged they'd had the right amount of that she made a sudden movement. The red silk ripped and her panties were off and being held at arm's length, an insubstantial rag of crimson which a moment before had been the only important thing between the men's eyes and the truly majestic spectacle of May in the buff.

With a slithering, swaying movement she turned and stuffed the last articles of clothing in the rucksack. She bent down with her legs apart, so they could see her tuft and the outlines of her quim lips in silhouette. If Mike hadn't been there, Murdo would have been unable to resist taking his cock out and putting it exactly where it appeared to be wanted most. If Murdo hadn't been there, Mike would have done precisely the same thing.

May turned with a smile, slipped on the robe which Mike was offering, and came over to Murdo's desk.

'Well? What did you think?' she asked.

Murdo just nodded.

The girl smiled again and went away to change back into her own clothes. Murdo pressed his intercom and asked the iceberg to fetch May's mother, Rachel.

'Rachel,' Murdo began. 'About your offer.'

Rachel crossed her legs. She was wearing a very short skirt.

'It's highly irregular, of course, and if our secret were ever to get out it would lose us a certain amount of credibility. In fact, in such a case, we would have to publish pictures of you, Rachel, to prove that I'd struck a worthwhile bargain.'

'That would be quite alright,' said the mother. 'I'm sure you can arrange a shadow or two to hide the blemishes.

Do you want to see me now with no clothes on?'

'I don't think that will be necessary. I'm sure we'll find, er . . .'

'What you're looking for? Yes. Well, I hope so.' Rachel uncrossed her legs and stood up. 'All we need now is a date, Mr Sinclair.'

'I'm afraid I can't offer you very much choice of dates,' he said. 'My schedules are almost impossibly tight. You and I will have to do our business this evening, and the restaurant outing with May will have to be tomorrow. The actual photo session for the Damsel spread can be later. Is that OK with you? Tonight, I mean?'

Rachel was a determined lady. She wanted her daughter to be a famous model and to have all the wealth and position she, Rachel, had never had. She was also determined that her daughter shouldn't make the same mistakes and get herself into sex and procreation too early. If Murdo had to be bedded tonight, then tonight it would be.

Chapter Sixteen

It was about ten o'clock in the morning, two days later, as Murdo sat at his computer terminal to write the article describing his night with May. He had a problem but it wasn't the usual one. Normally he'd be scratching his head to imagine what the sex should have been like, or trying to bring in exciting experiences from elsewhere to bolster the fairly mundane and short-lived encounter of the Red Knight with his Green Damsel.

Murdo's puzzle today was how to cram a quart into a pint pot. Rachel, May's mother, had arrived at his flat as promised and had proved to be a delightful, skilful and energetic bedfellow. Then, the next night, Murdo had gone through the restaurant routine expecting that to be that.

Instead, the incredibly beautiful, young and totally fanciable May had made it plain that her mother's protective measures regarding her daughter's virginity were somewhat superfluous – or, as she put it herself, she didn't mind having a little bit. If Murdo liked he could have another Damsel for supper, this time the real one.

In two consecutive evenings, therefore, Murdo Sinclair had been to nirvana and back, first with a mother and then her daughter. It was true that the mother knew more about it, but the daughter's body was astounding and her attitude eager and co-operative. They had been remarkable nights.

The secretary-iceberg brought him his coffee and his packet of Gitanes. He lit one and drew heavily on it, trying to work out where to start. He'd already decided to amalgamate the two nights as if they were one, cutting out about half the business so that he wouldn't appear to be boasting unduly about having a Damsel eight times in one session.

His readers would be expecting to read about what happened when he called to pick May up. Usually he and the Damsel did a turn then, before going out. In this case he hadn't even thought about it. He would have to write about his opening experience with Rachel as if it were May, and after that he might as well take it in turns. Murdo stubbed out the Gitanes, lit another, and began tapping.

Every month I seem to tell you that my dirty Damsel delights have been even more stunningly pungent than before. Every month we seem to find a girl yet more sumptuously gorgeous than the last one, and never has there been an end to it.

Perhaps, finally, we have reached the peak. Turn over the page and imagine where we can ever find a girl finer looking, more lissome of figure, more tasty and relishable than this month's Damsel, May?

Where is the girl to follow May? No doubt we shall be able to bring you one, and another, and another, but I have my fears as to whether any girl in the known and available universe could be more fetching, whether any breasts on earth could show nipples more enticing than the darling buds of May.

As is my wont, I turned up at May's hotel a little early, hoping that she might be in the mood for some pre-prandial scandal, something tasty, as it were, au dehors of the oeuvre. Well, I have to tell you that when I arrived and knocked on her door, *she wasn't there*!

Not there? For her editor? For Murdo? Unthinkable. I knocked again. No reply.

My usual equanimity was beginning to ripple. My urbane serenity was becoming sfumato (it means 'having a hazy outline', for those of you less erudite than myself). And then, of a sudden, all was well. Here she came, trotting down the hotel corridor, entrancing in a pure white tracksuit.

She had been, she told me, for her daily run and had got herself lost in the unfamiliar streets of the metropolis. May, you see, comes from Truro, where the chaps say 'Ooh-arr' as she jogs past them. In London they say 'Cor, strike a light' or something very similar.

She unlocked her door and ushered me in. She was contrite. She was abject in her apologies. Not only had my esteemed and illustrious self been kept waiting and unoccupied outside her door for four or five unwarranted minutes, but the same amount of time would now put us under some pressure to be ready to go out in time – that is, she said, if we were thinking of doing anything else other than simply getting ready.

I pointed out that I was already ready. It was she who would be under pressure.

'I'm so sorry,' said the despondent Damsel, lying on her back on the settee and pulling down her jogging trousers. 'Perhaps you had better give me what a naughty girl deserves.'

With this she swung her feet up and over her shoulders, supported her hips with her hands, and offered me her bare pink botty for spanking. It was pink because of her exertion and the sight of it, with its inviting black tufty outcrops at certain central points, made me forgive her immediately for being late and for any other misdemeanour she had ever committed or would ever commit in her entire life.

I knelt on the floor beside her. May shifted her position, raising her bountiful buttocks a little more in the air. I gave them a light tap with my palm.

'Come on, Murdo!' she cried. 'Give it a bit of wellie.'

So I did. I smacked her splendid, perfectly formed arse-cheeks six times, using as much of my strength as was reasonably appropriate.

It brought tears to her eyes. She bit her lip. A single pearly drop welled from its corner and coursed down her peaches and cream.

'May,' I said in alarm, 'have I . . .?'

'Oh yes,' she said. 'You have. Now hurry up and get your knickers off, dear heart, because I'm panting for it.'

She lowered her legs so that her heels were now tucked under the aforementioned cheeks. She spread her knees wide. Her darkly afforested pocket was laid open, its lips beckoning me in. I needed no further encouragement. In an instant I was on her, my cock plunging deep inside her hot wetness.

Her body was still damp from the exertions of her run. Stopping for a moment in my thrusts I unzipped the tracksuit top and laid bare the contents. I didn't know where to begin. I had never seen two such tremendous tits.

I placed one hand on each and buried my face in between them. She hugged me to her and shifted her legs. Her heels were on my back now. She was pulling me ever into her. I bucked and heaved and pushed and jumped, and within moments she was shouting out with pleasure.

My cock was going fifty to the dozen, and my hands were massaging her mighty melons with more enthusiasm than I, a hardened old fucker, could have thought possible. My darling May went into autopilot mode, her body jerking with its own primaeval impulses while her brain floated away on a magic carpet of sensations.

There was no need, I thought, for her to dig her fingernails in quite so deep as she came, but never mind, she was worth it. I gave her another twenty or thirty pumps to get my own juices flowing and she was almost out for the count by the time I sighed with satisfaction and stopped moving.

I looked at my watch. She had thirty minutes only

to get ready for our evening out. While she dived in the shower I summoned the hairdresser and make-up girl on the room phone and between us – I helped adjust her necklace so it fell perfectly across her upper breast – we got her fit in time.

Salim, my chauffeur, was his normal imperturbable self. I'm sure he is moved by the sight of these girls but he never shows it. I can only assume he goes home and gives his wife an extra couple of inches.

We were eating that night at a new place which is rapidly spinning to the top of the social whirl, the Uptown Top Ranking, a Caribbean restaurant where the food blows your brains out.

Now, you know me. I'm the one for Château Lafite with the thinly sliced, pink-roast duck breast, and the deep golden Sauternes with the wild strawberries. I'm not usually your man for chicken gumbo with gelignite – but I've been told by my very lovely deputy editors, Staz and Frenchie, that I'm becoming a boring old fart with all my poncy haute cuisine. Apparently I ought to get my nose into something more ethnic and less stuffed-shirt or, as my sweet Staz so eloquently put it, imagine I was eating with my knob end.

The restaurant was hot, sweaty and smoky, and fairly dark. There was reggae on the sound system, Red Stripe lager to drink, and no menu. This enormous black chap with hair like a bead curtain laughed at me when I asked for the bill of fare, and stopped laughing when May put her hand on my thigh.

Anyway, you get what you are given at the Uptown Top Ranking, and we were given something called Puss Prayers to start. These are avocado halves with a kind of salty, spicy smoked fish filling, and they are absolutely delicious.

May, who, as you can see in the pictures, was wearing black shoes, black tights, a white mini skirt and a white crocheted top with nothing underneath it, was the subject of everyone's attention. Perhaps, I thought, she has gone a bit too far. Her nipples were clearly visible poking out of the crochet.

Soon after we finished the Puss Prayers I thought I might be in the unfortunate position of having to defend May's honour against twenty men with ten-inch erections, so I gave the head waiter my card and invited him to May's photo session. Order was kept from then on.

You can see this head waiter in the photograph on the next page. Anyone who feels so inclined can ring his door bell and run away, but I'm not going to.

Next we had some more Red Stripe and something which I was told the chef had developed from an original recipe by Bob Marley. He called it Rasta Pasta, and it consisted – as far as I could make out – entirely of pasta shells, pickled pigs' foreskins and minced chilli peppers. And the greatest of these was the chilli peppers.

May, who seems to be quite used to this sort of thing, took it in her stride. I needed three more cans of Red Stripe.

It was a jolly evening, once the initial terror had worn off, but I must confess that I have catalogued it along with broken Greek plates and Turkish belly dancers as unnecessary and surplus to the proper requirements of a good dinner. Next month I'm going to L'Etoile or Wheeler's or somesuch, whatever Staz says.

Back at the apartment I made May stand in the middle of my sitting room while I walked around her. She is enough to raise the eyebrow of Buddha. And those nipples jutting through the crochet . . .

I poured myself a large one. I think it was a Talisker, but it might have been a drop of my own label, the Sinclair Malt, which is distilled solely for my family and which you will never have consumed.

Neither will you have had the eye-popping experience of May kneeling at your feet, unzipping your fly and bringing your quivering cock out into the ambient temperature.

Briefly, she gave it a lick and then, from a small pocket in her skirt, produced – of all things, go on, have a guess, there, I knew you'd be wrong – a sachet of salad cream.

She'd lifted it from a vulgar little plastic basket on the table at the restaurant. With her teeth she opened it at the corner and then squeezed a cool, thin, pale yellow line of Messrs Heinz's 57th variety right down my cock. There was some left so she swirled it around the end.

Looking up briefly with that heavenly smile she explained that she loved mayonnaise on her chips but salad cream would have to do. With infinite care she licked every drop from my rigid member and by the time she'd finished she needed to do very little more before she got her seconds.

Her last lick of Mr Heinz's creation was followed by an encirclement of my rampant tip by her pliant lips and with three or four short bobs of the head she received my own offering, a warm cream manufactured in secret recesses with, as per the abovementioned proprietary emulsion, no artificial colouring or preservatives.

I had been fondling May's fantastic bosom through the crochet while she knelt at her business, and now I raised her to her feet and removed the garment, its previously pristine whiteness somewhat grubbified with my sweaty palms.

To show me her tits better, May put her hands behind her head. That was a sight to behold. Keeping my eyes glued to their incredible wonder I undid her skirt, pulled it down, then pulled her tights and knickers off. She stood before me, naked, hands on head, her youthful beauty stating in definitive terms what the perfect photographic female is.

Placing my hands on her waist I turned her through one hundred and eighty degrees and pushed her towards the bedroom door. Still with elbows up and akimbo she tripped towards the threshold, bottom-cheeks jigging, while I filled our glasses. When I reached the bedroom she was lying on the bed, face down, legs slightly apart.

I needed no second invitation, no foreplay, no preamble whatever. Placing our drinks down on the bedside table I lay on top of her, pushed my member between her thighs, found her sweet nest and rammed home.

What bliss was mine, that time and the next. If only my dear beloved deputy editors, in charge for a while, had not cut my article to 2,500 words to make room for their own scarcely credible debauchery, I should have had room to tell you about May, a little bit drunk, deciding at midnight to make some real mayonnaise with egg yolk and olive oil.

Were the laws governing such matters more lax, I might even have been able to tell you what we did with it when she'd made it. Also I could have mentioned a few details about her going down a flight of stairs to knock on my neighbour's door to borrow a cucumber, and what we did with that. Then there was the best of all, a stand-up job, she with her clothes on, me in my dressing gown pulling her skirt up around her buttocks, in my doorway as we said goodbye the following morning.

But I can't tell you about that. No room. You must imagine it. Turn the page for photographic assistance.

Murdo sat back and lit a Gitanes. That was five Damsels in the bag in a fortnight. He had two days off which were to be spent playing in a pro-celebrity golf tournament (how he hoped his pro wasn't one of the top women golfers) and then it would be down to serious work with Jenny on the manual.

They had worked out it would take them about six weeks to do the photography, including the location shots

– parks, cliff tops, lovers' lanes and Jenny had insisted on a beer garden of a busy pub.

Then they would have it to write, for which they gave themselves another six weeks. This left a further six weeks for proofing, corrections and so on, before he would have to dive back to the magazine to do another Damsel.

They'd decided on the title, with Auntie Sheila's approval. It was punchy and to the point and Sheila said it summed up the pair of them perfectly. It was to be called 'Shameless'.